Praise for the Celebration Bay Mysteries

Independence Slay

"With one occurrence _____
ing together somehow.

"*Independence Slay* . . . _____
to the beach, and not j _____
has humor mixed in with a full story line that will have you
guessing with each page."   —*Fresh Fiction*

"Liv and her delightful Westie companion, Whiskey . . . prove
to be intelligent, witty, and genuinely likable enough to per-
severe through the eccentricities of this delightful holiday-
themed town."   —*Kings River Life Magazine*

"Shelley Freydont skillfully manipulates the story and the
characters for a perfect example of a small-town traditional
mystery with an amateur sleuth."   —*Lesa's Book Critiques*

Silent Knife

"A wonderful winter cozy that you can curl up with any time
of the year."   —*Escape with Dollycas into a Good Book*

"Freydont is a skilled writer . . . The dialogue is funny and
fast, and the plot carries the reader along swiftly . . . [A]
very enjoyable series."   —*Kings River Life Magazine*

"Shelley Freydont's holiday mysteries are perfect for seasonal
reading . . . You'll want to include it in a Christmas mystery
collection. After all, you do want to know what happens to
Santa Claus, don't you?"   —*Lesa's Book Critiques*

continued . . .

Foul Play at the Fair

"Event coordinator Liv Montgomery is doing her best to squash any obstacles to a successful Celebration Bay Harvest Festival, and when a body crops up, she's not going to let her plans be plowed under."
—Sheila Connolly, *New York Times* bestselling author of the Orchard Mysteries

"All the charm of a Norman Rockwell painting, but with a much more colorful cast of characters!"
—Cynthia Baxter, author of the Reigning Cats & Dogs Mysteries

"Celebrate Shelley Freydont's new mystery series in Celebration Bay, a city of festivals where the event coordinator plans everything. Except solving murders."
—Janet Bolin, author of the Threadville Mysteries

"*Foul Play at the Fair* is a fun romp of a story about Liv Montgomery, who gives up her irritating life of handling bridezillas and finds the perfect job in Celebration Bay, New York, with her Westie, Whiskey. A delicious read filled with interesting characters and good times."
—Joyce Lavene, coauthor of the Missing Pieces Mysteries

"I fell in love with Liv Montgomery and the citizens of Celebration Bay from the very first page."
—Mary Kennedy, author of the Dream Club Mysteries

"The fun first Celebration Bay Mystery is an engaging whodunit starring a burned-out protagonist who, though she fled the city, remains in a constant state of stress."
—*Genre Go Round Reviews*

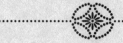

Trick or Deceit

Shelley Freydont

BERKLEY PRIME CRIME, NEW YORK

BERKLEY
PRIME
CRIME

An imprint of Penguin Random House LLC
375 Hudson Street, New York, New York 10014

TRICK OR DECEIT

A Berkley Prime Crime Book / published by arrangement with the author

ISBN: 978-0-425-28147-5

PUBLISHING HISTORY
Berkley Prime Crime mass-market edition / September 2015

PRINTED IN THE UNITED STATES OF AMERICA

10 9 8 7 6 5 4 3 2 1

Cover illustration by Robert Crawford.
Cover design by Lesley Worrell.
Interior text design by Tiffany Estreicher.

Penguin
Random
House

Chapter One

....

Liv Montgomery stopped at the bottom of the town hall steps to button her jacket. A year before, she'd moved to Celebration Bay, New York, from Manhattan, complete with a totally new "country" wardrobe of corduroy, plaids, comfortable shoes, even a hat with earflaps. Now she only brought out the earflaps when it was below ten degrees, which, being early October, it wasn't, and her jacket had finally lost its shiny, right-off-the-racks-at-L.L.Bean look.

And she was getting a lot fewer digs about being a city girl. Actually, since she'd taken over the duties of town event planner, attendance at activities had tripled, and she was becoming an accepted member of the community, most of the time.

Her assistant, Ted Driscoll, a tall, lean man of a certain age and an untalked-about past, tucked up his collar, then took her elbow. Beneath the jacket he was wearing a black pullover with a bat knitted onto the front.

Ted loved his holidays, and the women at the Yarn Barn kept him in festive sweaters, scarves, vests, and hats. He had a good singing voice, adored Liv's white Westie, Whiskey, knew his way around a computer, and had nerves of steel.

In a word, he was the best assistant Liv had ever had.

It was late afternoon and already dark, except for the lights from restaurants and shops and the wrought iron lamps that lit the paths through the park.

Being a family-friendly destination town, the inhabitants of Celebration Bay had the changeover from one holiday to the next down to a science. On September thirtieth, the Harvest on the Bay Festival transformed into Halloween, literally overnight. Town-wide decorations of colorful leaves and fall vegetables turned into broomsticks and bats. Gourds and pumpkins were carved into grimacing jack-o'-lanterns. Bales of hay that had offered respite to weary tourists were now the property of skeletons and witches.

They crossed the street and joined the scores of people headed toward the band shell at the far side of the village square, where the mayor would shortly announce the winner of Celebration Bay's first ever haunted house contest.

"So who do you think will win Best Haunted House tonight?" Liv asked.

"I think Barry Lindquist's Museum of Yankee Horrors takes the cake. My unofficial opinion, of course."

"It is pretty impressive," Liv said. "I knew about Hester Prynne, Lizzie Borden, and the Headless Horseman, but there were a bunch of crimes I never realized took place in New England."

Ted coughed out a laugh, sending a cloud into the air. "In true Celebration Bay style, Barry played loose with some of the more sordid efforts. Al Capone? I mean, since when did Chicago belong to the northeast?"

"I did wonder about that," Liv said. "Anyway I think it's a toss-up between his museum and Ernie Bolton's Monster Mansion."

"You screamed loud enough when that skeleton popped out of the coffin."

Liv grimaced. "I wasn't expecting it."

"That's the whole point. Now, do you want to find a seat or do you want to stand in the back surveying the assembly and looking for potential screw-ups, unexpected snafus, and sloppy crowd control?"

"Let's stand in the back, but only because I've been sitting all day."

"Uh-huh." Ted maneuvered them to a place right behind the last row of folding chairs.

"No really. I'm going to delegate a lot more this year. And exercise more."

"Uh-huh."

Liv pointed to the band shell, where five chairs and a lectern had been set up and where a row of jack-o'-lanterns lined the front of the stage. "Are those electric or candlelit?"

Ted shook his head. "Not to worry, they're battery powered. The pumpkins are ceramic and were donated by the Garden Club last year."

"Oh."

"And the folding chairs passed state folding chair inspection just last week."

"Very funny."

"Relax."

"I am relaxed. Just vigilant." It was her job. Event planners not only planned but were responsible for making sure that everything ran smoothly.

Ted chuckled. "Here we go."

Five people came onto the stage and sat in the chairs without mishap.

"See?" Ted said. "Safe and sound."

Liv rolled her eyes at him.

As soon as they were seated, Mayor Worley joined them and stood behind the lectern. He held up his hands to quiet the audience, which didn't have the slightest effect. It never did. He tapped on the microphone. A mechanical screech broadcast through the audience. They became quiet.

Gilbert Worley had been mayor for at least ten years, mainly, Liv guessed, because no one else wanted the job. He was short, portly, with black hair gelled back from his forehead and showing gray at the temples when he was behind on his Grecian Formula touch-ups.

He held up his hands again. "Ladies and gentlemen, boys and ghouls . . ."

The crowd groaned.

"Isn't that how he started last year's speech?" Liv asked.

"The last ten, at least."

The microphone squealed and the mayor stepped back. "Welcome to this year's Halloween kickoff. Tonight we have a special honor to award and a surprise to announce.

"As you know, the community center is in search of a new building, and the best way to insure success is by a fund-raising campaign—"

More groans from a few in the audience.

"It's for a good cause," someone yelled.

Most of the crowd agreed, loudly.

The mayor looked at the lectern as if he might find his gavel there, but this wasn't a town meeting; it just sounded like one.

"As you know, our community center has lost its lease. The center provides an important service to our young people, families, and seniors. In order to keep the center functioning, the board has taken a three-pronged approach that will hopefully enable us to find a permanent building and organizational operating expenses that will include . . ."

Beside her, Ted stifled a yawn.

"Donations have already been coming in, and we've applied for a community improvement grant from the VanderHauw Foundation."

Ted leaned toward Liv. "Never amazes me how Gilbert manages to take credit for everything, even though your contacts and grant application were what got us on Vander-Hauw's radar."

Liv shrugged. "As long as it gets the community center up and running, I don't care who takes credit for it."

Mayor Worley cleared his throat. "In addition, the board came up with the idea of holding a contest to decide what design would become the official Celebration Bay Haunted House, whose official opening will kick off this year's Halloween festivities. We had a whopping one hundred entries, with all entry fees going to the donation fund. A panel of five judges adjudicated every entry, no matter how small.

"I'd like the judges to stand." The mayor gestured to where three of the four town trustees—Rufus Cobb, Roscoe Jackson, and Jeremiah Atkins—were sitting in a row. As usual, the fourth trustee was AWOL.

"Chaz didn't even manage to get here for the community center?" Liv asked, disgusted.

Ted looked over the crowd. "I expect he's here somewhere. See. Over there, standing in the back opposite us."

Liv looked to where Ted indicated and came eye to eye with Chaz Bristow, owner and editor of the *Celebration Bay Clarion*. Liv's nemesis . . . and sometimes her reluctant partner in crime solving.

He grinned at her and she looked away.

"And two members of the business community." The mayor gestured to two well-dressed women sitting side by side at the end of the row. "Janine Tudor and Lucille Foster . . . Ladies." The two women waved.

Chaz Bristow slipped up beside Liv.

Liv felt the jolt of interest that she always tried to ignore when she was around him. He was too good-looking for his own good, at least according to Liv's landladies, Ida and Edna Zimmerman.

He was handsome, all right, with straight features, a firm if sometimes unshaven jaw, and blond hair that would be more appropriate on someone who lived outdoors in the sun instead of someone who preferred sleeping under a newspaper on the couch in his office.

Tonight he was wearing a light hunting jacket, a plaid scarf, and no hat. His blond hair looked less groomed than usual in the uneven light. But there was definitely something charismatic about the man.

He was infuriating; yo-yoed between out-and-out smarmy wastrel and intense, justice-seeking reporter, always with a serious surfer dude attitude. Infuriating, but appealing—

Appealing? When she was out of her mind and hallucinating.

Liv pulled herself together. "Why aren't you up there with the other trustees?"

"Three reasons."

"Really. What are they?"

"Because I own and run the local paper. I can't appear to take sides."

"Ha. You mean you just didn't want to be bothered."

Chaz shrugged.

"And the other two?"

He nodded toward the stage. "You're looking at them."

Liv frowned.

Ted leaned over. "He's talking about Lucille and Janine."

"Yep," Chaz said. "Amazing that the two of them can sit side by side without tearing each other's eyes out. The mayor must have a death wish. I sure don't."

"I take it they don't like each other."

Chaz gave her a deadpan look.

She turned to Ted.

He managed an even more deadpan expression.

"And now I'd like to introduce Lucille Foster, chairwoman of the judging panel. Lucille?"

Lucille stood gracefully; Janine remained seated with a tight smile on her face. Lucille was tall and elegantly dressed, in an off-white Burberry trench coat with a burnt orange paisley shawl looped over her shoulder. And the highest heels Liv had seen—or worn—since Manhattan. Hers were now residing in the deepest, darkest corner of her closet.

The highest and *the most expensive,* Liv thought as Lucille's red soles caught the light.

The chairwoman edged the mayor over and spoke into the microphone. "Thank you, Mayor Worley. I am so honored to be a part of this great fund-raiser. We here in Celebration Bay care about our town and about each other. That feeling is what makes us so special, and you've shown your caring by your donations to this worthy cause—the Celebration Bay Community Center."

While Lucille began explaining the guidelines of the contest and how the entries were judged, Liv looked over the crowd. It was small in the scheme of things. Mostly local people who supported the need for a new community center.

Liv had hoped that Jonathon Preston, director of development for the VanderHauw Foundation, would make it for the ceremony, but as it was he'd had to sandwich them in between a trip to a daycare center in Thailand and an afternoon music program in Detroit.

Too bad. Jon would have gotten a kick out of the spectacle. And Liv would have gotten a kick out of his enjoyment. Jon was a former colleague of hers from her Manhattan days, and they'd briefly been something more than friends. He was great to work with, indefatigable and energetic. They'd had some fun times, and Liv was looking forward to seeing him again.

". . . by the generous donation of . . ." Lucille Foster began to read off a list of people who had agreed to match the prize money offered to the winner of the Official Celebration Bay Haunted House. "All proceeds to go to the new community center. Already we have raised twenty thousand dollars."

Applause, and a few *woots.*

"Ten thousand will go to the winner of the contest to help offset expenses and operating costs. All ticket proceeds for the first Halloween will go back into the community center donation fund. Each of the runners-up will win five hundred dollars to use as they see fit.

"I want to thank everyone for their generosity and let you know that donations may be dropped off at town hall, sent to the mayor's office, or dropped in one of the many receptacles around town. Now, Mayor Worley, if you'll announce the three finalists."

The mayor stepped back up to the lectern as Lucille returned to her seat.

Mayor Worley cleared his throat. "There is one more person I would like to thank particularly . . ."

Lucille paused, then turned back to the podium, her smile managing to appear gracious and humble at the same time. It was impressive.

"Mrs. Amanda Marlton-Crosby," the mayor continued.

Lucille froze in place, her smile unwavering. Then, recovering herself, she smiled more broadly and sat down. Beside her, Janine Tudor didn't even try to hide her surprise or her delight that Lucille had been superseded by another.

"Amanda," the mayor continued, "has generously donated the full ten thousand dollars for the prize money so that the community center can keep all of the proceeds gathered thus far."

Applause and whistles followed. The three male judges exchanged looks. Janine sat ramrod straight. Next to her, Lucille crossed her legs and continued to smile, but her foot jiggled with perturbation, the red soles of her expensive shoes blinking like a stoplight among the ceramic pumpkins.

"Wow," Liv said. "Why didn't we know about this?"

Ted shrugged. "Does it matter?"

"No. It's just really a surprise."

"From the look of things," Chaz said, "a surprise to the judges, too."

The mayor stretched out his arm. "Amanda? Will you come up and present the check to the winner?" The mayor applauded into the microphone and everyone joined in as Amanda Marlton-Crosby climbed the steps to the stage.

She was in her thirties, Liv guessed, with spare, plain features and brown hair pulled back in a ponytail. She was wearing slacks and a red plaid car coat. Not how Liv would have chosen to dress if she had been a wealthy heiress, especially next to Lucille and Janine, who always dressed for the occasion. Maybe Amanda Marlton-Crosby had gone for a totally different look knowing she couldn't compete.

The mayor adjusted the microphone so that Amanda could speak into it.

"Thank you, Mayor Worley," she said in a voice so low that the entire audience leaned forward to hear. The mayor moved her closer to the microphone. "It is my honor and my pleasure to be here tonight and to be able to support the contest and its admirable goal of aiding the community center." She had none of the panache of either of the other two women onstage, but evidently she had money to spare.

"But I know you're all anxious to get out of the cold so . . . Mr. Mayor?"

The mayor fumbled inside his pocket, checked another, and finally pulled out an envelope. "Had you going, didn't I?" Chuckling, he opened the envelope.

"The three finalists are . . . Patty Wainwright of Miss Patty's Learn and Grow Center, for her Family-Friendly Ghosts and Goblins."

Cheers, whistles, and applause.

"Ernie Bolton's Monster Mansion."

More applause and several woots.

"And Barry Lindquist's Museum of Yankee Horrors."

"Way to go, Barry," someone yelled, followed by more applause.

The mayor smiled and nodded as the three finalists climbed the steps to the stage and stopped in a line, looking hopeful. All three were dressed in Halloween colors: Patty Wainwright wore a black skirt and a pumpkin-colored car coat, her hair plaited in two braids, Addams Family style; Ernie wore an orange and black striped sweater and bright orange earmuffs; and Barry Lindquist had added a jaunty orange tam to his dark green jacket and jeans.

The mayor held up his hand for silence, which for once everyone obeyed. "And now . . . the winner of ten thousand dollars and the title of Official Celebration Bay Haunted House—"

"Devil worshippers!"

The mayor broke off midsentence. "Who yelled that?"

"Repent, ye idolaters, or face eternal damnation!"

Everyone looked around for the source of the rant.

Off to the side, there was a discreet movement as three men dressed in plainclothes surrounded a man dressed completely in black.

"Burn in—" The rest of the sentence was cut off as the men surrounded him and moved just as easily out of the crowd, taking the miscreant with them. Shocked silence reigned.

"They are efficient," Ted whispered to Liv.

"Very," Liv agreed. Bayside Security. Liv had hired the security firm months ago on a permanent basis. They were good, inconspicuous, kept an eagle-eye watch over the growing crowds attracted to the town's events, and worked quickly to prevent disruption and remove troublemakers.

And with their military training, they had disappeared as quickly and as stealthily as they had appeared.

"Shades of Big Brother," Chaz intoned.

Liv ignored him, but had to admit their efficiency sometimes bordered on the spooky.

"Well, well." Mayor Worley laughed nervously. "Some of our folks are starting trick-or-treating early this year." The mayor cleared his throat. "Now, where were we? Oh yes. And the prize of ten thousand dollars goes to . . ." He handed the paper to Amanda Marlton-Crosby.

She leaned into the microphone. "Goes to Barry Lindquist for his Museum of Yankee Horrors."

Applause, whistles, and yells followed.

Barry Lindquist stepped forward, bowing and smiling. The mayor stood by as Amanda presented Barry with an envelope.

"Congratulations, Barry," the mayor said, pumping his free hand. "The Museum of Yankee Horrors is Celebration Bay's official haunted house."

The mayor announced the second- and third-place winners and presented them with checks.

"And now Joss Waterbury of Waterbury Orchards is serving free hot cider and donuts on the town hall steps."

While the mayor and Amanda Marlton-Crosby congratulated Barry and posed for publicity photographs, the other two finalists left the stage and the crowd began to disperse. A few people stopped by the stage to offer congratulations.

"Why aren't you taking photos for the newspaper?" Liv asked.

Chaz shrugged. "Oh." He looked around like he'd misplaced his camera, then reached in his pocket and pulled out his cell phone. He held it out toward the band shell and snapped a photo. "There," he said, and slid it back into his pocket.

Liv cut a look to Ted.

"When are you going to learn? He's probably already set up something with one of the other photographers."

"You're no fun," Chaz said.

"Let's go congratulate the winner and the finalists and thank Mrs. Marlton-Crosby."

By the time they reached the front, a crowd had gathered around the winners. The judges were chatting with the mayor and Amanda Marlton-Crosby.

Patty Wainwright was accepting congratulations for third place. "Isn't it neat? I'm going to keep the Happy Haunted House open for the younger kids. They need a fun, less-scary place to celebrate Halloween."

Ernie, however, stood off to the side, where he was clenching and unclenching his fists and glaring at the judges, Lucille in particular. He seemed hardly aware of the people who stopped to congratulate him on a job well done.

Mayor Worley motioned Liv over.

"Liv, I don't believe you've met Amanda Marlton-Crosby."

"Not formally. Thank you for such a generous gift, the kids and seniors will really appreciate it." Up close, Amanda seemed even smaller and more nondescript than she did on the stage, but Liv could see that although her clothes were rather simple and shapeless, they were designer.

The two women touched hands. "It's my pleasure. Now I must really go. I have a guest staying with me for the weekend. Rod should be around somewhere."

On cue, Rod Crosby, tall and athletic, appeared out of the dispersing crowd and came to stand at his wife's side. There couldn't be a wider contrast between husband and wife, her mouse to his dark-haired Adonis.

Liv didn't know Amanda's husband. She knew he oversaw the running of the fish camp where many of the locals kept their boats. The camp had once been the Marlton family's private marina but was now open to the public. It seemed like an odd thing for the husband of a multi-bazillion-dollar heiress to do. But fishermen, Liv had learned, were a large and diverse group.

Still, she had to stop herself from thinking that he must have married Amanda for her money. That was such a cliché. Maybe they were madly in love. And considering the way he put his arm around her shoulders and leaned in to kiss her cheek, Liv knew she should make an adjustment to her first impressions.

"It's getting chilly, dear. Let's get you home."

For a nanosecond, it looked like Amanda might demur, but then she just smiled and the two of them walked away.

Liv turned back to the others, who were all talking animatedly. Amanda Marlton-Crosby had just dropped ten K and wandered off into the night. And no one seemed to have noticed.

Weird, she thought, and turned her attention to the winner, Barry Lindquist.

"Congratulations, Barry," Liv said.

Barry smiled, showing big teeth. He was a large man, barrel-chested, but fit. Fortysomething and generally congenial. He'd been divorced for several years and was an object of interest among some of the single women in town. "Thank you. Thank you. It was a haul. But I'm real proud of the way it turned out."

"Well, you should be."

Liv smiled at the big man, who smiled back.

Finally Ted broke in. "Where did you get hold of all those mannequins?"

"Here and there. Heck, that was the hardest part, except finding shoes that would fit, especially for the real old-fashioned scenes. Those people sure had little feet."

Ted nodded.

"And the fun just goes on and on," Chaz said under his breath.

Liv shot him a look.

"Well, you did a beautiful job," Lucille Foster said.

Next to her, Janine looked bored. And maybe even perturbed at her fellow judge, Liv suspected.

Janine was used to being the center of attention, and made a point to be the best dressed at every function. But she'd been topped by Lucille Foster tonight. Next to Lucille's trench coat and Louboutin shoes, Janine's camel-colored three-quarter-length coat and three-inch black heels looked uninspired.

The way Janine looked at Lucille as she held court among the male judges, the mayor, and Ted and Chaz made Liv cringe. She had cause to recognize that expression. It had been aimed her way on more than one occasion.

"Ernie," Ted said. "Come on over so we can congratulate you, too. Excellent job."

"Yes, Ernie, very good," Lucille said.

Ernie shuffled over from where he'd been standing off to the side. "If it was so good, why didn't I win?"

Everyone stared.

"Really, Ernie . . ." Ted began.

Ernie turned to Lucille. "You said I was going to win. You promised."

Lucille shook her head. "I never said that, Ernie. I said you had a good chance of winning. And you did. You came in second out of over one hundred entries. That's something to be very proud of."

"Anyone with a pumpkin on their porch entered the contest to help out the community center. *I* went all out."

"And you can keep Monster Mansion open to the public, too," the mayor added.

"For all the good it will do me."

"Ernie." Lucille stepped toward him. "Don't be like that. It was a difficult decision, but the judges agreed."

"I'm sure they all did. But I know why Barry won."

"Hey, it was fair and square," Barry said, and pushed out his chest.

"Oh Lord," said Ted, but Chaz beat him to the two men, stepping in between them just as Ernie raised his fist.

Chaz caught him by the wrist and held him fast. "Just cool it, Ernie."

"Get your hands off me. I'm leaving." Ernie yanked his arm away and spun around. As he did, his shoulder bumped against Lucille, who staggered backward into the other judges. The shawl draped across her shoulders fell to the ground.

Ernie didn't slow down.

"Are you alright?" the mayor asked.

"Yes, I'm perfectly fine," Lucille said in a silkily calm voice. "Unfortunate that he feels that way, but we all agreed on the winner."

"True," the three male judges agreed.

The men had formed a semicircle of concern around Lucille. Janine stood by, looking ready to spit nails.

As the only person who seemed to notice the scarf was

still on the ground, Liv picked it up and brushed it off. It was a soft pashmina wool, and while it had just looked burnt orange at a distance, up close Liv could see an intricate pattern of gold and brown. She took a peek at the label. *Missoni.* Liv pushed down the little geyser of envy she felt erupting in her shallow little heart.

She handed it back to Lucille, who looked surprised. "Oh, thank you, hon."

Behind her, Chaz made a face.

"Not at all." *Hon,* Liv added to herself.

"Well, I had better get going," Jeremiah said. "Bankers' hours. Can I see you to your car, Lucille?"

"Or I can accompany you?" the mayor offered.

"Why, thank you both, but my husband, Carson, is here. Oh there he is now. Good night, all." She struck off across the park.

All the men stared after her.

Janine rolled her eyes.

Liv and Janine never agreed on anything. Janine didn't even like her. It was heartening to think that there was someone in town whom Janine liked even less.

"Are you guys going back to work?" Chaz asked Liv and Ted. "Or are you going for cider?"

"Both," Liv said. "And I want to find out what happened to the heckler."

"I'm sure your big marine has him being tortured in the basement, never to see the light of day."

"A.K. is not *my* marine, he's the head of Bayside Security, and I might point out, he's been doing a creditable job."

"Has he now? I love it when you use all those big words. So why don't we ditch the free cider and all go over to the pub for a burger?"

Liv was going to say no, but her stomach growled at the mere mention of food.

Ted laughed. "That sounded like a yes to me."

They walked around the band shell to the street, and

reached the sidewalk just in time to see Rod and Amanda standing by the passenger door of a silver Mercedes that was idling in the street.

"Really, Amanda?"

Amanda Marlton-Crosby shrugged and looked at the ground.

"Just get in," Rod said, and opened the car door. "I won't be long," he said. "You two will just gab about the good old days all night. Have fun. I'm going to have a couple of beers with the guys and I'll walk home. 'Night, honey."

He practically pushed her inside and closed the car door. Stood by while it drove away, then walked off down the street in the opposite direction of McCready's Pub.

"Guess he's not going to the pub," Liv said.

"No," Ted said.

"But we are," Chaz said, and hustled them across the street.

"Fine," Liv said. "And while we're there, you can tell me why Ernie only went after Lucille instead of the other judges, and why no one told me about the ten-thousand-dollar donation from Amanda Marlton-Crosby."

Chapter Two

....

McCready's Pub was right across the street from the back of the band shell and on a corner of one of the side streets that ended at the square. Since it was on the main drag, the owner had accentuated the Irish look with surface timbers and stucco. A neon sign hung like a marquee over the entrance.

It was a local hangout, loud, boisterous, and occasionally the scene of a good old-fashioned Yankee brawl. Generally late at night when the vacationing families with children were all safely tucked away in their hotel rooms. Fortunately, it was still early on a weeknight.

Even so, the bar was filling up pretty quickly.

"The Monster Mash" was playing at manageable decibels when they entered the pub, and a string of light-up skeletons and pumpkins danced across the mirror behind the bar. Someone had made little beer bottles and placed one in each skeleton's hand. Liv never ceased to be amazed at the lengths that Celebration Bay residents would go to celebrate holidays.

"Wow, I expected the place to be packed," Liv said over the music.

"It will be, as soon as they run out of free cider and donuts at town hall," Chaz said. "Let's grab that table in the corner."

As soon as the three of them sat down, a bar waitress sidled over and smiled at Chaz. He was like the pied piper to waitresses. They nearly fell over themselves to wait on him.

They each ordered burgers and beer even though it was only six thirty and normally Liv would try to get in another couple hours of work before calling it a day.

"What a night," Ted said as soon as the waitress had gone.

"Poor Ernie," Liv said. "He's over there at the bar all by himself. I don't get why he went off on Lucille. It was a committee decision."

"Maybe," Ted said. "But she was the chairwoman."

Chas laughed and exchanged a look with Ted.

"What's so funny?" Liv asked. "Is there something going on that I should know about? I noticed a few undercurrents . . ."

"You call that undercurrents?" asked Chaz incredulously. "Looked close to full blown to me. First there was Janine stuck in her seat while Lucille struts her stuff across the stage. You could practically see the smoke coming out of her ears. Then, out of the blue, Amanda Marlton-Crosby waltzes on, obliviously upstaging Lucille. I thought Lucille would have a diva attack right there onstage. I swear it was worth the price of admission."

"It was free," Liv pointed out.

Chaz looked surprised. "Yep, and that's about what it was worth."

The beers arrived, and while the waitress took a second to make eyes at Chaz, Liv took a sip of her beer. It was malty and cold, a product of a local microbrewery that gave Liv, a wine drinker by choice, a new appreciation for the foamy drink.

The door opened and two of the judges, Roscoe Jackson and Rufus Cobb, walked in and stopped by their table.

"Great evening," Liv said.

"Yes, it was," Roscoe said. "And Amanda Marlton-Crosby's donation has really started off the fund-raising with a bang."

"Would you like to join us? We can pull up an extra chairs."

"Thank you, but we just stopped in for quick drink," Rufus said. "I have to get back to the B-and-B."

They made their way over to the bar and took the two seats next to Ernie Bolton, who looked at them and moved away farther along the bar.

"Oh, Ernie, don't be such a poor sport," Rufus said. "Coming in second is an honor in itself."

Ernie glared at the two newcomers. "It was a setup. Barry's people don't even move. They just sit there like the dummies they are."

Ted sighed. "Oh Ernie, Ernie, Ernie."

Ernie pushed off the stool and confronted the newcomers. "Who did he get to? Lucille? Janine? Thinks he's some big stud. Which one was it?"

Roscoe slid off the stool and turned to face Ernie. He had to look up, since he stood just over five feet and Ernie was close to six.

"There were five of us judges. So it's no use blaming one of the ladies. You might as well blame me."

"Or me," Rufus added, jumping off his stool and coming to stand beside Roscoe.

"You two didn't vote for me? And you call yourselves friends?"

"The voting was confidential."

"Maybe somebody's vote was more important than the others."

"That's a dang lie," Rufus said. "Nobody outside the panel of judges knows how the vote went. Barry's entry won by a majority. So there's no use in blaming anybody."

Ernie fisted his hands, ready for a fight. "If I find out that no-good Barry Lindquist bribed the judges . . ."

"You'll do what?" Roscoe asked.

Beside him, Rufus chewed on his mustache, something he did when he was nervous, worried, or upset.

Ted groaned. "Not tonight." He stood up, but Mike Mc-Cready was already coming around the bar.

"Ernie, I don't want no trouble in here. Go home. Cool off."

Ernie's nostrils flared and he reached into his coat pocket. Liv braced herself, but he merely pulled out his earmuffs, shoved them over his ears, and stormed toward the exit door.

"Another disaster averted," Ted said.

"What was all the innuendo about Lucille and Janine?" Liv asked. "Or dare I ask?"

Chaz choked on his beer, and Ted said, "Let's just say they aren't the best of friends."

"I got that part. But why?"

"Beside the fact that Lucille's giving Janine a run for her money?" Chaz said.

Liv's mouth opened. "In real estate?"

"In men, my dear." Ted shook his head. "They nearly had a knock-down-drag-out at the manicurist's last week."

"Are you kidding me?" Liv asked. "But Lucille is married." She didn't ask who the fight was over, though Janine had been after Chaz for as long as Liv had lived in Celebration Bay.

The waitress appeared at the table. "Now who wants another beer?" The guys ordered another round. Liv stuck to the one she had. The waitress winked at Liv. "Have you ever noticed how guys sometimes make the best gossipers?"

"I'm noticing tonight," Liv said.

"Hey," said Chaz. "We consider that 'news' around here."

The waitress gave him a saucy look and went to get their beers.

"Yeah," Liv said. "It must be a slow day at the Four-H if you're reporting catfights."

Chaz shrugged.

"So how does Ernie fit into the mix?"

"Don't know that he does. Except . . ." Ted shrugged. "Ernie really needs the prize money."

"But it wasn't Lucille's fault he didn't win."

"No, but he might blame her husband."

"How so?"

"Because Ernie is broke, and when he tried to take out a loan, First Celebration Bank turned him down. So he went to Lucille's husband, Carson Foster. Carson is the CEO of the Mercantile Investment Trust."

"I never heard of it," Liv said.

"Because it's an *investment* bank." Chaz grinned at her. "Got any major funds to invest?"

"I might," Liv said. "No." She sipped her beer.

Ted shook his head. "Don't feel bad, Liv. Neither does Chaz."

"All my capital is tied up in the newspaper."

His two companions just looked at him.

"What there is of it . . . which isn't much . . . Well, it's hard to support myself and my paper and my numerous charitable endeavors by taking people out fishing. Especially when some of them stiff me."

He smiled complacently at Liv.

"I told you I would pay you."

"Too late. I'm already broke."

"You're always broke," Liv pointed out.

Chaz shook his head. "But not as broke as poor Ernie."

"Anyway," Ted said. "That's the reason we're losing the community center building. Ernie owes back taxes. He has to sell the building and his mother's house across the street from it, where he constructed the Monster Mansion. But without a loan, he can't pay his taxes and he can't sell unless he pays them or finds someone to pay his asking price *and* his taxes."

"Or wins ten thousand dollars in a haunted house contest," Liv said.

"Exactly," Chaz said. "And that opportunity just flew out the window."

"Pretty much," Ted agreed. "Unless Barry defaults before the official opening next weekend, and that seems unlikely."

Famous last words, Liv thought, and knocked the underside of the wooden table.

The pub filled up and they ate their burgers without much talking since the decibel level rose with the onslaught of patrons.

They left to the pulsing rhythm of "Thriller," and stopped at the corner.

"I guess you guys will be working tomorrow even though it's Saturday," Chaz said.

"It's one of our many busy seasons," Ted said. "Besides, Liv is a taskmaster."

They parted ways, Ted to pick up his car at town hall, Chaz to wherever he was going, and Liv to walk home.

That was one of the things she liked most about living in Celebration Bay. She could walk almost anywhere, anytime, without dealing with car exhaust, rattling subway noise, or muggers.

The Victorian house where her landladies lived was dark. It was later than Liv realized and they must have already gone to bed. Which meant they had probably dropped off Whiskey at Liv's carriage house at the back of the drive.

The sisters loved to babysit her Westie terrier, Whiskey. They'd happily take him every day, but Liv didn't want to take advantage of their generosity. Besides, she loved taking him to work with her. And Ted would complain, since he and Whiskey had become best buds.

Liv walked down the driveway, fishing for her key in her messenger bag. Before she even opened the door, she could hear Whiskey on the other side.

As soon as she opened it, he bounded forward like he'd been ignored for days.

"You don't fool me," she told him as he bounced around

her. "You're spoiled rotten. I hope you appreciate all the attention you get."

"Aarf," he said, and took off for the shrubbery. He came back a minute later and trotted inside.

Liv followed him in. "I'm beat. How about you, big guy? Have a perfectly pampered day?"

"Aarf," Whiskey said.

"I thought so." Liv hung up her coat and tossed her keys on the foyer table, then went into her cozy living room, where she fired up her iPad and checked her email. Whiskey snuggled down on her feet and, with a huge yawn, went to sleep.

When Liv's alarm rang the next morning, the sun was streaming through the window, making a dappled pattern across her down comforter. Whiskey was asleep on his plaid doggie bed. He looked so content Liv felt a pang knowing that she was about to trick him into going running with her.

Whiskey loved to run, could run for hours, but only on his own terms. A quick circuit of asphalt with no stops for smelling or claiming territory was not in his game plan. But a girl needed her exercise, and she was getting less and less of it as the winter holidays grew closer together.

Liv pushed the covers away. Whiskey opened an eye, snuffled, yawned, and pushed to his feet before padding out of the bedroom to wait for her by the kitchen door. She followed him down the short hall and let him out to a postage-stamp garden behind her landladies' well-tended perennial borders. Then she retraced her steps to the bedroom to dress in fall running gear.

When he barked at the back door, she greeted him with a dog biscuit and his leash.

If dogs could roll their eyes, Whiskey would have. As it was, he just looked forlorn, then sat and allowed her to attach the leash to his collar.

Two minutes later, they were on the sidewalk, Liv stretching

and Whiskey exploring the shrubbery at the front of her landladies' house.

They started off down the street, Liv concentrating first
on her stride and breathing, then letting her eyes roam over
the decorated houses as they passed. It was an occupational
hazard, multitasking when you didn't even want to task at
all. But this was the perfect way to get in exercise and an
overview of the upcoming festivities all at once.

The residents' enthusiasm for holidays and special events
never seemed to flag. This morning in the full daylight, the
decorated houses looked colorful and inviting with their cornstalks and hay bales, many recycled from the harvest festival.
Elaborately carved pumpkins sat on every porch. Grinning
scarecrows rubbed shoulders with grinning skeletons and black
cats with arching backs. Ghosts hung from the bare branches
of trees. Gravestones littered the yards. They all looked benign
in the morning light.

But each afternoon, as soon as it grew dark, the strings of
orange lights would come on, jack-o'-lantern candles were
lit, and witches were set in motion while ghosts danced in the
wind.

This morning the sky was blue and all was calm. Whiskey trotted along beside her. Since she'd chosen the middle
of the quiet street for her run, there wasn't that much to stop
and smell, but when she turned the corner, the loyal dog
rebelled. This was new territory for him, with new things
to sniff and claim. Usually they went the other way to work
or to run, but today their route would take them past the
winning haunted house entry, just so Liv could take a closer
look and make sure everything was in order.

Not that she was a control freak or anything. It just paid
to be prepared.

Liv slowed down for Whiskey but kept jogging until she
came to Barry Lindquist's Museum of Yankee Horrors two
blocks later.

It was the perfect-looking haunted house, complete with

gables and turrets covered in graying, weather-beaten shingles. Once a boardinghouse, it had sat empty for the past several years, Barry being either unable or unwilling to sell it. Liv imagined the knee-high wrought iron fence was original, and the even higher weeds were very effective. But she'd contracted for the land surrounding the house and parking lot as well as a vacant lot behind the parking lot to be mowed, and apparently the landscapers had not been by. The weeds had only gotten higher.

Ambiance was one thing, but unsightliness and neglect were something else. She came to a stop, unzipped her arm pocket, and extracted her phone. Let the leash out so Whiskey could snuffle at leisure while she took a couple photos of the overgrowth.

There had been caution tape over the entrance to the newly repaved parking lot the last time she'd been here. Now half the tape was lying on the ground.

She stepped over the tape and walked along the edge of the parking lot, taking photos as she went. Nothing had been done. She'd have to have a little talk with the landscapers.

She'd reached the back of the property and was taking a last photo of the vacant lot when Whiskey yanked on the leash.

"All right. I'm done. Let's get going."

Whiskey barked and strained at the leash, but in the opposite direction.

"Oh, all right, two more minutes, but if you get burrs all stuck in your coat, don't complain to me when you have to go to the Woofery for grooming."

She let out the leash again and Whiskey, ignoring her threat, pranced happily into the brush to ferret out unsuspecting small animals or discarded fast-food wrappers.

Sure enough he came back a minute later with something in his mouth. Something huge. A bone. An arm. A human arm.

Liv's eyes widened and her stomach lurched—she froze to the spot as Whiskey lovingly laid the arm at her feet. She swayed even as she realized that it wasn't a real human arm, but a mannequin.

"What the heck?" she said, miffed at herself for being so gullible, and outright angry that someone was using the lot as a dumping ground.

She looked back at the house. Had Barry ended up with extra parts and dumped them rather than disposing of them properly? Or . . .

A much worse thought struck her. Ernie had been pretty angry last night, but surely . . . Ted's words rang in her mind: *Unless Barry defaults . . .*

"Heel." She shortened the leash and walked to the edge of the empty lot. She could see what looked like a clothed torso farther in. And a boot not too far from that. Not a dumping ground for garbage. It looked like the museum might have been looted. She walked along the side of the house, practically pulling a recalcitrant Whiskey with her. No signs of a break-in.

They continued around to the back of the house. And there it was: a shattered window leading to the cellar. It may have been broken before, or more recently—like last night. Either way it needed to be repaired. She climbed the back steps and knocked on the door.

She knew Barry didn't live on the premises, but she also didn't want to surprise any looters or squatters that might be inside.

No one answered, so she turned the knob. The door opened. Damn.

She stepped back, closed it again, and went down the steps. Didn't stop until she was back on the sidewalk out front. No way was she going inside alone. One year of living in Celebration Bay had taught her more about staying safe from lawbreakers than an entire lifetime in Manhattan. Go figure.

She opened her contact list, found Barry's home number. He answered on the fourth ring.

"Yeah."

"Barry, this is Liv Montgomery. I'm at your museum. Did you leave any mannequin parts out in the vacant lot?"

"What? Why would I do something like that?"

"I don't know, but on further investigation I noticed a cellar window was broken."

"Somebody broke in? So help me, if that Ernie Bolton has vandalized my museum— I'll be right over. Stay there." He hung up.

"Yes, sir," Liv said to her disconnected phone. "I think we might have woke him up, Whiskey. He sounds kind of cranky. If it's a false alarm, we'll buy him breakfast."

At the sound of breakfast, Whiskey sat and looked at her expectantly. "Sorry, guy. There's been a little change in plans."

Barry Lindquist's truck pulled up to the curb five minutes later. He jumped out and began riffling through a huge ring of keys as he hurried toward Liv, who was waiting on the front steps.

Definitely woke him up, she thought. His chin was covered in red stubble.

"Did you call the cops?"

"Not yet. I thought we should check to see if someone had really broken in. The back door was unlocked."

"What? No way." He leapt up to the porch and unlocked the front door.

Liv and Whiskey followed him inside.

The foyer was suitably eerie, especially with the lights off. Even when Barry flicked the lights on, it was still pretty macabre. There was a skeleton clothed in rags sitting in a rocking chair, a knife dripping blood sitting in her lap.

Psycho? Wasn't the Bates Motel in Oregon? Evidently not anymore.

Spiderwebs draped over the banister of what once must have been a lovely staircase; now its dark wood was dull and dry looking. Liv made a mental note to have Ted check with the fire marshal that the building had passed all safety inspections.

A little late now. The mayor had decided on this contest as a way to raise money for the community center and had convinced the other trustees to go along with it before he'd consulted Liv. Which was fine, but Liv would have rather been consulted during the planning session instead of playing catch-up ever since.

Barry was tromping toward the parlor, so Liv left the entry skeleton and prepared for whatever she might see in the next room.

It was a disaster. What had been set pieces days before were now mere shambles. The upholstery was slashed, and the mannequins dismantled and strewn across the room.

Barry let out a howl. "I'll kill that so-and-so! I swear he'll be sorry he ever messed with me."

He spun around, nearly knocking Liv over, and disappeared into the next room. The dining room had been a scene right out of classic horror movies and, more recently, the *Beautiful Creatures* movie, with a table that spun around until the diners whirred into blurs. It had been very cleverly staged and mechanized; there were no diners now.

The table at least appeared unharmed; the chairs were overturned, but whatever body parts hadn't been bolted to the seats had been ripped literally limb to limb and were nowhere to be seen. Which meant there might be a lot more mannequin bodies out in the vacant lot.

"I'll call the police. They might be able to find some clues as to who the perpetrator is if we don't touch anything."

"Oh, I know who did this, all right. That . . . Well, he won't get away with it. If he thinks he'll win by default, that dirty, low-down— Well, he won't. I'll get this place back up and running if it's the last thing I do."

"Still, I think we should wait outside." Liv maneuvered Barry onto the front porch while she made the call.

He didn't stop but strode straight across the parking lot.

"Barry, wait!" Liv hurried after him while she waited for

the police dispatcher to answer. She gave her information and hung up just as Barry stepped into the vacant lot.

The weeds came nearly to his waist. He leaned over, disappearing for a moment, then reappeared carrying a torso wearing a union army coat. He laid it carefully on the ground and started back in.

"I don't think you—"

Barry waded through the grasses, ignoring her.

An old town car passed down the street and turned right into the parking lot of the old theater that was directly across the street. Henry Gallantine, former child star and director of the current production of the Celebration Bay Players, got out. Seeing Liv and Barry, he waved, then came across the street and over to where Liv stood.

"You two are out early this morning. What's afoot?"

"Someone broke into Barry's museum and vandalized the place," Liv said.

"Oh, dear. And threw the pieces outside?"

"So it appears."

"Is it salvageable?"

"I don't know. I've called the police. Not that there's much they'll be able to do."

"No, not usually with these breaking-and-entering cases."

"Barry is in shock and angry, but he said he's going to get the museum up and running again."

"Then he will. You can't keep a good Yankee down. I'll be right back." Henry trotted off in the direction of the theater. He was still very fit. Insisted he had always done his own stunts and was ready, willing, and able to do them again if his agent called. Which so far hadn't happened.

He went inside the theater and Liv turned back to see Barry bringing out several legs, some still wearing shoes, some bare.

"They're everywhere," Barry said. He sounded close to tears. "What am I going to do?"

A commotion down the street made Liv turn around. A group of people had just come out of the theater, pushing two platform handcarts.

Leading the troupe was Henry Gallantine, and right behind him was Liv's assistant, Ted Driscoll. There were several other people, who Liv guessed were cast members.

"Yankee ingenuity," she said. Even though she was nowhere near being considered a local—her best friend BeBe had been here for nearly thirteen years and she was still considered an outsider—Liv's heart swelled with pride at her neighbors.

"The cast of *Little Shop of Horrors* has come to your aid!" Henry announced.

Barry's jaw dropped. "Uh, thanks, Henry."

"Now, careful troupe, treat these somewhat historically accurate figures as if they were your own parents." The group spread out, and Henry began placing the parts they had already gathered onto one of the handcarts.

One of the actresses hesitated. Unlike the others who were wearing jeans and sweatshirts, she was dressed in a blue fifties prom dress beneath a gray hoodie. They must have gotten her in the middle of a fitting.

She frowned at Henry. "I thought we were going to run through the first act this morning."

"Yes, indeed. Rehearse away while you work." Henry made an expansive gesture. "All the world's your stage, Marla Jean. Use it as you will."

"What if there are wild animals in there?"

"Many hands make light work," he said, ignoring her concern, and pushing her toward the vacant lot. As they reached the edge of the pavement, he lifted his head and followed her into the weeds.

"I don't know which one of his movies he's channeling, but this is the most energy I've seen out of this group since rehearsals started," Ted said.

"You're in the play?"

"Guilty as charged." Her assistant grinned at her. This

morning he was wearing a leather jacket and a brown fedora with an orange band and feather.

"You didn't say anything. I know you have a great singing voice." He'd taught Whiskey to sing every holiday song there was. Unfortunately, Whiskey's idea of singing never passed the yowl stage, as far as Liv was concerned, but it only egged Ted on. And what Whiskey lacked in ability, he made up for with his enthusiasm. "Can you act, too?"

"Need you ask?"

"I guess not." So far she hadn't seen anything Ted couldn't do.

"I'm just the voice of the narrator. Actually, it's going to be taped for the performances, but I told Henry I would help out when I had the chance. But I draw the line at gathering body parts from a vacant lot. You never know what you might find back there."

Liv shivered. "Don't."

"I was thinking skunks and other vermin."

"Still, eww."

They stood on the tarmac watching the group while waiting for the police. The carts filled up with body parts—arms, legs, heads—piled on top of each other. One of the young men carried the pantalooned and stockinged legs of a character that Liv couldn't even guess at. *Bluebeard?*

Another young man waltzed out with a torso dressed as a pilgrim.

He twirled around and placed her upright on the pile of limbs, then bowed and turned a cheeky grin on the others. "I thought I'd give her a little thrill. God knows those puritans had no fun."

A police cruiser stopped at the curb and Officer Meese jumped out.

"Heard there was a break-in," Meese said to Liv and Ted since no one else paid him any mind. "What are these people doing?"

"There was a break-in at the Museum of Yankee Horrors."

"The contest winner?"

"I'm afraid so," Liv said. "The whole place has been vandalized, the mannequins were dismantled and thrown out in the grass. Some people from the theater group came over to help gather whatever they could find. Barry's hoping that he'll be able to reconstruct it before the official opening on the weekend."

"Huh." Meese looked over the group that had filled the first cart and was working on the second. "Wow."

"That's almost all of them," Henry Gallantine announced. "Shall we start returning them to the house?"

"Wait, sir. Please," said Officer Meese. "Mr. Lindquist? Can you tell me what happened?"

Barry stepped toward the officer. "I'll tell you what—"

A bloodcurdling scream rose from the grasses.

Liv jumped. "Holy moly. What was that?"

Another scream.

Ted chuckled. "Marla Jean Higgins. I'd recognize that scream anywhere. She's been practicing for weeks. She probably saw a mouse."

A third scream, this time even louder and more bloodcurdling.

"But maybe we should go see."

Liv and Ted struck off toward the lot, where the rest of the actors were still combing through the grasses.

Henry joined them. "That girl takes her role very seriously. Can't act her way out of a paper bag, but her scream is superb. It's the sole reason she got the part." He gestured for them to precede him down the path of trampled grass made by the volunteers, then called out, "Marla Jean, very nice, dear, that will do."

"Girl, ha," Ted said. "Marla Jean is forty if she's a day. She just acts like a time traveler from a bobby-sox movie. Shall we?" Ted gestured for Liv to follow Henry.

Several yards into the empty lot, the actors were gathered in a perfect semicircle, looking at something in the brush.

Marla Jean had stopped screeching and was sobbing into the sweatshirt of one of the male actors. He looked back at Henry, his face white as chalk.

"What a tableau," Henry muttered.

Ted put out a hand. "Henry, I think you and Liv should stay here." Henry nodded and Ted motioned Meese to follow him.

The two of them approached the group, then both knelt down, their heads disappearing from view, and Liv got a sudden sinking feeling that she knew what they were looking at.

"They seem to have found a live one," Henry said, and shuddered dramatically.

The group parted.

"Perhaps, not exactly alive, but . . ." Henry turned away.

Not a mannequin in period costume, but a woman in an off-white trench coat.

Officer Meese reached for his cell phone. "Folks, if you'll just stand back, I think I'd better ask the sheriff to take over."

Chapter Three

....

"Who is it?" Henry asked.

Liv recognized the trench coat from the award ceremony, but she couldn't imagine why Lucille Foster would be lying dead among a field of dismantled dummies. If it was Lucille.

She moved closer and peered over the shoulder of one of the actors. She could just see the woman's face. It was Lucille, all right.

"Good heavens," Henry said from behind her. Liv jumped; she hadn't realized he'd followed her. "Is that Lucille Foster?"

"Looks like it," Liv managed.

"What happened?" Barry asked, coming closer. "What's she doing here?" His voice climbed an octave.

No one answered. Ted knelt down and stuck his fingers on Lucille's neck. Waited for a few seconds, stood up. Looked at Liv and shook his head.

"Shouldn't we at least try—"

Ted leaned close to her. "Already cold," he whispered.

Liv shivered. She was feeling the cold herself. Her teeth began to chatter but she wasn't sure if it was from the weather or from shock. She wished the sheriff would hurry up. "Do you think she had a heart attack?" *Please say yes.*

"There was a bruise on her neck. It's possible she was strangled," Ted said. "Of course, that's just my unqualified opinion."

"Strangled? But what was she even doing here? Why wasn't she at home. It doesn't make sense. Why would she vandalize the museum? She was one of the judges."

"Liv, keep your voice down. Take a deep breath and regroup. I don't know any more than you do."

"I know, sorry. It's just . . ."

Ted patted her shoulder. "I know." He sighed. "And after such a peaceful Harvest Festival."

Liv sighed, too. "I knew it was too good to last."

"You think you're disappointed," Henry said. "Imagine the poor victim."

Liv didn't have to imagine. Lucille Foster was dead, possibly strangled. And only last night she'd been celebrating the winners of the contest and the success of the fund-raiser.

The actors stood close together, still holding mannequin parts. They didn't seem to realize what they were doing. Occasionally a sob would escape from Marla Jean, or a nervous laugh from one of the others, quickly cut off. It was a little surreal. Even with the gruesome reality just feet away from them—a real dead person—they looked like a crowd scene on *CSI*.

Barry just stood looking down at the body, wringing his hands, and mumbling, "I don't understand, I don't understand."

Liv heard a car door slam. It was the sheriff, Bill Gunnison. At least he'd had the good sense not to use the siren. Not that the news would be kept secret for long. The main form of entertainment in Celebration Bay was Monday Night Football, arguing in the pub, and listening to the police band on ham radios. And not necessarily in that order.

Ted, Henry, and Liv turned to wait for Bill. Barry didn't wait but ran up to meet him and began gesticulating and pointing to the field, while the sheriff nodded and kept walking.

Bill Gunnison was in his fifties, tall and big boned, with grizzled graying hair and twinkling blue eyes, even when he was angry.

Normally this was the season for his sciatica to act up, but he'd signed up for a yoga class in September and it seemed to be doing a lot of good. He was barely limping. He'd received a lot of grief from Chaz and some of the other guys about what he looked like in yoga pants, even though he assured them he wore sweats. But he took all the ribbing in stride. He didn't excite easily, which made him a good sheriff. Henry Gallantine couldn't have cast him in a better role.

Liv shook her head. Her mind tended to wander when she was freaked out. Which she was now.

"Liv, Ted," Bill said. "I suppose I shouldn't be surprised to see you both here."

"I was just helping Henry out at the theater," Ted told him.

"And I was jogging by," Liv added. She sighed. "Except that I stopped to take a photo of this lot that was supposed to have been mowed—"

Bill held up his hand. "Just hold that thought until I can deal with the crime scene. Barry, I know you're upset, but these things take time. If you will please stand here with the others, I'll talk to you as soon as possible."

Barry began to protest.

Ted placed a hand on his shoulder. "We'll get everything sorted out. Not to worry."

"Don't worry? My museum has been destroyed, Lucille Foster is dead, this is a disaster. Just a disaster."

He walked over to talk to Officer Meese. Whiskey attempted to follow him, but Liv made him sit.

"Just a few more minutes," she said. *Maybe.*

Bill and the young officer began moving people back to

the parking lot, urging them to walk single file and keeping them a distance from the body. But Barry refused to move.

Finally Bill had to take his arm and steer him back to the parking lot. Ted, Liv, and Henry followed.

"If you will all stay right here for the moment, Officer Meese will take your statements."

The actors added the last mannequin parts to the handcart and stayed there, striking another tableau, huddled together next to a pile of arms, legs, and torsos waiting to be carted away. It was a gruesome scene, something fit for the Museum of Yankee Horrors itself.

Liv tore her gaze and her thoughts away. She concentrated on watching Bill, who had returned to the overgrown lot and was peering into the grasses. She wondered what he was looking for. And if they had trampled any evidence the culprit might have left behind.

She shivered again and hugged herself. Under Armour was great as long as you kept moving, but between the shock and the morning chill, Liv was feeling extremely uncomfortable.

Liv pulled out her phone and checked the time: 9:20. All this had happened in a little over an hour. She should have been home, dressed, and on her way to work by now. Ted, too. She'd barely been aware of the passage of time. The sun hadn't come out. The day was raw and overcast. It looked like they were in for some weather. Hopefully no major storms that would destroy decorations or rain on their scheduled weekend activities.

Then Liv remembered that for one person there would be no activities ever again. She knelt down and scratched Whiskey's ears. He put his paws on her knee and licked her face. She nuzzled her face in his fur and felt a little better.

Whiskey had been content to sit at her feet for the first few minutes, but when Liv stood up he moved over to Ted and looked expectant.

"Sorry, fella, not the time or the place right now." Ted held his hands open. "No song, no treat."

Whiskey sat there a few seconds longer, then stood and shook himself. He'd been patient, but now he was ready to go home to his breakfast.

He barked once, to get her attention.

Liv let out his leash just enough to give him some wandering room without getting in the way of the investigation.

Whiskey trotted over to the group of actors, where he was an immediate hit. Marla Jean leaned over and hugged him. Two of the guys scratched his back and ears.

Therapy dog, Liv thought, remembering how he'd helped calm more than one upset young person since they'd moved here. And from the way everyone was petting him and talking nonsense, he was working his magic on the dismayed actors.

The crime scene truck and ambulance arrived. Bill motioned them into the grass. There was a brief discussion, then they all began whatever it was they did.

"How did this happen?" she asked. "We saw her last night. Saw her go meet her husband. When did she come down here? And why? Surely she wasn't the one vandalizing the museum."

"It doesn't seem likely," Ted said. "Maybe she saw something, and stopped— But no. She would be too smart to try to stop them herself. She would have called the police and reported it."

Liv huffed out a sigh. "One would think."

Henry looked around, then leaned in to listen.

"But we saw her leave with her husband," Liv said. "So where is he? You don't think that he could be—"

"I certainly hope not." Ted's brow knitted. "I remember her saying, 'There's Carson,' and leaving, but I didn't actually see him, did you?"

Liv thought back. "I . . . No, I guess I didn't. But why would she—"

"Aha, the plot thickens," Henry said, sounding delighted.

Liv gritted her teeth. He couldn't help it, poor man. Everything in his life was a line to be delivered and a part to play. But sometimes it really got on her nerves.

Another squad car arrived and two more policemen got out. Right behind them, a black Humvee pulled into the lot.

A.K. Pierce's "stealth mobile," as Chaz called it, came to a stop at the side of the official cars and A.K. got out.

A.K. Pierce was as powerful looking as his vehicle. Big, brawny, tough, with a shaved head and a steady eye that said take no prisoners. Though Liv had seen him almost smile on several occasions. He was thrilling, and a little scary. And totally intriguing.

He strode up to them. "Ms. Montgomery, Ted, Mr. Gallantine." The men all looked suitably stoic and solemn.

"Did Bill call you?" Liv asked.

"Heard the dispatch. Thought you might need some crowd control. I stationed cars at each end of the block to discourage gawkers."

Or attract them, Liv thought. But she knew he'd done the right thing. By now a third of the town must know a body had been found. Soon half the town would know who it was.

They'd all come to depend on A.K. and Bayside Security for crowd control and extra security. It was his men who had skillfully disposed of the ranting soapbox speaker. He'd become Bill's unofficial right-hand man. Liv didn't know if that was totally legal.

The town usually depended on the county law enforcement. Celebration Bay being a rather small town—at least between holidays—didn't as yet warrant its own police force and relied on the county sheriff and his staff. But with the influx of tourists each holiday, they didn't always have enough men to cover the town's needs.

It meant Bill had to do a lot of running around, and the crime scene van and coroner weren't always readily available. Today they had come right away, for which Liv was grateful.

A.K. was used to being in charge, but he never seemed to mind playing backup to Bill's forward guard.

He shook out a black jacket that he'd carried from the car and draped it over Liv's shoulders. "Thought you might be cold, once you stopped running."

"I was, thanks."

Ted lifted his eyebrows.

Bill saw A.K. and motioned him over. A.K. nodded slightly to Liv, before striding across the tarmac. A man in control. One who didn't suffer from sciatica. And who probably looked darn good in yoga pants.

Liv shook herself. Her thoughts were ricocheting all over her brain. She needed to focus on the problem at hand. She needed to relive the past hour or so, go over her movements of the morning, not let random inappropriate thoughts bushwhack her when she should be concentrating on what was happening and planning triage.

Barry began to pace. Finally he wandered over to the carts and picked up a piece. It appeared to be an arm, with flowing material hanging from one end—the wrist, Liv guessed, though the hand was missing. Barry began to pull the material up the arm. It must have been a sleeve that got torn when the mannequins were wrenched apart.

As soon as Barry got one side up, and let go to bring the rest up, the first pieces fell down. Finally he gave up, tossed the arm back onto the pile, and stood staring across the weeds of the vacant lot.

Liv hurt for him. He'd spent so much time and effort on the mannequins, not to mention expense. And they'd been truly interesting. But she didn't see how he could ever get the displays back together in time for the grand opening, even if the police released them in time.

And that meant the prize money would go to the

runner-up—Ernie Bolton. The same Ernie Bolton who might be angry enough to loot and destroy his competition. But would Ernie be desperate enough to commit murder? Liv just couldn't believe it.

She wanted to ask Ted's opinion, but Bill stepped out of the grasses and everyone turned their attention to him.

"When can we go, Sheriff?" one of the actors asked. "I have work in a couple of hours."

"And my mom needs me to take her out to the mall. She'll have a fit when she finds out what's happened," said another.

The others agreed and began talking at once.

Bill held up his hand. They kept talking.

"Quiet *en scene*!" Henry roared.

Immediate silence.

"Now, Sheriff, if you would continue."

Bill blinked. "If you will proceed over to the theater, you can all give your statements to Officer Meese. We may need to talk to you again." He looked around the group. "Which one of you found the body?"

No one spoke. Had it been a group sighting?

Finally a hand went up. "I did," Marla Jean said. Her mouth twisted. "I thought it was a mannequin and I picked up her hand." She finished the confession with a wail. Her friends surrounded her and tried to soothe her.

Beside Liv, Henry groaned and rubbed a hand across his face. "I've created a monster."

"And what did you do next?"

Marla Jean stopped wailing. "I dropped it, of course, and screamed."

Bill nodded.

"And everyone came to see what was the matter . . . and she was just lying there in the grass."

The others nodded agreement.

"And after that?"

"Mr. Gallantine and the other two came to see. And he"— Marla Jean pointed to Meese—"called you."

"And no one else touched the body?"

"I did," Ted said. "Her neck. To determine if there was a pulse. When I didn't find one, I stepped away. And no one has touched her since."

"I see. Meese, take these folks across the street to the theater. There's probably some coffee or hot chocolate in the green room you can make, right, Henry?"

Henry nodded and tossed Meese a key ring. "The one with the green plastic edge."

Meese nodded, looked back at his gaggle of actors, and herded them away.

Whiskey came back to sit beside Liv.

"It looks a little like the reign of terror over there," Ted said under his breath.

Liv nodded. "I was thinking the same thing. The bodies piled on carts to be taken away." Especially with Barry standing guard over the cart of mannequins like a modern-day sansculotte.

"I'll be here a while longer," Bill said. "If there are no more details you can point out, I'll see you at your office later. Unless you have something to add, Henry, you can return to the theater and give your statement to Officer Meese, too."

"Thank you, Sheriff." Henry started to leave, then changed his mind and went over to Barry. "Now, Barry," Henry said in his best stage voice. "I know things look bleak now, but if you decide you want to remount your museum, my small band of players is at your disposal. And we have a costume room and several sewing machines. Just give the word. We'll be yours to command."

Barry just stared at him, and finally managed, "Thanks," and with a half bow, Henry strode through the parking lot and down the street.

Bill slowly looked back to Ted and Liv. Opened his mouth and shut it. Closed his eyes, opened them. Said, "I'll see you two later," and without a look, went back into the now not-so-empty lot.

"Well, I guess I'll drop by the theater," Ted said. "See if we can at least get the rehearsal started, then let's meet at the office for a little damage control. You want to pick up coffee?"

"Sure. I'll just run home and get changed. See you in a few." A few *if* she got home, showered, changed, *and* managed to get past her inquisitive landladies, the bakery, and the coffee shop before news got out about the murder.

Not a chance.

Chapter Four

....

Liv made it back to her carriage house unseen. She fed Whiskey and let him out while she showered and dressed.

Less than half an hour later, they left for work—and had almost made it to the sidewalk when someone called, "Good morning, Liv."

Whiskey barked a greeting and dragged Liv over to Ida Zimmerman, one of Liv's landladies. Miss Ida was holding a broom, but that didn't fool Liv. She was out for information.

"Morning, Miss Ida." Both Ida and her sister, Edna, had been schoolteachers in town before retiring, and everyone called them "Miss." They didn't look at all alike: Miss Ida was small boned, demurely spoken, and tended to twinsets and sensible shoes. Miss Edna was tall and bigger boned, spoke her mind freely, and had hung up her twinsets the day she retired, changed into slacks and pullovers, and had never looked back.

They were both dears and they'd taken a shine to Whiskey and, by association, Liv. They, like most local residents, listened to the police band for their entertainment, enjoyed a little gossip, and were always ready to help with an "investigation."

The fact that Liv was an event planner and not a detective made absolutely no difference to them—or to anyone else in town. They expected her to do her part in bringing justice, and were more than willing to do their own parts to help.

"I heard there's a commotion over at Barry Lindquist's new museum. Nothing was damaged, was it?"

Liv was tempted to say she didn't know anything about it. But that would be useless. Everyone would know all the details before Liv had paid for her coffee, and the sisters' feelings would be hurt if she didn't tell them first.

"Well . . ."

"Wait for me, you two." Miss Edna came barreling through the front door and down the front steps. "I just heard on the police band that the coroner was summoned," she said. "Just what happened over there, Liv?"

Liv gave up her last shred of hope that she would get away without revealing the whole story.

"Whiskey and I were out running . . ."

"And you found a body?"

"No, Whiskey found the arm of a mannequin in the weeds."

"You clever little man," Ida said. She dug into her pocket and pulled out a biscuit, which she gave to Whiskey.

"Barry's museum had been vandalized and there were mannequins all over that vacant lot next door."

"We've been telling the trustees to have somebody clean up that lot for months now," Edna said.

"I called Barry, who came over, and sure enough, the place was wrecked." Liv went through the morning, organizing facts as she spoke. She knew she'd be telling the story again. By the time she made it through town and to work, she'd have it down pat.

Of course she could drive to work, but she walked to work every day, and everyone would know she had driven just so she wouldn't have to talk to them. And, like the sisters, their feelings would be hurt.

"Who died?"

"Lucille Foster."

"Lucille?" Ida echoed. "Edna and I were just talking about her yesterday"

Edna shook her head. "And the whole town will be talking about her today. What a shame."

"What on earth was she doing over there?" Ida asked.

It was exactly what Liv had been wondering.

"Well," Edna said. "It wasn't to see Barry Lindquist. Of that we can be sure."

"They don't like each other?" Liv asked.

"I have no idea," Edna said. "But we heard tell he lost a bundle of money in a hedge fund that Lucille's husband, Carson, talked him into getting involved in."

"You don't think she saw someone vandalizing the museum and had a heart attack?" Ida looked concerned.

"Ida, I don't think it was natural causes. Did the sheriff say?" Edna looked expectantly at Liv.

"He didn't say. It was all so weird and horrible. Some poor girl in Henry's play found the—found her. Thought she was a mannequin and tried to pick her up."

Edna cracked a laugh. "Sorry, but what a ridiculous situation."

"It was pretty macabre and one of the actresses let out a scream to end all screams."

"Were there any signs of foul play?" Ida asked.

"I confess I was so stupefied that I wasn't thinking much of anything. I'd already called the police over the break-in. So Officer Meese was there when they found the—Lucille. Now, I had really better get to work."

"I expect you'll have to move to Plan B," Edna said and shook her head. "Everyone said Barry's exhibit was so professional looking and the mannequins looked real."

"And taught a little history, too," Ida added.

Liv didn't burst Ida's teacherly bubble by telling her that Barry had played fast and loose with history in the typical, time-honored Celebration Bay way.

"I'm sure you both will know more than I will by the end of day."

"Drop by and we'll compare notes," Ida said. "Do you want to leave Whiskey with us today?"

"Thanks, but I'm hoping I won't be long."

"Well, you have a nice day," Ida said.

"And keep your ears open," Edna added.

"Will do," Liv said, and she and Whiskey headed to the town square for coffee and pastries and a little gossip.

The sun made a brief appearance. And if Liv hadn't been concerned about murder and how the vandalism would affect the rest of the festival, she would have enjoyed the crisp fall day. The leaves that hadn't fallen were brilliant red and yellow. There was an icy chill in the air; seriously cold weather would be sweeping in on them soon. And then the snow.

But before Liv had gone two blocks, the sun had vanished and she began making contingency plans. She would have to talk to the mayor first thing about what, if anything, to do with the prize money. It would be a diplomatic nightmare. She didn't see how Barry could get his museum back up in time for the official opening at the end of the week. How long would they wait to transfer the prize to the runner-up?

And if Ernie Bolton had vandalized Barry's exhibit, would he still be given the first-place prize money and official recognition for his haunted house? If that failed, it would have to go to Miss Patty for her friendly ghost house. A worthy effort on Miss Patty's part, but not Liv's idea of an official site.

She would have to check with the mayor about that, not a duty she was looking forward to. Gilbert always got hysterical when things hit a bump.

A bump? Liv just hoped Ted had been wrong and Lucille's

death was natural, though for the life of her, Liv couldn't come up with a scenario that placed Lucille Foster at the scene other than ones involving foul play.

Her first stop was the Apple of My Eye Bakery, owned and run by Dolly Hunnicutt. Her husband, Fred, ran the business end of the bakery and was permanent traffic committee chair for all the festivals and events.

The bakery, like all the stores on the square, was decorated for Halloween. A witch's hat sat atop the pink cupcake wall clock. There were pumpkin and black cat centerpieces at the three tables the bakery kept inside.

Dolly, like her husband, was stocky and good humored, generous and totally serious about holidays. Today she was wearing an orange and black polka-dot apron detailed in orange rickrack and an orange mobcap. Beneath it Dolly's rosy pink complexion looked a little out of place.

There were a couple of people ahead of her, but Dolly saw Liv and gave her a knowing look. She'd already heard, which meant that Liv would be stopped by questions and speculations down the entire block to town hall, where the event office was located.

As soon as Liv reached the front of the line, Dolly said, "Did you hear about the break-in?"

Liv nodded.

"You were there?"

"I was just running by and Whiskey discovered one of the mannequins."

"Oh dear. Is it an awful mess?"

"I'm afraid so. The mannequins were all dismantled and thrown out into the vacant lot next door."

"What will happen now? Do you think Barry can put it back together?"

"It looks like a major undertaking, though Henry Gallantine offered the cast of *Little Shop of Horrors* to help reconstruct the scenes."

"That was sweet of Henry. Ever since he started that

theater group, he's stopped being such a recluse. He's like a changed man."

Liv nodded, though if you asked her, Henry was more in his element than he'd ever been. Back in the theatrical saddle again.

"Do they know who did it? Everyone in this morning said that Ernie was really unhappy about losing. So unlike him."

"He was pretty upset," Liv agreed. "But so far the police haven't considered the possible suspects. At least as far as I know."

"Well, Bill certainly can't think Patty Wainwright would do such a thing," Dolly said. "She's the sweetest soul."

Liv thought that was what neighbors always said about serial killers—"he was always such a nice quiet boy"—but in this case she had to agree with Dolly. The preschool teacher and caregiver would hardly break into a house and destroy the competition. Besides, the panel had chosen her in order to have a child-friendly haunted house in town.

"I'm sure Bill will get to the bottom of this," Liv said.

Dolly nodded. "I'm sure he will. Now, what would you like? I have orange breakfast rolls this morning."

"Those rolls on the tray oozing frosting?"

"The very ones."

"I shouldn't, but I will."

"Ted shouldn't either, but he loves them."

Liv laughed. "We both love everything you bake. I've had to start running twice as far just to keep from gaining weight. And Ted? I think he must have a hollow leg."

"Why, listen to you, Liv Montgomery. I bet you never talked about hollow legs in the corporate event world."

"Huh, how about that."

"We'll make a country girl of you yet."

They'd certainly made a holiday girl out of her. Today she was wearing black slacks and a black sweater and jacket and felt right at home. Of course she'd always worn black in the corporate event world; the difference now was the smiling jack-o'-lantern that took up most of the sweater front.

"And for you, my favorite dog, a black cat doggie biscuit."

Whiskey barked. He recognized the word "cat;" he had an ongoing love-hate relationship with the cat from the bookstore, two doors down. All love on Whiskey's part, all hate on Tinkerbelle's, who wasn't really friendly to anyone (which had earned her the nickname Tink the Stink).

"Ever since you started baking your Dolly Doggie Treats, he's on a new exercise regimen, too."

Dolly slipped it into the bag, then leaned over and made kissy noises to Whiskey. "Is Liv making you run, too, sweetie?"

Whiskey cowered on the floor.

"I swear he understands what we're saying."

"He certainly knows a few words," Liv agreed. "He's also a sly manipulator. But we love you anyway, don't we?" Liv rattled the bag at him and Whiskey immediately perked up.

Liv thanked Dolly and was turning to go when the door opened and BeBe Ford ran through the door. BeBe was a lush thirtysomething, half country girl and half urban entrepreneur left over from her former life. She was Liv's best friend in Celebration Bay. BeBe owned and ran the Buttercup Coffee Exchange, made a mean latte, had ridden shotgun on some of Liv's wilder exploits, and was responsible for Liv and Ted's caffeine well-being each morning.

"Did you hear?" BeBe stopped mid-step. "Oh, hi, Liv. I wondered if something was wrong. I guess you heard about the contest-winning haunted house."

"She was there," Dolly said.

BeBe looked to the ceiling. "Of course you were. Spill."

Liv told her about Whiskey finding the arm, calling Barry, and discovering the house had been ransacked.

"Were you still there when they found the body?"

"What body?" Dolly asked and came around the counter. "There's a body? Who was it?"

Liv sighed. Looked around. All the customers had left. "Lucille Foster."

Dolly stared. "Was it an accident? What was she doing there?"

Liv shrugged. "I don't know and I don't know."

"Did Bill come?" BeBe asked.

"Yes. But he said he'd talk to me and Ted later. So you probably know more than I do, since I went home to shower and come here."

"Well, it wasn't a heart attack," BeBe said. "At least that's what I heard. They took photos and enclosed the area in crime scene tape."

"No-o-o," Dolly said. "Really?"

"There *was* a crime," Liv said. "Someone threw all the mannequins in the vacant lot. Doesn't mean it was . . ." Liv lowered her voice. "Murder."

"Or manslaughter," BeBe said. "She might have been driving by and saw someone breaking in and tried to stop them."

"Maybe," Liv said. Except she realized that there hadn't been any cars parked in the lot or on the street, just the ones in the theater parking lot, which Liv assumed belonged to the actors. Besides, if Lucille had been trying to stop a burglary, why would she have gone down the street to park?

"Liv? Did you think of something?"

"No. I don't know what she was doing there. Or why someone would want to kill her."

"Maybe we could pin this one on Janine," BeBe said.

Dolly pursed her lips. "That's not funny. Janine is a pain in just about everybody's patooty, especially Liv's. But she wouldn't murder Lucille just because of what Lucille did."

"I noticed last night that Janine and Lucille weren't on friendly terms. What did she do?" Liv asked.

"Well . . ." Dolly looked around the empty shop. She moved even closer. She smelled like pumpkin pie. Between that and the coffee aroma wafting from BeBe, the combination was enough to make Liv's stomach growl. Which it did.

"What did she do?" Liv urged.

"Yes, please hurry up, Dolly," BeBe said. "Before someone comes. I had a party of six waiting for my assistant to make their Monster Mocha Macchiatos. They're on their way here next."

"Well," Dolly continued. "Some people, not me mind you . . ."

"Go on . . ."

"Some people say that Lucille caused Janine's divorce."

"Lucille Foster?" Liv asked. The woman hadn't struck Liv as the town vixen.

"No one would ever say anything. Carson is well respected in this town." Dolly pursed her lips.

BeBe snorted. "Plus he owns mortgages on everything that isn't held by First Celebration Bank. Not to mention a bunch of money that he's invested for anyone with two pennies to rub together."

"Wait," Liv said. "How did his wife cause Janine's divorce?"

The front door opened; the little bell that welcomed newcomers made the three women jump apart. Like three co-conspirators. Or witches in a Shakespeare play.

Dolly grimaced before moving behind the counter and smiling at the newcomers. "May I help you?"

BeBe and Liv waved good-bye and walked next door to the Buttercup Coffee Exchange, passing six coffee-cup-wielding tourists on their way. The coffee bar was empty except for Quincy Hinks, owner of the Bookworm, taking his morning break. He was bent over a hardcover book, oblivious to the world and the grinning skeleton that was sharing his table.

He didn't even look up when Whiskey, recognizing his favorite cat's roommate, trotted over and sniffed Quincy's shoes.

BeBe held up a finger to Penny Newland, who was working part time at the coffee bar, and pulled Liv around into the back room.

"I heard that Janine's husband and Lucille were having an affair, and Janine found out about it. Janine and Lucille evidently had been best friends before that. I don't have any details. That's just what I heard. I didn't know them, but from what I've heard . . ." BeBe lowered her voice. "Well, Carson may be well respected as a man and an investor, but I heard he was a pretty boring husband. So Lucille looked elsewhere." BeBe smothered a laugh.

"That's interesting, but I don't see how it could have anything to do with the vandalism."

"Me, neither. Not exactly a killing offense." BeBe frowned. "Plus it was years ago. Well, let's get your order. I have to get back to work."

So did Liv. It had taken her a good twenty minutes to make the three-block walk from her house to the Buttercup, and she still had a whole block of shops to go.

"I know Mocha Macchiato isn't your thing," BeBe said. "Want to give Witches Brew a try? Just a dash of licorice."

"BeBe," Liv said.

BeBe huffed. "I know, double-shot latte, no whip cream, no cinnamon. Don't you ever want to expand you horizons?"

"Yes, just not with coffee."

BeBe had just finished steaming the milk for Liv's latte, when Dolly ran into the coffee bar. "Fred just called. The police picked up Ernie Bolton for questioning."

"It was inevitable," Liv said, though she was surprised they'd moved this fast. "He seems the most probable culprit for the vandalism."

"But murder, Liv?"

A cold shiver ran up Liv's spine and she gripped Whiskey's leash a little tighter. "Did Fred say they thought it was murder?"

"No, but what else could it be?"

"I think we should just wait and see. Now I have to run, Ted will be screaming for sustenance." And she still had to make it down the rest of the block.

She took the cardboard tray with Ted's tea and her no-frills latte in the other hand.

BeBe ran to open the door. "Let us know the minute you learn anything."

"You, too." Liv looked out the door. Coast clear. What were the chances she could make it to work without having to tell her story again?

She made it past Bay-Berry Candles and was almost clear of A Stich in Time, but hesitated to admire the quilt that hung in the window. It wasn't constructed in the usual orange and black colors of Halloween, no witches on broomsticks and black cats or the other decorations. This quilt was pieced with dark grays and greens, with a silver five-pointed star that covered most of the quilt and was surrounded by strange exotic symbols. Even looking at it through the window Liv could feel its power, same but different than the other Halloween quilts that shared the display.

She'd have to ask Miriam about it later, when the news of Lucille's death wasn't heating up the rumor lines and Liv's coffee wasn't getting cold.

"Liv! Did you hear?" Miriam Krause slipped out the door of the fabric and quilting shop and closed it behind her. "The quilting club is meeting and we're all in shock. Lucille Foster was found dead this morning."

"I heard," Liv said, drawing her attention from the quilt. "You know, that's an amazing quilt. Did the club make it?"

"Heavens no. It's on loan from Yolanda Nestor."

"Yolanda Nestor? I don't think I know her, but her name is familiar. Is she from around here?"

"She just took over the space where the Pyne Bough used to be."

"Oh yes. Now I remember. At the end of the summer. I've been so busy I haven't even been inside to welcome her."

"It's an amazing shop. Takes a little getting used to, but she joined the quilting group. She's here now, would you like to meet her?"

"I would, Miriam, but I'm really late for work."

"I guess you already got all the details from Dolly and BeBe."

Liv nodded.

"Sometimes I feel that I'm missing out being the farthest down the block."

Liv laughed. "Well, going the other way, you're one of the first ones on the block."

"True," Miriam said. "I'll tell Yolanda you admired her quilt."

"Please do."

Liv was just thinking, *Whew, almost home free*, when a cry arose from the park across the street.

"The end is near! Repent, you worshippers of the devil. Fall on your knees and repent your wicked ways. You sinners, you harlots, you forn—"

"Okay, that does it." Liv shoved her drinks and her carryall at Miriam.

But before she even stepped off the curb, the door to A Stitch in Time flew open. A woman wearing black yoga pants and an oversized black sweater tunic swept out and onto the sidewalk. She didn't slow down but strode straight across the street and stuck her open hand up to the man's face.

He ricocheted back, stumbled, and fell on his butt.

"Oh dear," Miriam said.

"She didn't even touch him," Liv said. "If he thinks he's going to sue, he's got another think coming."

As she watched, he scrambled back, somehow managed to get to his feet, and ran.

The woman watched him go, then turned and came back across the street. "How long has he been here?" she asked Miriam.

"I don't know. Liv?"

"I saw him for the first time last night at the award ceremony."

"Well, I'm getting a little tired of the likes of him."

The woman turned slowly, and Liv got her first good look at her face. Late fifties, or maybe sixties, with black, black hair and even darker eyes in a roundish face. She wore a heavy silver necklace with a medallion that looked familiar. Liv looked from the woman to the quilt in the window and back to the necklace. The same five-pointed star.

"Liv," Miriam said. "I'd like you to meet Yolanda Nestor."

The woman stuck out her hand. "Proprietor of the Mystic Eye, and purveyor and practitioner of all things metaphysical."

Chapter Five

....

"She's a witch?" Liv asked incredulously.

Ted looked up from where he was teaching Whiskey *The Addams Family* theme song. "Interesting woman. Watch this. *Da do da do da dooo do.*"

"Ar roo Ar roo Ar roooo roo," Whiskey repeated.

Ted grinned and snapped his fingers twice.

Whiskey bounced on his front paws.

"Now he not only sings, he dances. We really need to take this on the road."

"Ted, you've already taught him a song for each season. Could you concentrate? We have vandalism, a death, possibly murder—"

"Definitely murder."

Liv groaned. "Vandalism, murder, a hellfire guy warning everybody who'll listen that the end is near. And a witch who owns a store in town held up her hand and made him fall down." Liv slapped her hand on her forehead. "No. What am I saying? It wasn't some kind of magic. She held up her hand, he stepped back and tripped and fell. And if he thinks he's going to sue—"

"Stop. Hand me the baked goods that must be in your carryall. I need my tea."

Liv handed him the tray of drinks and reached in her bag. The pastries were smushed.

"Witch?" Liv reiterated. "Are you serious? We have a store run by a witch now?"

"Yes but evidently a good witch."

"Ted, if you're making this up . . ."

"No, not at all, and she'll be great for business."

"For Halloween maybe, but what about the rest of the year?"

"Oh ye of little faith. There's tarot, and Ouija boards, herbs, and oils and jewelry and—"

"You've been to her store?"

"Of course. Someone had to welcome her to the neighborhood."

"Where was I?"

"In the big city begging for money for the community center."

"I wasn't begging. Oh no, Jonathon Preston is coming next weekend to see our wholesome, friendly little town in need of big bucks for a community center. Jon loves a good spectacle as much as the next person, but I think he'll draw the line at murder. Thank God he's stuck in Bangkok for an extra week. Maybe Bill will have solved the case, brought the perpetrator to jail, the museum will open as intended, and . . . And that crazy man will be gone. Ugh." She huffed out a sigh and walked into her office where she slumped down in her desk chair.

"Where did I go wrong?" she asked to the empty room.

"You're doing everything right," Ted said, carrying in two flattened orange rolls and their coffee and tea on a silver tray.

Whiskey trotted behind him, growling and shaking the black cat biscuit in his mouth.

"This may not bode well for the neighborhood felines," Ted said as he put down the tray. "Whiskey took one look at that biscuit and I was afraid he was going to take my hand with it."

Liv looked up horrified. "Really?"

Ted laughed. "No, but he definitely recognized it for what it was. His nemesis Tink the Stink." He handed her a plate with a pastry on it. "Where shall we start?"

Liv glanced at the stack of folders on her desk that hadn't been there when they'd left the night before.

"How did you beat me back to the office? I thought you were rehearsing."

"Meese took too long with his questioning. Poor man, he didn't have a chance. He's probably still there."

"What do you mean?"

"They're actors. They're terribly detail oriented, they generally make good witnesses, but you can't expect them to tell a story without a little blocking, a bit of elaboration and gesticulating, and pulling out every emotional stop. Meese may be there for a while."

"Did they say anything useful?"

"Just what we already know or saw. But you missed everyone's interpretation of Marla Jean's scream."

"Not funny."

"I know. But a little comic relief never hurts."

"Did they find her car?"

"Who's— Oh, Lucille's." He thought, shook his head. "Not before I left. I'm not sure they were even looking for it. What made you think about her car?"

"When I was talking to BeBe. She thought that Lucille might have been driving by and saw the break in and tried to stop it."

"Seems unlikely. She would have driven to the corner and called the police from her cell. But why would she be driving along that street? They live on the opposite side of town."

Liv opened the tab on her latte cup. "No one would break

in until the crowds were gone, and that would be pretty late, long after the ceremony was over. Why was Lucille out that late? And where was her husband?" She took a sip of coffee. "They didn't find his body, did they?"

Ted shook his head. "Not that I know of."

"So why wasn't he with her? And if he dropped her off somewhere, how did she end up there?"

"And why?" Ted added.

"And what are we going to do about it?"

Ted stared at her. "Are you actually suggesting that *we* investigate?"

"What? No! I mean the other stuff. Like what do we do about the haunted house situation? According to the rules, if the winner is unable to fulfill his obligation, the prize and the title go to the runner-up. Do you think Barry can get his exhibits back up and running? Should we tell Ernie to stand by?" She stopped. "Fred called Dolly to say that the police picked Ernie up for questioning."

Ted put down the pastry he'd just picked up. "Aah, the Celebration Bay gossip hotline."

"Well?"

"Hmm. Ernie might be angry enough to indulge in a bit of vandalism. But murder? I don't know."

"Why would he do something like vandalize Barry's museum? He has to live in this town. Did he think no one would find out?"

"I don't know, Liv. He's always been a straight-up guy. Rented his machine shop to Pastor Schorr for the community center fairly cheap. But he has to sell. He has to pay back taxes or face jail. He's between a rock and a hard place. Maybe losing to Barry just pushed him over the brink. But . . . we don't know that he did any of it."

"Who else?"

Ted took his cup and leaned back in his chair. "That I don't know."

They both sat studying their cups.

"Edna said that Barry lost a lot of money because of Lucille's husband."

"Ancient history."

"A dish served cold," she reminded him.

"Revenge?" asked Ted.

Liv shrugged.

"Okay, just for argument's sake, let's say he lures her into his horror museum and kills her, then wrecks his own display, for which he just won ten thousand dollars."

"He loses twice," Liv said. "First from the investment and then from his prize money. Hmm. Maybe he caught her vandalizing the displays."

"Why would she do that?"

Liv sighed. "I don't know. None of it makes sense. And you know Gilbert will be coming through that door any minute now, wringing his hands in a panic and wanting to know what we're going to do about it."

"We're going to let Bill find the killer. We're going to tell Ernie to stand by, unless Bill has evidence that we're not privy to, and in that case, we'll have to make sure Barry gets back up and running and in less than a week." Ted shuddered. "I refuse to go to a haunted house where all the accoutrements are made for munchkins and I'm greeted by Casper the Friendly Ghost."

"Oh," said Liv, "and we also have to find a way to get rid of that end-of-the-world guy before he starts accosting families and scaring them away."

"I'll call down to the permit department and find out if he's legal."

"I don't care if he is, he's not going to yell doom and gloom during our Halloween activities."

Ted grinned. "We could always have Yolanda and her sisters scare him away."

"She has sisters?" Liv asked, horrified at the thought of a family of witches running a business in town, even if they were good witches. Someone was bound to complain.

"Of the sisterhood variety."

"Oh."

"I think they're planning to have their Samhain around here somewhere."

"You're kidding, right?"

Ted shook his head and took a large bite of orange roll.

"How many?"

Ted shrugged. "Are you one of those people who thinks witches worship the devil?"

She gave him a look.

"I didn't think so. So what's the problem?"

"Right after a murder isn't a great time to introduce the occult into the neighborhood. People might freak and run them out of town."

Ted finished chewing and brushed off his fingertips. "Or figure out how to exploit them for the rest of the town's events."

"That would be even worse. I guess I'd better get over to the store and introduce myself properly and welcome her, belatedly, to town."

"Good idea, but wait until we figure out how to deal with the . . . kerfuffle, and get a plan before we have to present it to the remaining judges panel. Which you know we'll have to do. And probably sooner rather than later."

Liv nodded and pushed her plate away. She wasn't looking forward to that. All these meetings, whether town council, or town wide, generally solved nothing. They only stirred up the inhabitants more than necessary and ended with the command for Liv to fix things.

She booted up her computer. "Okay. Where do we start?"

Two hours later, the only plan they had consisted of crossing their fingers that Barry would get his house back together in time. And wondering what was taking Bill so long.

Liv drummed her fingers on the desk. "BeBe said Lucille was responsible for Janine's divorce."

Ted stretched back in his chair. "If you ask me, Janine was responsible for that. But yes, I've heard Lucille might have had a part in it."

"Did it create a scandal?"

"Not really. No one much liked Janine's husband anyway."

"So Lucille might really have had an affair with the man?"

"Sure."

"Wait. You sound like you're not even surprised. Was Lucille known for having a roving eye?"

Ted choked out a laugh. "If only it stopped there."

"You mean there was more than one?"

Ted nodded.

"A lot?"

Ted shrugged.

"I hate it when you withhold information." Not getting a reaction, she said, "You don't think Lucille and Ernie . . ."

"No."

"Lucille and Barry?"

"Not likely. Considering his history with the investment bank."

"Revenge?"

"Not Barry's style. Besides, his attitude would not be appreciated in all quarters. A lot of people have their money tied up in investments that Carson steered them to. And have done well."

"So he wouldn't win any friends by attacking Carson."

"Exactly. And even if she was meeting Barry for some reason, why did she die in a vacant lot?"

Liv grasped at her last straw. "Maybe she had a heart attack and he panicked and dumped her body."

"In the weeds next to his museum?"

"Maybe they saw someone had broken in and went to investigate and she collapsed in fright, and he panicked, et cetera."

Ted raised his eyebrow and one side of his mouth, his that's-so-farfetched-it-pains-me expression. "Then went home, crawled in bed, fell asleep, and waited for someone to notice that he'd been burglarized, and give him a call? Where he proceeded to act like a crazy person over the loss of his exhibit? Liv, he worked hard on that haunted house. It may sound stupid, but he put his heart and soul into it. Besides, I don't think it was a heart attack."

"Aneurism?" Liv asked hopefully.

"Give it up, Liv. Let's just wait for Bill."

They both fell silent. Neither of them wanted to say the obvious, that Lucille had been murdered.

They went back to working on Plan B.

They were still at it when a weary sheriff walked into the office that afternoon.

"Have a seat," Liv said. "Can I get you some water? Coffee? Tea?"

"I'm coffee'd out. I want my breakfast, lunch, heck, I'd settle for an early bird special at Buddy's Place." He held up a hand. "Don't even suggest we go out for dinner. I've still got a bucket load of work to do."

"I'll order take out and have Ginny send over the special," Ted said. "Liv, you want anything?"

Liv shook her head. "I'm fine."

Ted went out into the outer office to make the call.

"Bill, can you just tell me whether Lucille died of natural causes?"

The look on his face said it all.

Liv's stomach dropped. "You mean . . ."

"I'm afraid so. But I won't know anything for sure until I get the coroner's report, which could be a while. Evidently they're really backed up at the moment."

Liv sighed. "Do you have to know how she died before you start investigating?"

"Heck no. But it makes it that much harder. Anyway, I'm pretty sure I already know how she died."

Liv leaned forward. Ted stuck his head in the door, the telephone still in his hand.

"Death by asphyxiation," Bill said.

"Meaning?"

"She stopped breathing," offered Ted wryly.

"Duh," Liv said. "I mean what was the method of asphyxiation?"

Bill winced. "I wanted to get statements from you before I start giving out details. Don't want to taint your memory."

"She was strangled, right?"

"How—" Bill slumped back in his chair. "Of course, you've been discussing this since you left. Don't you know—"

"Yes," Liv assured him. "We know not to discuss things until we give our statements, so we don't monkey around with the facts by mistake. But you took a really long time. Besides, we didn't really get very far."

"Well, that's one good thing that's happened today."

"Did something else happen besides the murder?" asked Liv. "And the vandalism, of course?"

Bill clasped his hands behind his head and stretched. "I had to notify Carson—no easy way to do that. And take him to identify the body. We all knew who it was, but it had to be done. Then I had to tell him he couldn't have the body until they finished with the autopsy. Ugh. Awful."

"So he wasn't with her last night," Liv said.

"Not according to Carson."

"He didn't pick her up at all?"

"Says he didn't."

"He didn't report her missing?" Ted asked.

Bill shook his head.

"Didn't you think that was weird?" Liv asked.

Bill glanced at Ted but didn't answer.

"If your wife didn't come home all night, wouldn't you call the police?"

Two blank expressions looked back at her.

"Ugh. Why am I asking two bachelors?"

"It's not that, Liv. It's, uh . . ." Bill shifted in his seat. She didn't think it was his sciatica making him uncomfortable. "I guess it isn't the first time she didn't come home at night."

"She—?"

Bill nodded.

"Did her husband know about her affairs?" asked Liv.

"How could he not," Ted said.

"But not from any one of us," Bill added.

"Is there a chance he'd finally had enough?"

Bill and Ted shook their heads simultaneously.

Liv saw it. The closing of ranks. Their locals to her out-sider. They wouldn't even consider that someone they obvi-ously liked and respected could kill his wife, even if she'd cheated on him more than once.

"Then," Bill took up the thread of his conversation, cur-tailing any excursions into the Fosters' marital problems, "Barry reamed me for not ensuring proper security. At which point A.K. said that it was Barry's responsibility to hire additional security, because it was on private property. I thought they were going to get into it. But I tell you, that A.K. is cool as a cucumber."

They'd obviously ended the discussion about Lucille and Carson Foster.

"We spent the rest of the morning trying to collect data from the most mucked-up crime scene I've ever seen."

"We didn't know it was a crime scene," Liv said. "I mean we did, but we thought it was just vandalism. And knowing there's not much the police can do if they don't catch the vandal red-handed, everyone just started helping out."

"They were being good neighbors," Ted added. "Good neighbors, not very good detectives and Lord, most of them can't act at all."

"Do you think Barry can refurbish the exhibit before next weekend?" Liv asked.

"He says he's going to try, and since all those dummies had already been handled, I told him to go for it. Hope I wasn't mistaken."

"Do you think it would be possible for us to go over and check on his progress? Or at least talk to him about his expectations?"

"Sure, at this point why not. Like you said, there's not much evidence to collect from vandals. We swept the house for anything out of the ordinary."

Liv wondered what, at the Museum of Yankee Horrors, he'd considered ordinary.

"We looked for any signs of a struggle, even though the body was not found in the house or even for that matter on Barry's property. The vacant lot is still off limits. But we're working quickly. Rain is on its way.

"If you'll just wait until I eat, I'll go with you."

Ted and Liv both gave their statements while they waited for Bill's lunch. Then they let him eat in peace—except for Whiskey, who was tired of being ignored, and came over to demand attention . . . or food.

Ted took him out for a quick walk, and they were soon all piled into the police cruiser. They made a quick detour to drop Whiskey off at home, then headed for the Museum of Yankee Horrors.

Bill pulled into the parking lot at the side of the museum. The vacant lot was cordoned off with yellow crime scene tape, but the crime scene and coroner's vans had left. A small knot of people stood across the street watching, though there wasn't much to see.

An officer was standing in front of the tape, guarding the pathway through the weeds they had created earlier that morning. Piles of garbage and castoffs littered the back of the parking lot. On closer inspection, Liv saw that the piles had been gathered and separated by the police force. Bottles in one pile, cans in another, paper, garbage, scrap metal, and what looked like pieces of clothing.

As soon as the cruiser came to a halt, Bill got out and

went over to talk to the officer. Liv tried to see if there was anything interesting in the piles of detritus, but either whatever might be evidence had been taken away or there was none to begin with. Probably destroyed by the helpful theater group.

Ted waited at a discreet distance, though Liv had no doubt he was on high alert. She certainly was.

After a brief chat, Bill came back, and the three of them went up the front steps to the house.

Henry had been true to his word. The cast members from that morning had been joined by several others. It looked like his entire cast was busy refitting arms and legs, and re-dressing mannequins into their proper clothes. Two sewing machines had been set up and Henry Gallantine was leaning over one.

"Amazing," Liv said.

Henry looked up at that, and gave a regal wave. "Needs must where the devil drives," he intoned in a theatrical baritone.

"Please, no more talk about devils," Liv said. "Which reminds me. Bill, that ranting idiot is still in the square."

Bill nodded distractedly. He was looking at Officer Meese, who was sitting on a kitchen chair frowning at the piles of clothing and body parts. "I told Meese to stay here and look out for anything that might be a clue. Not that I expect you people left anything possibly recognizable."

"Doesn't look like he's found anything," Liv said.

A skill saw started up from somewhere out back, followed by hammering.

"Structural damage?" Liv asked Barry.

"Some, not too bad, mainly where the jackass yanked the figures from their moorings. Wrecked some parts though. Hope I can get replacements quick."

"So do I. Do you think you can make it?"

Barry looked daggers at her. "You think I can't?"

Ted stepped up next to her. "Barry, if she knew, she

wouldn't be asking. Can you get it up and running by the weekend?"

Barry turned away, looked from one scene to the next. Some of the scenery, like the Salem pillory, had been partially rebuilt. Liv had shuddered the first time she'd seen it during the judging. A puritan scene of a man whose head and hands were stuck through holes of a wooden yoke and a magistrate leaning over to nail his ear to the wood. That had been a shock, especially with the accompanying recording of the man's screams.

Today he had been returned to the pillory, though his legs lay unattached on the floor below him, while the two people working on the exhibit paused for a soda. The daylight did nothing to soften the experience. Today was all the more frightening since the magistrate, fully clothed in colonial gear, a hammer in one hand and a nail in the other, was as headless as the Horseman of Sleepy Hollow. And a lot more real looking.

"The Grave Diggers of Salem" was completely missing except for the red velvet ropes that kept the audience at bay.

It looked like an impossible job to reconstruct all of the scenes. Anything that could be torn down had been demolished, like someone had done it in a fit of rage, which didn't bode well for Ernie Bolton. He was the only person they knew of who had been angry that Barry won.

Partial displays were everywhere. Tests of sound systems fought in the air until the shrieks drove Liv back to the foyer where she found Barry gazing up the staircase, his hands shoved in his overalls.

"Well, at least he missed the ghost on the staircase," Barry said dejectedly.

She looked up the staircase where a track ran along the ceiling, and from it hung a frame with a diaphanous gown. At the preview Liv had attended, the "ghost" had swept down the stairs, blown by the wind from a fan and sparkling in the theatrical lighting. It had greeted them as they'd

entered. It had been pretty impressive the night of the judging. Today it just looked like a piece of fabric on a coat hanger.

"You'll make it," Liv said and patted his arm. But she
didn't have much hope. It was too bad. Ernie's Monster Mansion had all the standard features of a haunted house—spooks,
and screams and wet spaghetti, and skeletons jumping out of
coffins—but the museum had been special.

"You'll make it," she said again and watched Barry wander off into the parlor. She continued on to the dining room
where half-clothed mannequins were being glued back
together. Two young women leaned over a table full of latex
masks that would have to be repaired and reapplied to the
mannequin's expressionless faces.

The future wasn't looking too rosy for Barry Lindquist.

Liv walked through the archway into the kitchen. Bill and
Ted were talking to Officer Meese, who still sat at the kitchen
table sorting odd bits of fabric and logging them into his
notebook.

She reached them just as Barry stormed down the hall, a
torso wearing a bloodied dress held under one arm and the
presumably accompanying stocking-clad legs stuck under
the other.

"Sheriff! We can't find Lizzie's shoes. They have to be
out there somewhere."

Bill looked to Meese, who consulted a piece of paper.
"We didn't find anything but what's in those piles over there
and what's left out in the parking lot. And that's mainly
garbage that's been there for I don't know how long."

"Then they must still be out there in the grass and your
men somehow overlooked them," Barry said. "When can we
get back in to continue our search?"

"Do you have to have those exact shoes? Can't you replace
them with something else?"

"No, they're crafted to look authentic. Cost me a load of
money."

Bill scratched his head. "Meese, take a couple of these folks out to the lot and let them search. But watch them and stop them if anything interesting turns up."

"Yes, sir." Meese motioned to two of the younger men and herded them out of the house. He'd obviously had enough of body part duty.

"Hold up," Bill said. "Barry, what exactly are they looking for?"

"They're brown leather, small heels, buttons up the side."

Bill turned to Meese. "Got it?"

Meese nodded. "Yes, sir, but sir . . ."

"Yes?"

Meese nodded to the sheriff and they stepped away from the others.

Liv watched Bill's expression turn from question to disbelief. He rubbed his hand across his face. Got out his phone and made a call. Hung up. He and Meese stood looking at the floor between them until Bill's phone pinged.

Bill swiped his finger across the screen, tapped it, and turned it for Meese to see.

Meese nodded and hung his head.

Bill came back. "Are these your missing shoes?" He turned the phone's screen so that Barry could see.

Liv and Ted looked, too.

"Yes, by gad, you took Lizzie's shoes as evidence?"

"You're positive? They were found with Lucille's body. We assumed they were hers."

"Of course I'm sure. They're eighteenth-century costume shoes."

Liv and Ted exchanged looks. And Liv knew they were both thinking the same thing.

If the police had Lizzie Borden's shoes, where were Lucille Foster's?

Chapter Six

....

Bill returned his phone to his belt clip. "They'll send Lizzie's shoes back as soon as they've been dusted for prints and released. It might take a day or two, so, Barry, you'll just have be patient." He turned to Liv. "Do you think you could recognize Lucille's shoes among those piles of shoes?"

Christian Louboutins? "Oh, I think so," Liv said. "I'll be glad to look."

"Barry, can you show her where the extra shoes are?"

Barry mumbled something and led her down the hall. "I don't know why the police took Lizzie's shoes in the first place," he groused.

"They must have been lying near Lucille and the police assumed they belonged to her." Though frankly, Liv didn't understand how they could mistake Lizzie Borden's brown button-ups for Lucille's spike-heeled, red-soled Louboutins.

"The shoes are in there," Barry said, and went off down the hall.

Liv stepped into a room that must have been a porch at

one time. A double row of shoes and boots were lined up along one wall. There were more than forty completed pairs and another ten or so still waiting for their mates. Liv could tell at a glance that none of them were Lucille Foster's.

She went back to the exhibition rooms and searched each half-assembled scene. She pulled up skirts, looked in corners and under chairs on the outside chance someone had unthinkingly tossed them out of the way. She found work boots and patent leather evening shoes, thirties pumps, shoes with spats, straps, pointed toes, metal toes, button-up, lace-up, slip-ons. She even found one bedroom slipper and a pair of cowboy boots, which turned out to belong to one of the actors who'd taken them off because they were scuffing the staging area.

But no designer heels.

She called the workers together and made a general announcement. No one had seen any four-inch Christian Louboutin heels. She got a few blank looks and several sounds of appreciation. One young man asked if there was a reward.

"No," Bill said. "But you won't go to jail if you turn them over."

The man made an over-the-top Pulcinella sigh and went down on one knee in front of Marla Jean. "And I was going to give them to you."

She jumped and slapped his outstretched hand.

Henry quelled them with an *ahem*.

Liv thanked them and they went back to work.

"Actors," Bill said. "You can never get a straight answer out of them."

"I think they would come forward if they'd seen the shoes though. Their fifteen seconds of fame," Liv said. "Which means the shoes must still be out in the vacant lot."

Bill rubbed his back.

Liv thought, *Please, don't come down with sciatica now.*

He saw her looking at him and dropped his hand. "I'm fine, but would you mind going with Meese to take another look around? I don't think these guys would know the difference between those Lamber—whatever those shoes were—and a pair of mocs. I know I wouldn't."

"I'll be glad to." What else could she say? Though she was tempted to send the smart-aleck actor in her stead.

Officer Meese took Liv out to the edge of the parking lot. The other patrolman pushed away from the cruiser he'd been leaning against. Liv went right to the piles that were accumulating on the tarmac. A cursory look revealed no shoes.

Suddenly, the unmowed lot appeared to stretch for miles instead of to the next street over. And Liv said a few choice words about what she thought of the landscaping service that was supposed to have cleared out the lot several days ago.

Well, as soon as the area was released, she was going to get them over here, if she had to drag them herself. She couldn't have any more bodies popping up during the Halloween entertainments.

At least she was dressed for mucking about in overgrown grass. After the morning's exploits some inner sense must have guided her to black jeans and her fleece jacket.

She explained what they were looking for. Meese and two others nodded solemnly. Meese handed her a stick with a point on it that looked a little like a harpoon. She'd seen prisoners picking up garbage along the highway with the same instrument

"So you don't have to use your hands," Meese explained.

Liv nodded. She had no intention of picking up anything with her hands.

They all went in the opening and spread out. Liv went straight through, headed for the far side. She didn't expect to find much. This morning it had seemed like whoever had stolen the mannequins had dumped most of them near the parking lot or only as far as he could throw them.

Still, it wouldn't hurt to keep looking.

They expanded the search to include the house, the grassy areas surrounding the parking lot, even the street.

They finally gave up when the sun began setting. They'd found a few more objects belonging to the haunted house display, but no shoes. And a lot of garbage. Not only was the lot neglected, it was clearly being used as a dumping ground.

Bill was sitting with Henry when Liv and Meese came back inside. The place was eerily quiet.

The sheriff eased himself out of the chair.

"No luck?"

"None. Where is everybody?"

"Breaking for dinner and enlisting other members of the cast, friends, and relatives to come to our aid," Henry said.

"Miriam Krause is coming over to see if there is work she and her quilting club can help with," Bill added.

"Bless her," Henry said.

Liv agreed. Miriam had helped them out before in a pinch. The town should send her a nice thank-you. She got out her phone and made a note to bring that up in the next board meeting. There was sure to be one in the near future—once the mayor found out about the death of Lucille Foster.

She shut off her phone. "Henry, is this going to interfere with your play rehearsals?"

"Not at all. We were working with a partial cast this morning. And our next rehearsal isn't until Wednesday night. I hope by then we will have a whole regiment of worker bees."

"Where's Barry?"

"We sent him home. The man was headed for a breakdown. The sheriff promised him the police would keep an extra vigil on the house until he can have a security system installed."

The sheriff nodded. "We always patrol the streets at night. No one reported anything last night. Ted already left. I told him I'd drive you home."

"Thanks. I wasn't looking forward to walking."

They said good night to Henry, who was staying to organize the night shift of players. Bill drove her home and stopped at the curb.

"Thanks, Bill. I'll just jump out before the sisters see you and invite you in for a sherry."

"Thanks. I want to see if any news has come in from the coroner or the crime scene people. I doubt it has. Even if it does, it will consist mainly of the crime scene boys complaining about how we didn't secure the area."

"We stopped cleaning up as soon as we found the body. I don't see what they have to complain about."

"Me neither, but I've seen them come down on EMTs for wrecking a scene, when they were just trying to save a life. This is a heavy, burnout, frustrating business sometimes."

"Well, we appreciate you all for doing it. Get some rest."

"You, too."

Liv made it as far as the driveway, when the Zimmermans' front door opened and Ida came out on the porch. "Liv, Whiskey is here with us. We saved you some dinner. It's warming in the oven. Bill?" She motioned him to lower the window. "Have you eaten? There's plenty."

"Thank you, Miss Ida, but I have to get back to the station." He smiled and waved and drove away.

Liv didn't need any urging to climb the steps to the porch of the Victorian house. She was tired and hungry.

Miss Ida opened the door for her. "You poor thing. You come right in and sit down."

After saying hello to Edna and making a fuss over her "poor neglected dog" (who was holding a new chew toy between his teeth), Liv excused herself to clean off the worst of her afternoon scavenger hunt, then rejoined the sisters and her dog in the kitchen.

"Does Bill have any leads?" Edna asked, pouring white wine into a cut-glass goblet and handing it to Liv. She held up the bottle to her sister.

"No, thank you, I have my tea." Ida brought a mug over to the table and sat down.

"I don't know," Liv said. "I don't think so. I heard they took Ernie Bolton in for questioning. He is the most obvious suspect. But Bill didn't say anything, so I guess it didn't pan out."

"Besides, Ernie wouldn't kill Lucille," Ida said. "They've been friends for years."

Edna poured herself a small glass of wine and sat down on the other side of Liv. "But you spent the day with him, didn't you?"

"Let Liv eat, Edna. She must be starving."

Liv cut a piece of chicken and chewed slowly. "This is delicious."

"Rosemary chicken. Edna got the recipe off the Internet."

Liv gave her a thumbs-up because her mouth was full.

While she chewed, she wondered how much she was at liberty to tell the sisters, who had probably learned as much from the police band, in the comfort of their sitting room, as Liv had after spending all day mucking about the crime scene.

"Besides," Ida continued, disregarding the rosemary chicken detour. "I don't believe for a minute that Ernie Bolton would kill anybody."

"Nor do I," Edna said. "But vandalize Barry's exhibit? He might, in a moment of—of temporary insanity."

"What does Bill think?" Ida asked.

"He hasn't said, at least not to me."

Both sisters leaned a little forward.

"What do you think?" Edna asked.

"I don't know what to think."

"Well, what do you know?" Ida asked, encouragingly.

Liv put down her fork. "That's just it. Not a lot. And I don't think the police know much more than I do. It's more a question of what we don't know."

"It always is, at the beginning of an investigation," said Ida. "Or at least I would assume so."

"So what don't you know?" Edna asked.

"Wait a minute, Edna." Miss Ida pushed away from the table and went of to the counter where she opened a drawer and took out a tablet and a pencil. She carried them back to the table.

"Since you don't seem to have your computer with you."

Liv scraped the last of the mashed potatoes off her plate and put down her fork.

"Would you like more, dear?"

"No, thank you, that was delicious."

"And from the Internet of all places," said Ida and whisked her plate away. She was back in a matter of seconds, Liv's plate squeaky clean and turned upside down on a drying rack, and Ida's attention focused on Liv.

"This is what we—I—know so far. You can fill me in on anything you learned over the airways." Liv really just wanted to go home to her little carriage house, take a long, hot shower, and curl up with the television remote. Instead, she opened the tablet of paper and drew a grid with headers at the top: Events, Time, People, Evidence.

"So this morning around eight thirty, I was out running with Whiskey."

At the mention of his name, Whiskey's head appeared from under the table, where he'd no doubt been in hiding, waiting to hijack a dropped morsel of food.

"I slowed down at the Museum of Yankee Horrors when I noticed that the vacant lot next to it had not been mowed." Liv explained to them about the landscape company and how she'd stopped to take a photo to remind them of their contract. While she was talking she wrote down, *8:30, Liv /Whiskey@ HM*, for Horror Museum, in the grid boxes.

"I let the leash out so Whiskey could explore a little bit and he came out with an arm in his mouth."

"The mannequin's," Edna said.

"Yes, but it did give me start."

She told them about seeing other parts of mannequins in the tall grasses, and about calling Barry. As she wrote she filled in more squares of the grid. When she got to the end of the day, she turned the paper around to show them.

"It looks like a lot but it doesn't tell us much. Just a lot of useless stuff."

"Well, I'm not surprised." Ida frowned at the page, then handed it to Edna, who nodded slowly.

"What?" Liv asked.

"To begin with, you left out last night."

"But I . . . oh." The sisters were absolutely right. Everyone had been so distracted by finding the body and getting the museum restored that no one had tried to trace Lucille's movements of the night before. Though she was sure Bill would get there eventually.

Liv took the tablet back. "At the award ceremony last night—"

"Now I'm sorry we didn't just bundle up and go," Miss Ida said.

"You're the one who said it was too cold."

"Besides, we didn't want to leave Whiskey by himself, sweet thing."

Liv heard a couple of tail thumps from under the table. She wondered when he was going to give up waiting for crumbs and come out.

"Ida, stick to the point."

Ida pursed her lips.

"Amanda Marlton-Crosby came into town to present her donation. A check for ten thousand dollars."

"So we heard," Edna said. "As well she should."

"You don't like her?" Liv asked.

"Don't know her."

"Knew her father though," Ida said. "Old money."

"They're from Celebration Bay?" Liv asked.

"No, no," Ida said.

"From everywhere but here," Edna added. "The family built that old manse back around the turn of the twentieth century. Fancied themselves part of the Gilded Age. Only summered here. And only occasionally, until Amanda's grandfather got the fishing bug, and passed it onto his son, Amanda's father."

"Which is why they keep the fish camp?"

"Yes. Amanda was her father's pet, and now that he's not in good health and can't come up, she keeps the old place open to humor him."

"Sort of a homage," Ida added.

"They've opened it to the public and have someone manage it in the summer," Edna said. "And someone to keep an eye on it off season. But not a close enough eye, if you ask me, because—"

"Edna!"

"Oh, don't be an old prude, Ida. Liv isn't a babe in the woods. Everybody knows fishermen aren't the only ones who stay overnight in those cabins."

"And sometimes not even overnight," Ida added, forgetting her prudishness.

"I see."

"Since Amanda's marriage," Edna continued, "she and her husband have been spending more time here. They used to leave right after they closed up the camp for winter and fly south with the snowbirds. I guess they decided to stay longer this year. So anyway, Amanda gave a check? Very generous, I must say."

"Yes," Liv agreed. "And everyone made a fuss over Barry, and Ernie was very upset. He even stopped by the judges to complain about the contest being fixed. Which is ridiculous. Then he stormed off, almost knocking Lucille off her high heels."

Liv stopped, wondering whether she should tell the sisters about not finding Lucille's shoes.

"What, Liv? Did you think of something?"

"Not really, but doing this really helps put things into

perspective." Bill hadn't said to keep the news secret. And knowing that bunch of amateur actors, everyone in town would be out on a shoe hunt.

And what about Lucille's car? No one had mentioned it. "Did you hear anything over the radio about anyone finding Lucille's car?"

The sisters looked at each other."

"No, we didn't," Edna said.

"They haven't located her car?" Ida asked.

"I didn't see it. And no one mentioned it. I should have asked."

"Well, just write it down, you'll remember to ask later."

Liv wrote it down. "There's something even stranger."

"Yes?" the sisters said together.

"They don't have her shoes."

"Her shoes?" Edna said. "Why not? Did they lose them?"

"No, they . . ." Liv must be tired because she felt the urge to laugh, and nothing today had been the least bit funny. "The police took the wrong shoes. They found shoes next to Lucille's feet and bagged them as evidence, but they— they—they belonged to Lizzie Borden." She clapped a hand over her mouth.

Edna cracked out a laugh. "But what happened to Lucille's shoes?"

Liv stopped laughing. "We don't know."

"Do you think she was mugged for her shoes?" Ida asked, wide eyed, and pulled her feet under her chair. "They do that kind of thing in the city."

"I doubt if that would happen in Celebration Bay," Edna said. "And thieves usually steal those expensive running shoes." She looked thoughtful. "Oh dear, you don't think it was a symbolic gesture, the killer took her shoes and substituted the shoes of a murderess to leave a message?"

"I hadn't thought about that," Liv said, impressed. "Lizzie purportedly killed her parents with an ax. But who would Lucille have killed?"

"She would never. The idea." Ida hmmphed her disgust. "Unless she killed someone's dreams." She looked at Liv.

"You mean maybe Ernie blamed her for 'killing his dream' of paying his back taxes?"

"It sounds senseless when you say it, but motives have been even sillier than that."

"Ida's right. And this sounds like a crime of passion, not sense," Edna said.

"True."

Ida pointed to Liv's notebook. "I think you'd better start a different grid for possible suspects and their motives."

It was a tribute to the Zimmerman sisters' tenacity that Liv didn't argue. When she had first moved here and was thrust into an investigation, she'd fought her involvement all the way. Now everyone in Celebration Bay just seemed to expect it from her. She planned all the major events in town. They came to her for all the problems associated with the events and more. They expected her to solve problems—all problems.

Even the sheriff consulted her.

The town somehow decided that since Liv was from Manhattan—which everyone considered the capital of murder and mayhem—she would have the right expertise to catch a crook. Even though Liv had never even witnessed a robbery, much less a murder, in her entire life in Manhattan.

As far as murders, Celebration Bay seemed to be holding its own.

"Liv?"

Liv turned to a new page. "First, let's make a timetable of events. That may eliminate some suspects to begin with."

"Do they know what time Lucille was killed?" Edna asked.

"Not that they're telling me," Liv said.

Ida shook her head. "I just can't believe someone would kill her. She was always so nice."

Edna rolled her eyes at that one. "She was always nice to us. But I think her husband might have a different story."

"Carson? That sweet man, how could anyone be mean to him?"

Edna huffed out air. "It's a good thing you were an elementary school teacher."

Ida nodded. "It's important to teach the fundamentals of scholarship and life in the formative years."

Liv smiled. She loved her landladies. Wacky, wonderful, compassionate people, not afraid of sticking their noses in places some people would say they didn't belong.

"Liv is trying to make a timetable, Ida."

"Yes, how can we help, dear? We didn't go to the festivities."

"Mainly just help me think." Liv thought back. "The award ceremony started around six thirty and took about a half hour, max. Then the finalists and the judges and Amanda Marlton-Crosby and the mayor and a few others stood around talking after that, say seven ten. Ernie got angry and knocked into Lucille as he walked away. But his anger didn't seem to be directed at her, just at everyone in general."

"Aha," Edna said. "And do we know where Ernie went?"

"As a matter of fact, we do," Liv said. "He went off to McCready's. Ted, Chaz, and I went over for a burger and he was still there, complaining to whomever would listen. He left a little after eight, I think. And I have no idea where he went after that."

"What about Lucille?"

"Pretty soon after Ernie left, Amanda said she had to go, she had guests at home. The mayor offered to walk her to her car but she said no, that her husband was meeting her. Which he did. Then pretty soon after that, the mayor asked Lucille if he could walk her to *her* car.

"And she thanked him but said Carson was picking her up, and then she said, 'Oh there he is,' and ran off in the opposite direction of Amanda."

"Carson," Edna breathed.

"Surely not," Ida said.

"Well, Ted pointed out a salient fact. We heard her say 'There's Carson,' and point in the direction of the sidewalk, but neither of us actually saw him." Liv frowned. "I don't know if anyone else saw him. I'm sure Bill must have asked the others."

"Well, you'd better ask him. Doesn't pay to make assumptions about what other people might or might not do." Edna cut a look at her sister. "Something that some people should remember."

"But why would she say she saw him, if she didn't?" Liv mused.

"Maybe she thought she saw him but didn't," Ida said.

"Or maybe she was just trying to get away from the mayor," Edna said.

Ida tittered, then clamped her hand over her mouth.

"Or," Liv said, "she was meeting someone who was not her husband and didn't want anyone else to know."

Chapter Seven

....

Neither sister had an idea about who Lucille might have been meeting. They knew about her liaisons, but like everyone else, they were loath to talk about them, even to Liv, whom they had goaded into investigating in the first place. Maybe it was just a case of no one wanting to cast the first stone.

Liv had several pages of notes but nothing that she sensed would lead them out of total guesswork. And that was the only conclusion they'd reached when Liv promised to meet them at nine forty-five the next morning for church.

Liv was so tempted to say, "I'm sleeping in." She needed the sleep. She wanted to be fresh and alert for Jonathon Preston when he arrived next weekend. The week ahead was bound to be long hours and little rest, and it was hard to wow anybody with your proposal when you were cracking giant yawns. And besides, she wouldn't mind him seeing her at her best.

But she also thought maybe the contemplative nature of

a sermon and a few hymns would restore some equilibrium. And then there would always be gossip at the Fellowship hour. She could restore her spirit *and* get a take on the climate of the community after Lucille's death.

"I'll be there with bells on," Liv said, and stifled a yawn.

She waited while Whiskey made a quick round of the garden, then they went inside, where Liv tossed her notes on her desk and went to take a shower and Whiskey made a beeline to his plaid doggie bed in the corner of Liv's bedroom.

The next morning, Liv was dressed and ready and drinking a cup of coffee when she heard the sisters come out to the garage.

She lifted her coat off the back of her kitchen chair and slipped it on as she headed for the door. Whiskey padded up to her, looking expectant.

"Just church, fella. I won't be long. Stay."

It was pretty cold for early October, overcast and bleak. Last year around this time she had lived in Celebration Bay for two months and was up to her eyeballs in damage control. And a year later here she was again performing triage. Murder had a way of impinging on one's best-laid plans.

While Liv waited for Edna to back the Zimmermans' old Buick out of the garage, she thought about Lucille Foster's shoes. They were distinctive with the trademark Louboutin red soles. Liv had actually crawled to the back of her closet looking for a pair of her old Manhattan heels this morning. But when she'd found them, then backed out to try them on, she realized how inappropriate to life in Celebration Bay they were.

And how totally inappropriate they were for an award ceremony in the park. Lucille had been even more overdressed than Janine. And Janine took delight in putting everyone else to shame, wardrobe wise as well everything else.

So Liv had kicked the offending heels to the back of the closet where they belonged and chosen a wider, lower, more comfortable Sunday shoe instead.

But she kept thinking about Lucille's shoes. Perhaps she had just come from some dressy affair and hadn't had time to change before the award ceremony. Or she was planning on going somewhere directly after the ceremony. With her husband? Or with someone else?

She'd have to ask Bill what he'd found out from Carson Foster. On one level it was none of Liv's business, but on another . . . She'd learned early in her career that it paid to be aware of every possible snafu and have a secondary plan in place.

Liv climbed into the backseat, and a few minutes later they were pulling into the parking lot across the street from the First Presbyterian Church.

Pastor Schorr was greeting his flock at the front door, dressed in his surplice. His light hair shone like a lamp of welcome against the gray day. The pastor was a young man with a booming voice, who, in addition to his pastoral duties, had founded and ran the community center that was the object of the current fund-raiser.

People were eager to get inside and the welcomes were quick, though a couple of people who saw Liv and the Zimmermans crossing the street lagged a little, probably hoping to hear some dirt. Liv was sure there would be plenty at Fellowship hour, but she would be listening for it, not handing it out.

Pastor Schorr took her hand and patted it like an older and wise man, but the look in his eye was more "here we go again." Liv smiled back at him and kept walking, straight to the pew where they always sat, where the Zimmerman family had been sitting for generations. BeBe was waiting for them and scooted over a little to make more room.

"I was beginning to wonder if you all were coming. Everybody's talking about the vandalism over at Barry's

Museum of Yankee Horrors. I wouldn't want to be Ernie Bolton right now."

Liv scooched in beside her. "What are they saying about him?"

"That he was a sore loser and broke in and destroyed Barry's exhibits."

Liv wasn't surprised. "What about the other thing?"

BeBe looked around and moved closer. "The verdict is split. Some say he did it, some not. Of the dids, some are saying it was probably an accident and he should come forward."

"Has anybody seen him?"

BeBe shrugged. "I doubt he'll be coming out in public for a while."

The choir came in singing "For the Beauty of the Earth."

As the music died away, and scripture was read, Liv wondered if Pastor Schorr would mention the death of Lucille Foster. As far as Liv knew, the Fosters weren't members of the congregation, but in spite of the hordes of tourists that visited each year, Celebration Bay was a small town through and through.

He talked about the fullness of harvest and the earth sleeping to replenish itself, and it seemed somehow appropriate, even though he didn't mention Lucille by name. Liv listened intently, ordered her mind not to wander, concentrated not to let her eye rove over the others and wonder if one of them was a murderer.

The morning service ended with a hopeful recessional, then the congregation broke into conversation as they headed for the doors or down to the Fellowship room for coffee hour.

Liv didn't even have to ask if they were staying. Liv and BeBe followed the two sisters down the stairs, where Edna and Ida headed straight for the refreshment table and Ruth Benedict, the town's most voracious, and sometimes most vicious, gossiper.

Liv and BeBe exchanged looks and decided to fortify themselves with coffee and cookies before joining the conversation.

By the time they made their way over to the ladies, two other ladies had joined them and were listening intently to Ruth.

"Open marriage," Ruth said and raised her eyebrows. "Well, at least on her side."

"I never," said one of the other churchgoers.

"Well, she did. And more than once." Ruth puffed up, sending a wave of navy blue rayon across her ample bust. "I wouldn't be surprised if one of her . . . men . . . did her in."

"Why on earth?" Edna said.

Edna of course didn't actually need to be told why a person might kill his or her lover; she may have never married and had lived in Celebration Bay all her life, but she knew what was what. No, Edna was priming Ruth's pump.

Ruth shrugged. "Jealousy? Maybe she was trying to break it off . . ."

"You don't think maybe Carson . . . ?"

"It's totally possible. Maybe he just couldn't take it anymore."

"I don't believe she was that bad. They always looked so happy together. And they were very generous in support of the children's clothing drive, the food pantry, and a dozen other charities."

Ruth snorted. "Maybe her charity should have begun at home."

"Ruth Benedict," Ida said, scandalized. "Remember where you are."

"I'm not saying anything that everybody else doesn't know. But the one thing I can tell you is my house looks out over Lakeside Road. And more than once I've seen Lucille's car going up and coming back, sometimes late at night."

"So what?" Edna said. "The Lakeside Diner is up there, and Dexter Kent's nursery and—"

"And those tacky cabins at the fish camp. You know what kind of shenanigans go on there."

"I'm afraid I've never been there," Edna said icily.

"Well, you know it by reputation. I see Chaz Bristow's jeep up there all the time, day and nighttime, too." Ruth cut a look toward Liv. "I've seen your car drive up that ways a few times."

"Ruth, everyone uses that road."

"It's not a direct route to anywhere."

"Don't be ridiculous. I've been up to Dexter's several times. The event office conducts a lot of business with him. And I've eaten at the diner and I've even been to the fish camp, for fishing. That's all there is to it."

"If you say so." Ruth didn't sound like she believed it. "But Liv, we all know what's going on between you and Chaz. And it's not just fishing."

"What? There's nothing."

"You don't have to answer to her, Liv," Edna said. "That's insulting, Ruth Benedict."

"I'm just saying what I saw."

"And you have a dirty mind," Ida added.

"Chaz didn't deny it," Ruth said smugly.

"Hmmph," Ida said. "I doubt if Chaz has ever talked to you."

Liv was moved to hear the sisters stick up for her. Even though there really wasn't anything going on between Liv and Chaz, or Liv and anybody, she was still learning how small towns could be. And she'd been very careful not to give people anything to talk about. Not that anything like the truth would stop people like Ruth Benedict, a woman with way too much time on her hands.

"Did you see anyone on Friday night?" Liv hadn't meant to ask, but she couldn't help herself.

Ruth put a finger to her chin. It didn't fool any of them. Ruth knew exactly what she was going to say. "Well, since I didn't come into town for the ceremony, I saw everyone who came and went. I saw Amanda Marlton drive down to town in her Land Rover, but I didn't see her drive home again." She raised both eyebrows and leaned closer to her audience. "But there was a silver Mercedes that came back late and pulled into the drive."

Liv didn't understand how she could make so much innuendo with so few actual facts.

"I don't think you know what you're talking about," Edna said. "It's dark by four thirty. How can you tell what cars go by?"

"Because," Ruth said smugly. "The county put in streetlamps just below my house. I can see every car that passes like it was daylight. And . . ." Her expression turned sly. "I wouldn't ordinarily say anything . . ."

Ha, thought Liv.

"Ha," said Edna.

"But I did see Chaz's old jeep follow the Mercedes up a while later."

Liv's stomach clenched. She wanted to say, "well not with me," but that was nobody's business.

"Ladies," Pastor Schorr said brightly, breaking into the group. "Such a lovely group of worshippers this morning."

Ruth smiled and nodded. "Oh, Pastor, I'm glad you stopped by. I wanted to talk to you about the poinsettia sale. I have a few ideas." She deftly moved him away from the group. Or maybe he had done the moving. Liv wasn't sure.

The other two women wandered off.

"Well," Edna said. "Spread out and see if you hear anything meaningful."

Liv and BeBe stayed together and mingled. But the most they heard was surprise at Amanda Marlton-Crosby's generous donation and a quick reference of "isn't it a shame about Lucille Foster."

It had been a singularly disappointing morning. And embarrassing. As they got ready to leave, Liv pulled BeBe into an empty hallway.

"Does eveyone think Chaz and I are having an affair?"

"Heck, Liv. They wouldn't talk about it around me if they did. And what do you care?"

"I don't."

BeBe gave her a look. "You're just mad because he let Ruth Benedict think you were."

"If he really did. I wonder if he's heard about the murder?"

Instead of returning home with the sisters, Liv decided to stop by the newspaper office to see Chaz. If he was even there. Maybe he was at the fish camp, fishing, or with one of his many admirers.

She didn't care.

Not a lot anyway. But she did need his help if she could convince him to listen. For a former investigative reporter he sure tried to keep his head in the sand about breaking news, defaulting to fishing stories and Four-H and Scouting endeavors.

At first Liv had thought it was sheer laziness, but lately she had come to realize that like most people Chaz was carrying around a few bruises from the past. Wounds that he would rather put to rest, but that all came back again every time he had to interest himself in an investigation.

Liv felt for him, but not enough to let him off the hook, to use a fishing term. Behind Chaz's lazy, flirtatious, sometimes infuriatingly smart-aleck attitude was a finely tempered mind.

But today she wasn't particularly interested in his mind. Today she had more personal business to conduct.

"I don't think you should go over there mad," Edna said.

"What you and Chaz do is your own business," added Ida.

"We're just friends," Liz said. "And sometimes we aren't even friends."

"I know he can be annoying, but he's a nice young man after all is said and done." Edna nodded to herself.

Liv gave up. "I'm not mad. I'm going to see if he has any ideas about what happened on Friday night."

"That's a good idea," Ida said. "He was always such a bright boy."

Liv smiled and headed up the block to give that bright boy a piece of her mind.

The *Celebration Bay Clarion* office was housed in a cottage, a block from First Presbyterian. It had once been a charming Craftsman, painted white with green shutters. At least when Liv had first seen it she'd thought it charming—until she got close to it. Then she saw the graying façade, the peeling paint on the shutters. The porch was sagging and the windows looked like they hadn't been washed in a decade.

The windows still looked pretty dirty, but the porch had new floorboards, and the shutters had been scraped and painted.

It still had a long ways to go.

Liv hesitated out on the walk. She was Ms. Organization, the quintessential event planner, in control, cool in an emergency, but Chaz Bristow made her rush into things without thinking. Like now.

She didn't know—or care, she reminded herself—how he spent his weekends, how he'd spent last night, or what he was doing this morning. Though maybe it would have been better if she'd called first.

Just as she was about to turn away, an upstairs window opened. Chaz's head stuck out. "If you're taking the census, you'd better come in."

Liv frowned up at him. "What?"

"Those shoes."

"What about them?"

"Very sensible. Like you might be going door to door. I picture you more as the four-inch-heel type."

"Still?" She'd gone out of her way to fit into the rural atmosphere of the town. "Anyway, that's what I've come to see you about."

"Shoes? Sounds promising."

"Lucille Foster's shoes. And some information about the fish camp."

"Oops. I never did, not with Lucille anyway."

"You know she's dead?"

Chaz just looked at her. "You better come in."

The door wasn't locked, it never was. A lot of people in town didn't lock their doors. It was one of the quaint things that Liv found appealing, not that she would ever leave her own cottage unlocked. Nor did she think Chaz should either.

He'd been an investigative reporter in Los Angeles and had witnessed things Ted said she shouldn't ask him about. That kind of life didn't sound like it would increase a man's trust in his fellow man.

She stepped inside the foyer. Groped for a light switch, thinking if he'd only wash the windows, the house wouldn't be so dark. Nothing much had changed since the last time she'd been here. The room had once been a parlor but whatever furnishings were left had been pushed to the far end to make room for a large kneehole desk and several wooden chairs that served as a reception area.

Two other rooms housed the newspaper proper. The upstairs was Chaz's living quarters, which Liv had never seen. If the downstairs was any indication, she had no desire to enter them, either.

Chaz padded barefoot down the stairs, pulling a T-shirt over his head.

He walked right past her and into the newspaper room. Liv followed him through another dark room, inhabited by several desks piled high with books and papers and several computers and screens of varying sizes. A sagging couch, also covered in papers, sat in the middle of the room.

Chaz didn't stop to turn on a light, but walked straight through to another room, which held more equipment, and into the kitchen.

Liv prepared herself and stepped in behind him. The last

time she'd been here it had looked like a garbage dump. Chaz had just gotten back from a trip to LA that he hadn't told anyone about, one that had really affected him, and not for the better.

It had taken work on everyone's part to get him back to his infuriating snarky self. Today the kitchen was spotless. It was also bare of any food or signs of eating.

Hmmm. "Am I interrupting anything?"

Chaz raised one eyebrow, and a slow smile spread across his face. "What do you have in mind?"

"Stop it. I came to get some information. Did you know that Lucille Foster was murdered sometime Friday night?"

The smile disappeared. "I need coffee."

"They took Ernie Bolton in for questioning. Do you know if they let him out?"

Chaz ran his fingers through his hair, leaving it sticking up in spikes. "Just wait until I have some coffee. You're not making sense. And I don't know anything. When I left you and Ted Friday night, I went up to the fish camp. I just got back last night."

Liv pursed her lips. That was something else she was going to find out about while she was here. Even though she really didn't want to know.

Chaz got coffee from the freezer, measured it out, poured water in the coffeemaker, and stood at the counter watching it drip into the carafe.

Liv sat at the table and waited. At last he reached into the cabinet and took out two mugs, filled them, handed one to Liv, and sat down across from her.

He stared into his mug between sips of coffee, but when he finally looked up, Liv saw a glint of what he called his journalistic addiction. "What happened?"

She told him about jogging and discovering Barry's museum had been vandalized.

Chaz didn't look at her but stared into the middle distance as if he were absorbing information and filing it as it came in.

He must be tired, because he typically surrounded himself in
BS and goofiness. And she'd have to drag him into helping.

He hadn't even told her to leave it alone, at least not yet,
and that was usually the first thing he said.

She told him about finding the mannequins in the weeds,
calling Barry, and finding Lucille's body; about being at the
bakery when they heard that Ernie had been taken in for
questioning.

She repeated her conversation with Bill and then told him
about discovering that Lucille's shoes were missing.

When she finally finished, she was out of breath.

Chaz looked up and said, "Lucille?"

And that's when Liv got worried.

Chapter Eight

....

Liv fought the buzzing in her ears. Ruth Benedict saying, "Chaz's jeep was at the fish camp Friday night." "You weren't—you didn't—?" She couldn't even form the words, the thought was so repellent. She changed tack. "There's speculation that Lucille caught someone breaking into Barry's museum and tried to stop them."

"Lucille?" This time he sounded more like himself. He rubbed his face with both hands. "Go back to the beginning and tell me everything again and give me more detail."

She did, step by step.

"Damn, it doesn't make sense."

"No, it doesn't. Lucille didn't strike me as someone who would do something so obviously futile, not to mention dangerous, just to stop a burglary." *Especially not while wearing those shoes,* she added to herself. They looked more like the kind of shoes you wore on a . . . date.

"She wasn't," Chaz said. "She would hire someone to do it."

Liv frowned. "But maybe if she saw that it was Ernie, and she thought she could talk some sense into him . . ."

"Liv, first of all, Ernie didn't leave the pub until after eight o'clock. The ceremony had been over for at least half an hour. And she'd already gone off with her husband."

"Did you see him?"

"No."

"Neither did anyone else."

"Was anyone paying attention?"

"No, I guess not, but Carson said he didn't pick her up, and regardless, the vandalism had to occur much later. Chaz, the whole thing was dismantled like someone was tearing the figures limb from limb."

"Hmm."

"It's only two blocks from the square. The movie house is half a block from there. People would be around until pretty late. Whoever broke in would have had to wait until the middle of the night."

"True," Chaz said. "And you're wondering what Lucille was doing driving around that late at night?"

"Yes. But there's one other thing. When I left Bill at the museum yesterday afternoon, they hadn't found her shoes or her car."

Chaz took a sip of coffee, beetled his eyebrows.

Liv could practically see his mind wake up, and she knew he was already putting events into possible scenarios. He was good. He just wasn't willing.

"Stop it," he said finally.

"That's my line," Liv said. "Stop what?"

"Sitting there like a puppy waiting for a biscuit."

"That was demeaning. I'm a woman waiting for you to decide to participate."

He looked at her, a slow smile curving his lips and working its way up to his eyes. "I'm well aware of the first, and it's not me who's indecisive."

"Chaz."

"Yeah, I'll take a look at the facts. Lucille wasn't a bad person. She just got bored easily and didn't always use the best judgment."

"So you know about her . . ."

"Yep. Everybody did."

"Do you think one of her, um, lovers might have killed her and not the vandal?"

"How the hell would I know?"

Liv gulped. "Not you?"

"For crying out loud, Liv. Are seriously asking me that?"

"Well, Ruth Benedict said she was always seeing Lucille's car up at the fish camp and that she saw your jeep there Friday night." Liv took a breath.

Chaz cocked his head. "That's because I went fishing. I told you that."

"Oh, right. Did you, uh, happen to see Lucille while you were up there?"

"No. And I haven't 'seen' her in the way you mean since I was fourteen and she introduced me to the mysteries of adulthood."

"She didn't."

"Here's to you, Mrs. Foster."

"TMI."

He chuckled. "Don't ask if you don't want to know the truth. I didn't see anyone at the camp. I was on my boat, on the lake. Besides, the camp is closed for a private party."

Liv rolled her eyes. "I can imagine."

"No, really, get this. Amanda Marlton-Crosby rented out the whole place—all eight cabins—to a bunch of witches for their Halloween ritual."

"Witches? Why would they come to the fish camp?"

"Beats me, but I saw Rod Crosby last week cleaning the cottages out and spiffing up the place. He said that Amanda had rented the whole thing out for three weekends. Guess they thought that field between the camp and the house would be the perfect place to dance naked widdershins or whatever they do."

"Stop it. Why do you keep doing that?"

"Being provocative?"

"Being obnoxious."

"I like to see you get all huffy."

"Well, stop it, and for your info, they don't dance widdershins, at least I don't think they do, I think widdershins creates negative energy." Liv frowned. "How did we go from Lucille being murdered to talking about witches?"

"Your rambling, eclectic, delicious mind."

"So before we leave the subject, why on earth did Amanda rent to them?"

"Amanda knows their leader, or whatever you call the head witch. She opened a store in town, but I haven't seen it yet."

"Oh, I met her yesterday, Yolanda Nestor. She rented the space that used to be the Pyne Bough. And she put a spell on the soapbox prophet."

"He's back?"

"I guess Bill has been too busy to pick him up. But I'm going to make sure we get rid of him by next weekend."

"Maybe this Yolanda can turn him into a frog."

"I don't think she's that kind of witch. She seemed really nice except for the knocking the soapboxer over thing. She says he tripped, but . . . When are they coming?"

"A few of them are coming sometime this week, according to Rod Crosby. . . to do the preparations and commune with the spirits or whatever. Then the whole lot is coming in for Halloween night.

"Rod was not pleased at all, he thought he and Amanda were going to spend the fall in Manhattan and the winter in Miami. Now she's talking about a white Christmas and chestnuts roasting on an open fire. Poor guy."

"They don't seem to like it here much. They hardly ever

come into town," Liv said. "And then she donates ten K to the haunted house winner. I didn't know she was even aware the community center needed a new space."

"She's just really shy. Rod's the people person. Maybe he told her about it."

Liv pulled out her phone and made a note to check out Yolanda and her coven, and make sure they were friendly and wouldn't cause too much of a disturbance in town. That's all Liv needed—anti-Halloween sentiment, which she'd heard had become a real concern in a few other towns. She was determined to keep her event fun and anger free.

Chaz got up and poured them more coffee.

"Well, first things first," Liv said when he was seated across from her again. "What are we going to do about Lucille's murder?"

When Liv left a few minutes later, they hadn't come up with any more of a plan than she had with Ted or the sisters. Normally that would irritate her, that Chaz had the acumen but not the desire to help. Now, she was beginning to see a pattern. Obstinacy at the beginning, then being slowly drawn into taking a look at the facts, then following the story, wherever it led.

And after having been around him for a year and pleading with him to help, she was beginning to realize when he was hooked, just like all those poor fish he hauled out of the lake. He could wriggle all he wanted to, but he would investigate.

She smiled to herself as she walked toward the street. It made her feel a little powerful—and kind of mercenary. She deflated a bit. Surely she shouldn't be enjoying the feeling of having just a little power over the recalcitrant newspaper editor.

"Hey," Chaz called.

She wiped off the smile and turned back to him. He was

leaning out the door, his hands braced against the frame. Celebration Bay's celebrated bad boy. An image he cultivated and probably deserved.

"When is your philanthropist coming?"

"Jon Preston? Not until this next weekend, thank goodness."

"I can see where murder might put a damper on your fundraiser."

"I know. I just hope this can all be resolved before he gets here."

Storm clouds swept in and Liv spent Sunday afternoon curled up on the couch with Whiskey and her laptop, trying to concentrate on the other events for Halloween—the new zombie parade, among others. So far sign-up had been going great. It was scheduled for Thursday afternoon, starting at the post office parking lot, circling the square, and ending at the band shell. Short and sweet.

Liv had insisted that it be held on a weekday afternoon and open to all ages. The last thing she wanted was a bunch of zombies staggering out of the pub and acting crazy. Maybe not the last thing; the last thing she needed was an unsolved murder and a killer running loose when hundreds of kids were about to go door-to-door trick-or-treating.

Her fingers itched to call Bill to see if there had been any breaks in the case, but she knew he was doing the best he could with the staff he had. He had to take care of the entire county, not just their town, and Halloween always brought an uptick in misdemeanors. She'd get in touch with A.K. Pierce first thing in the morning and have Bayside Security beef up their presence on the street.

Maybe A.K. could figure out a way to keep that soapboxer out of town square. He was bound to cause trouble.

Halloween might be dedicated to costume parties and handing out candy, but Halloween Eve was often an excuse for people to misbehave. Whether you called it Cabbage Night, Mischief Night, Devil's Night, or any of the other sobriquets, it was a night of egging and toilet-papering people's shrubbery, and it sometimes led to vandalism and theft.

Liv sighed. Someone in Celebration Bay hadn't waited, and he'd thrown in murder as an added insult.

By the time evening rolled around and it was time for Liv to meet BeBe for their weekly dinner, she'd worked herself into a first-class funk. The weather wasn't helping. Rain was coming down in sheets, and Liv thought of all the bales of hay getting saturated and the decorations hanging limp and torn.

Thank goodness they'd gotten all the mannequins out of the lot yesterday. She wondered how Ernie Bolton's haunted house was faring with Ernie held for questioning. His wife would not be able to cover everything to protect it from the rain. Liv looked at the time on her laptop. Maybe BeBe could pick her up early and they could swing by to see if she needed help.

She made the call. "I'm on my way," BeBe said, and hung up.

Liv stood up.

Whiskey jumped off the couch, shook himself, and looked at Liv before he shot off down the hall to hide.

"You're in luck. You get to stay here. But if you want to go out, it's now or much later." She walked down the hall to the kitchen and stood at the door. After a few seconds Whiskey came out of hiding. Liv opened the door.

Whiskey looked out, looked back at her.

"I know, just get it done."

Whiskey shot out the door to the shelter of the bushes. He was back and shaking off the rain a minute later. Liv grabbed a towel she kept for just that purpose and gave him a good rub.

A treat quickly snatched from her hand and he was headed back to his doggie bed.

Liv did a quick cleanup and put on boots and her rain slicker.

BeBe's Subaru pulled into the driveway a minute later. Liv opened the door and made a dash for the car.

"That was fast," Liv said as she slammed the front door.

"I was bored stiff. I'm afraid I've become a workaholic, and since hiring a staff, I have several hours a week with nothing to do." She looked over her shoulder to back out to the street. "I guess I have to retrain myself to enjoy doing nothing."

"Yeah, I can relate."

"So, it's crazy about Ernie, isn't it? I don't think he would kill anybody, even for all that money. It would be smarter to kill Barry. Though I'm not condoning that, either."

"I don't think so, either. Even if Lucille caught him wrecking Barry's museum, why didn't she just drive to the corner and call the police?"

"Exactly." BeBe turned up the wipers. "Maybe *he* caught *her* vandalizing and tried to stop it? And her death was an accident?"

"What motive could Lucille possibly have to destroy the display?"

They had to drive past Barry's museum on their way to Ernie's Monster Mansion. There were lights on inside, but only one car that Liv could see through the rain. Barry was probably camping out there to prevent further breaking and entering.

Three blocks later they turned onto Baxter Street. The community center was dark, only two security lights burned at the corner of the building. Across the street, Ernie's haunted house was also dark, except for one light upstairs, and a dim porch light.

Just enough light to see two shadowed figures moving about the displays in the front yard. The rest of the street was deserted, and for a split second Liv thought it might be another case of vandalism. But when BeBe pulled up to the curb, Liv saw that it was two women, pulling tarps over the Halloween decorations. And not having too much success.

Liv and BeBe both jumped out of the car and ran up the walk to help.

"Mrs. Bolton, we came to help," BeBe said. "What can we do?"

Liv had never met Ernie's wife, really only knew Ernie through the community center. From what she could tell, Harriett Bolton was a dumpy, middle-aged woman with dark hair hanging wet and limp in the rain. The other woman was younger, and looked vaguely familiar. Probably a relative.

Harriett thrust one end of the tarp at BeBe and motioned for her to pull it over Dracula's casket. Between them the four women managed to cover the wooden casket and tuck the tarp into the bottom. That's when Liv noticed the electrical cables still attached and getting wet.

An accident waiting to happen. The second woman was already in the yard shaking a plastic drop cloth, attempting to open it up. Liv grabbed the other end and they covered most of the gravestones, Ernie must have cut some corners toward the end, because while the majority of the stones were made from polyresin, a few were nothing more than foam board and had already begun to disintegrate.

When they had covered everything in the yard, Liv and the other woman joined BeBe and a frowning Mrs. Bolton back on the porch.

"I think it's salvageable," Liv said optimistically.

"Don't matter. But thank you for coming. I don't know what we're gonna do now. They took my Ernie away, saying he killed that Foster woman. But Ernie's not like that. And he didn't wreck Barry's house, neither. Guess we'll have to pack it in and go stay with my mother 'til they let Ernie go. If they don't get him on back taxes. Then we will be in a fix."

Beside her the other woman let out a wail.

"Hush up, girl," Mrs. Bolton said.

Liv recognized that screech. "Marla Jean?"

The woman looked up, and sure enough, it was Marla Jean Higgins. Liv could see a Greek toga beneath her transparent rain coat.

"You know my daughter?"

"Your daughter?" Liv tried to smile. "We met briefly yesterday. I'm Liv Montgomery. I'm the town's event coordinator."

"I'm Ernie's wife, Harriett. Glad to meet ya. Though I know who you are. Just never had call to say hello before now."

"Well, I'm sorry it isn't under happier circumstances."

"I am, too. Especially now that Marla's back at home."

Marla turned and fled inside.

"She always had self-esteem problems," Harriett confessed. "Then she just up and married that Eddie Higgins, and wouldn't you know it, he took off less than a year later . . ." She sighed heavily. "You want to come in for some coffee or something? That's about the best I can do."

"Thank you, Mrs. Bolton," BeBe said, "but we have dinner plans."

Harriett Bolton nodded, like it was inevitable that they would have dinner plans.

"I'll try to get by tomorrow and see what we can do to help you get this back up and running," Liv said.

Mrs. Bolton nodded again.

Liv and BeBe got back in the car and drove away.

"That was depressing," BeBe said as soon as the house was out of sight.

"No kidding. And no wonder Ernie was so desperate to win that money."

"Desperate enough to destroy Barry's entry?"

"I don't know, but it is kind of weird that Marla Jean was at the play rehearsal yesterday morning and helped collect the damaged parts and clean up the mess. Barry was blaming Ernie at the top of his lungs and she didn't say a word." Liv paused. "Actually, she was the one who found the body."

"Yikes, that must have been horrible."

"Yes," Liv said. "Horrible, very loud, and—coincidental?"

BeBe cut into her Buddy's Place homemade meat loaf. "You think maybe Marla knew the body was going to be there? That's psycho. Though she is a little weird."

"She's definitely into costumes. Saturday morning she was wearing a fifties cocktail dress and tonight a toga."

"A lot of people in town are into costumes." BeBe smiled at their waitress, who was wearing a cat ears headband and painted whiskers. "There's a long way between being a little weird and being willing to kill."

"True," Liv said.

Buddy's was a diner luncheonette crossover eating experience. Home cooking with a wine and beer license. Genny Parsons—proprietress, hostess, sometimes waitress, and self-professed chief cook and bottle washer—set down her mug of coffee and slipped into the booth beside Liv.

"Just sent the other two waitresses home." She reached for the sugar packets. "The rain is keeping everybody away. It's like that TV show about fashion designing. One day you're covered in customers, the next . . ." She looked around.

There were two guys sitting at the counter and an older couple sharing a piece of lemon meringue pie.

"You have us," BeBe said.

"And I love you both for it. But you didn't get this wet running from your car to the diner. What have you two been up to?"

"We went to check on Ernie's Monster Mansion."

"Terrible news. You don't think he did it, do you?"

Liv shrugged. "I have no idea."

"So what happened over there?"

"Harriett Bolton and her daughter, Marla Jean, were trying to cover up everything. We stopped to help."

"It was Liv's idea."

"Why am I not surprised. Just like Liv to mix doing a good deed with a little light sleuthing."

"No," Liv protested. "It was purely selfish, in case we need Ernie's haunted house as backup. I had no intention of sleuthing. Though I was sort of surprised to find Marla Jean there. I had no idea she was Ernie's daughter."

"I went to school with her," Genny said. "We were in the same chemistry class. But we were never friends. Had an odd kick in her gallop."

"Still does," BeBe said.

Genny snorted a laugh. "Liv, you're looking shocked. Is that because I look young for my age?"

"You do," Liv said. "I just . . . Mrs. Bolton said Marla Jean had just gotten out of a marriage."

"Now that's a story. And I hate to talk out of school, but Eddie Higgins was a flimflam man. We used to call him Fast Eddie when we were in high school. He could con the socks off you without you even taking off your shoes. I don't know how Marla caught him even for a couple of months."

"So what did he con Marla Jean out of? Certainly not her looks or her youth. She's got to be forty if she's a day."

"Forty-mmmph-mmmph," Genny said, mumbling the last number so that it was unrecognizable.

"Let's just say early forties," BeBe said.

"Anyway, Fast Eddie made her life a misery for a few months, and when she finally got that he didn't really love her, she hauled her butt back home. That was a couple of years ago. They say Ernie's fortunes began to go the way of all flesh after that."

"Why? Did he have to pay Eddie off?"

"Eddie conned him into giving him a little strip of land that belonged to Ernie's mother, rest her soul." Genny paused to drink some coffee.

"And?" Liv coaxed.

"And it was right near the highway. Ernie had been holding on to it for years in case the highway department ever decided to widen the road. Wasn't worth two nickels. He thought he was getting off easy to get rid of that parasite. Of course what Ernie didn't know was that some folks were interested in building some condos nearby and they *were* going to have to widen the road that ran right past Ernie's property."

"So Fast Eddie turned around and sold it," Liv said.

"Yes, he did, to Carson Foster. And he made a pretty penny off it. Dumb skunk. If Eddie had held on to it for a few months longer, he could have sold it for a lot more. Now, Carson, *he* made a fortune off it."

"What happened to Fast Eddie?"

Genny shrugged. "Nobody's seen him since."

Chapter Nine

....

Liv didn't see how the cheating and absconding of Fast Eddie Higgins could have anything to do with the current vandalism and murder. It was just one of those strange phenomena of small towns that she was still trying to understand and get used to.

Sometimes it seemed like everyone knew everyone else, and most of them seemed to be kin to each other. Thousands of tourists came through their town each year and yet Celebration Bay was still the quintessential small town.

Liv liked it but she wasn't always comfortable with it. And Monday morning was no different.

She'd left Whiskey with Ida and Edna that morning. She was sure there was going to be fallout from Lucille Foster's murder, starting with the mayor. Liv didn't understand why he hadn't already made an appearance or at least phoned.

She picked up her usual pastries and drinks but didn't stop to talk to Dolly or BeBe. She hurried past the other stores on the block, though she did make a mental note to stop around the corner to the new occult store and say hello. Made a second note to get rid of the soapbox spouter who had moved across the street to place himself in front of the Corner Café and next to the alley that abutted Yolanda Nestor's new store.

She handed Ted their morning tea, coffee, and pumpkin sunflower seed muffins and went straight to her office.

"What's the rush?" he called after her. "It's not even ten o'clock."

"I'm calling downstairs to Permits and Licenses to find out if that nutcase in the park has a permit to . . . to . . . rant."

She picked up the phone.

Ted came in a minute later, bearing a silver tray with their muffins on little china plates. The tea and coffee he always left in cardboard in case of a sudden emergency. Emergencies generally required on-site caffeine.

Their office of two ran on enthusiasm, energy, and copious amounts of coffee and tea.

"I already called. They said they hadn't been sure what to do and asked the mayor. He said to give the guy a permit to set up in the park."

Liv drummed her fingers. "But he's moved to the sidewalk across the street."

"You don't think he adds a little drama to the occasion?"

"I think he's bound to cause trouble."

"True. I'll go down and see exactly what his parameters are. Maybe we can get him on a technicality. But more importantly, I was hoping you would bring Whiskey to work today. I was going to ask you if he could be in the zombie parade with me."

Liv stared at Ted. "Why am I always surprised? The candy cane socks and red bow tie I can live with, I even got used to the green striped vest with the cloverleaf tie, but somehow the image of you painted gray and dressed in rags as you stumble down Main Street is going to be a little difficult."

"I'm going to be a sophisticated zombie. And I need a

dapper dog." He set one of the plates in front of Liv along with a napkin and fork. "The muffins are a little delicate."

He sat down on the other side of her desk. The office did seem quiet without Whiskey, not that he ever barked or bothered them. He was just good company.

She sighed. "Well, if we don't get—"

The phone rang. Ted stood. "I'll get it. You drink your latte before it gets cold."

"Thanks." She flipped the tab off her cup and sipped. Exhaled as she fell into her morning routine. Pinched off a corner of her muffin. Dolly never let them down. Everything she made was delicious, and the reason Liv was having to exercise more than she usually did.

She took another bite out of the muffin. She could hear Ted on the phone in the outer office. She wondered who was calling this early and hoped to heaven it wasn't more trouble.

He came back in and sat down. Picked up his tea. "That was your VanderHauw Foundation rep on the phone."

"Jon Preston? What did he say? Is he back from Thailand? He isn't cancelling, is he?"

"Not only is he back, but he's here."

"What? He's here in Celebration Bay?" Liv looked down at her everyday work clothes.

When she looked up again, Ted was grinning at her.

"And he's hoping you'll have time to have lunch with him today at the inn. I graciously accepted for you."

"Look how I'm dressed."

"You look like you do every day. Absolutely superb."

"Thanks, but Jon might be expecting something a little more . . ."

"Sexy?"

She glowered at him. "Businesslike."

"You look fine. Now drink your coffee."

"But he wasn't coming in until Thursday. Do you think this is a good sign?" Liv slumped. "Or do you think he's heard about Lucille's murder and is going to wig out? How did he sound?"

Liv knew that was a stupid question. She hadn't lived and worked with the movers and shakers without knowing and learning not to ever give anything away—including opinions—until it was necessary.

"Only lunch will tell. Now, where were we?"

Liv thought back. "I was about to say we need to get rid of the doomsday prophet and figure out this murder before the zombie parade. I was hoping it would all be cleared up before Jon's arrival. Mayor Worley will have a coronary. And where is he? I thought he'd be here wringing his hands first thing."

The outer door opened and closed.

"Perfect timing," Ted said, and took a bite of the moist muffin. "DHL should model their delivery drones after him."

Gilbert Worley whisked through the door and into Liv's office without slowing down.

Liv braced herself.

Ted said, "Good morning, Gilbert."

"Good? You call a murder of one of our finest citizens good?"

"You'll be happy to know our taxpayers' dollars are at work, and Bill has already taken Ernie Bolton in for questioning," Liv assured him.

"Ernie?" Gilbert's black brows snapped together. "Ridiculous. Ernie is no murderer. Has Bill Gunnison lost his mind?"

"Ernie had reason to vandalize Barry Lindquist's Museum of Yankee Horrors. Lucille's body was found with the other . . . um . . . bodies."

The mayor pulled up a chair, collapsed into it, and began kneading his hands. "This job is making me old before my time."

Liv and Ted exchanged looks. Middle age had come and was quickly exiting; politics could do that to a person. He had worry lines, his jowls were beginning to sag, and the

Grecian Formula that kept his brilliantined hair black could not stop it from receding from his forehead.

His job did make for a lot of pressure, even though as mayor he mainly ran meetings, voted on tied ballots from the board of trustees, and spent most of his energy getting reelected.

He was an alarmist and dramatic, but was loyal to his town.

"What are you going to do about it?" The mayor eyed their pastries.

"Care for a bite?" Ted asked innocently.

"No, and I don't see how the two of you can sit there eating when a murder has been committed and the winning entry of Amanda Marlton-Crosby's generous donation is in shambles.

"She'll be appalled. What if she withdraws her offer? And what about that fellow from that grant organization? How do you expect us to qualify for grants if we keep killing people off?

"I want this solved before he shows up. Understand?"

Liv and Ted traded looks.

"Gilbert, calm down." Ted turned in his chair to face the mayor, who was rapidly turning purple. "How many reports from Bayside Security have you sat through? We have one of the lowest incidences of crime of any destination town this size."

"But other people don't know that."

"I'll have Chaz run an article showing the statistics," Liv said. "Will that set your mind at ease?"

"You have to do something!"

Neither Liv nor Ted pointed out that murder investigation was not their responsibility. It would be a hopeless argument. The event office organized most of the town's business lives, brokered deals, arbitrated arguments, and kept the town running smoothly as its numbers swelled and abated with each passing holiday.

The mayor heaved out of the chair. "Well, I can't wait around for Bill Gunnison to do his job. I'm calling an emergency meeting—"

"No!" Liv and Ted said simultaneously.

"The last thing we—you—need is a horde of people with little information and lots of questions at a town meeting," Liv said. "Give Bill a chance to get to the bottom of things."

"It will be too late by then."

Too late for what? Liv wondered. Gilbert Worley was a master of stirring up a tempest in a teapot, and though Liv took murder very seriously, she didn't think histrionics would do any good.

"I'll have to call the judging committee at least. I want you two there, too, and we'll have to insist that Chaz do his duty."

"Chaz wasn't on the committee," Ted pointed out.

"Only because he refused to do it. His father was the same way. Didn't give a hoot about his civic duty, just spent his time stirring up trouble."

"Yes, and printing the truth," Ted added.

Liv sat quietly and waited for them to finish. They had been fighting this battle long before she arrived in town. She groaned inwardly. An emergency meeting of the judges, one of whom was Janine, Liv's nemesis. And possibly Lucille's.

Maybe this could be an interesting meeting after all.

"And I want to be kept abreast of everything that is happening from now on." The mayor turned on his heel and strode out the door, nearly knocking over the two people who had just entered.

The mayor stumbled back and stammered. "Amanda, what brings you here this fine morning?"

Liv didn't hear her answer because she had just seen Mrs. Marlton-Crosby's escort: Jonathon Preston. Handsome, intelligent, dressed like he'd just stepped off Fifth Avenue.

Liv's breath escaped in a whoosh and she stood, smiling

and looking gracious as she walked around her desk while fervently hoping that she didn't have crumbs on her sweater.

"We heard the news about the museum being vandalized," Amanda said. "So we came right down to see what the situation is."

The mayor gulped audibly. "Yes, yes, very unfortunate. These things happen—but uh, not here in Celebration Bay. They happen in other places, but here we have very strict security, hire our own company to interface with the police and—"

"Amanda," Ted said, coming forward and cutting the mayor off. "So good to see you. We didn't get a chance to talk, Friday. You know Liv Montgomery, our events co-coordinator?"

"Of course." Amanda Marlton-Crosby offered her hand. Liv shook it.

"And we're old friends," said her companion. "How are you, Liv?" Jon took her by the arms and kissed both cheeks.

"Jon, what a surprise. I wasn't expecting you until the weekend."

"I know, but I returned to New York early and came up right away. Thought I'd take a couple of days to catch up on my reports. If I stayed in the city, they'd have me working nonstop on the next project. Besides, Amanda's family and mine go way back, so I came to say hello before you and I got hot and heavy into the grant proposal. Should I go away until Friday?" His eyes twinkled.

He was like a burst of intense vibrant air. A shot of adrenaline. He was *on*. You always had to be on in Manhattan. Liv was afraid she might have lost some of her cutting edge.

She took his arm. "I'm delighted that you're here. This is my assistant, Ted Driscoll."

Ted nodded formally as the men shook hands. But Liv didn't miss the assessing look he gave the newcomer. "And I don't know if you've met Mayor Worley? Jonathon Preston."

"Haven't had the pleasure until now." Jonathon shook hands with the mayor.

"Ah," the mayor said, galvanized into speech. "Be sure Liv shows you all our lovely sights. We have an annual influx of tourist numbering—"

"Yes, your portfolio was very precise and very informative." Jon glanced at the mayor, but he was smiling at Liv. They both knew whose work the portfolio was.

"Ah, well, yes."

"Actually, we came into town for Amanda to say hello to an old schoolmate of hers. She's just opened a store in town."

"Yes," Amanda said. "Yolanda Nestor. Have you met her?"

"We met briefly the other day over one of her beautiful quilts. I've been meaning to visit her store."

The outside office door opened again and A.K. Pierce, head of Bayside Security, strode in, but stopped in the outer office.

He nodded abruptly, then stepped back out of the way, and stood feet parted, hands behind his back, in what Liv had come to recognize as his relaxed stance.

"Excuse us." Ted took the mayor's arm and trundled him out the door, closing it behind him.

"Will you sit down?" Liv asked, gesturing to the two chairs while trying to stand in front of their breakfast remains.

Amanda smiled graciously. "Thank you, but we just came to get an update on this terrible news. Poor Lucille. Do they have any idea what she was doing there?"

So much for keeping the story under wraps. "I'm afraid not," Liv said. "But Bill Gunnison has his men working overtime on it, and the gentleman who just came in is the head of our security team."

"He looks very formidable," Jonathon said, still with that twinkle in his eye and a characteristic half smile on his face.

"He is, and he runs a very tight and efficient team."

"Will Barry Lindquist be able to restore his entry in time for it to open next weekend?" Amanda asked.

"We have every hope," Liv told her. "A group of volunteers have been repairing and restaging the displays."

"Already? That's wonderful. Oh, Jon, I hope you get to see it. So clever."

He smiled at her, a smile tender enough to have Liv wondering what their relationship was. Then she remembered Amanda was married. Not that that seemed to stop some people in town.

"Anyway," Jon said. "I didn't want you to see me in town and think I was here early to spy on you.

"Of course not," Liv said, though they both knew that surprise visits could make or break an event or a fund-raising campaign.

"You don't mind if I borrow him for the morning, Liv?" Amanda posed it as a question, but Liv read it as a fait accompli.

"Not at all. I was just running out on an errand. Why don't I walk out with you?"

Liv needed to talk to A.K. about the permit for the soapbox orator. But Ted could bring him up to speed. If he wasn't already. A.K. Pierce seemed to have eyes everywhere. But right now she needed to make sure Amanda and Jon weren't accosted by the doom and gloom man.

"Let me just tell Ted I'm leaving."

She went quickly into the other room, where Ted and A.K. were talking quietly, their heads bent.

"Change of schedule, it seems. I'm going to walk out with Jon and Amanda. I don't want them running into the eyesore on the corner on their own."

"He's got a permit," A.K. said. "Or I would have had someone see him to the county line."

"Yes. Ted, could you talk to the mayor about that?"

Ted nodded.

"And then make sure he does something about it?"

"Check and check."

"Great, thank you." She started to go back into her office but turned to Ted. "Do I look okay?"

"Divine," Ted said.

A.K. nodded brusquely.

Liv grabbed her coat and went to get the others.

Ted waylaid the mayor as they left the office, and Liv and Jon and Amanda made their way outside.

Walking down the steps of town hall, Jon slipped his arm around Liv's waist and leaned over until his mouth was close to her ear. "You look like a real country girl."

Just what she had feared; she was losing her edge. "Fits the venue."

"Now there's my Liv. Though I must say, there's something really appealing about you in corduroy and Fair Isle knit."

"And totally out of place standing next to you."

"Oh, I brought my casual weekend clothes. I just wanted to wow you on my first day here."

Liv laughed. If he only knew—and she was sure he did—that he was the one they hoped to wow.

They crossed the street to the park where a man was leaning against the hood of a dark green Land Rover. He saw them coming and stood up. He was tall and well-built, with dark wavy hair and a chiseled chin and cheeks. Amanda's husband, Rod Crosby.

"Oh, there you are, Rod," Amanda said. "Did you have trouble parking?"

"Just had to go round the block a couple of times." He leaned over and kissed Amanda's cheek.

Jon gave Liv his most sardonic look before he leaned close and said, "A real piece of work, that one."

Oh, thought Liv. Jonathon Preston, international philanthropist and distributor of charity and goodwill, did not like Rod Crosby—at all. She wondered why.

Rod was good looking but didn't hold a candle to Jon, if you like a more refined look. And Jon in his Savile Row bespoke suit and Armani loafers actually managed to look less out of place than Rod in his khakis and polo sweater. And infinitely more interesting.

Amanda took her husband's arm and the four of them struck off toward Yolanda's store.

It was a clear, crisp day after the rain. A perfect fall day in Celebration Bay. But Liv wasn't conscious of the weather. As they strolled down the sidewalk, she kept her eyes open for the prophet who was no longer standing on the corner.

Maybe she could get them to Yolanda's store without being accosted.

They were walking past the Corner Café, and Liv was thinking they were home free, when the doomsday prophet jumped out of the alley, waving his hands. He was dressed all in black and his face was thin and pale and his eyes were bloodshot. Liv thought he must be drunk.

"Save yourselves, flee Sodom and Gomorrah before it's too late. End to all devil worshippers!"

Liv gritted her teeth and kept the others moving.

"Is this part of the entertainment?" Jon asked.

"No, he just showed up on Friday. Evidently someone gave him a permit to stand there. We're working on having it rescinded. Not the family-friendly Halloween we celebrate here."

Jonathon chuckled. "He's not nearly as good as the ones on Thirty-fourth Street."

"No, but he's just as persistent. Hopefully he'll be gone by this afternoon. Please try just ignore him." Liv looked over her shoulder. He was gaining on them.

"They shall fall like—"

Ahead of them, the door to the Mystic Eye opened and Yolanda Nestor stepped out. Today she was wearing harem pants and an ankle-length, flowing vest over a burgundy scoop-necked blouse. The outfit made her look quite exotic,

which Liv assumed lent ambience to the store and was probably good for business. Yolanda saw them and hurried over.

"Amanda! I didn't know if you would make it in today.
The girls just called and they're only a block away." The two
women hugged.

"The girls?" Rod said.

"Members of my . . . ?" Yolanda lowered her voice.
"Co-o-o-o-ven."

Her tone ran goose bumps up Liv's arm.

"You'll love them," she said in her normal voice.

"Witch, witch, burn in hell!" the protester yelled, but Liv
noticed he was keeping his distance from Yolanda.

"Okay, that's enough." Liv pulled out her phone and
speed-dialed A.K., who she bet was still upstairs with Ted.
"We have a situation down here on the street."

"We saw it and we're on our way." On his words the door
to town hall opened and A.K. came running down the steps,
followed by Ted.

"Go back to Hades, you witch!" The man shook his fist
at Yolanda. Today he seemed more menacing than annoying.

"You know, I'm getting awfully tired of you," Yolanda said.

A.K. was already at the corner when a maroon, soccer-
mom minivan pulled up in front of the store.

Liv fervently hoped there would be no violence to scare
the tourists away.

All four doors opened at once, and four women who
looked just like suburban housewives got out of the car and
swept forward like avenging angels.

The Four Soccer Moms of the Apocalypse, Liv thought.
Go for it, girls.

They surrounded the heckler and began to chant, and
with the chant they grasped hands and began to circle. Not
widdershins, Liv was glad to note.

Across the street, A.K. and Ted had stopped in their
tracks and were staring in fascination.

"Back, you Devil's handmaids—!" His words ended in

a gurgle. The circle opened in between two of the women and the protester fell backward. A.K. was there to cart him away.

"Well," said Jonathon. "You certainly know how to entertain a guy."

Yolanda stretched out her arms. "Perfect timing as always, girls. Let me introduce you all to four of my sisters. Maddie, Gilda, Susanna, and Christie. Welcome to Celebration Bay and the Mystic Eye."

"Hi," Liv said. *Always something new in Celebration Bay.*

Yolanda introduced everyone, including Ted, who had joined them. There was some squealing and laughing as the women all crowded into the store, leaving Rod, Jonathon, Ted, and Liv on the sidewalk.

"Whew," Rod said. "What a bunch of crazy women."

Jonathon raised an eyebrow. "I really wouldn't say things like that in front of Yolanda," he said. "She's bound to take offense."

"I'm sure I don't care. If Amanda hadn't insisted on opening up the fish camp cabins so they could do their hocuspocus on our property, we'd be in Miami by now."

Jon's jaw tightened, but he said nothing.

Rod shrugged. "I'll wait by the car." He strode off, hands in his trouser pockets.

Liv saw A.K. coming toward them, empty-handed.

"What happened to the, uh . . ."

"Handed him off to a couple of my operatives. They've taken him to the mayor. Let him deal with the man."

Ted snorted politely behind his fist. A.K. looked completely bland.

"But will he—? Maybe I should go see."

"A.K. and I will take care of it," Ted said. But he and A.K. just stood there.

"Listen," Jonathon said, slightly amused. "I didn't come early to throw your schedule off. Go take care of what you need to and meet us over at the inn at one. Will that work for you?"

Liv glanced at Ted. "Absolutely. See you then."

"I think I'll go move Amanda along or she'll be in there all day. Until lunch then." He gave Liv his most charming smile.

Ted and A.K. watched as Jon walked to the door. He stopped on the threshold, turned back, and winked at Liv, then nodded to both Ted and A.K. and shut the door.

Liv turned to face Ted and A.K. They were both still staring at the door.

One look at their solemn faces and Liv tried not to smile. "We're just friends."

No change in their expressions.

"Really, guys. He's just amusing himself."

Nothing.

"Really. That wink? He's playing you."

She just hoped he wasn't playing her.

Chapter Ten

·····························

A.K. and Ted waited for Liv to walk past them and then they fell in step beside her.

She glanced from one to the other. "What?"

"Nothing," A.K. said.

She switched her focus to Ted.

He shrugged. "Nothing."

Liv wondered what was up. Had they expected trouble? But why?

She stopped. They stopped. "How did you guys get here so quick?"

Ted shrugged. A.K. didn't even twitch.

"You were already leaving the building when I called you." Liv glanced up to her office window, down to the corner where the protester had stood. "You were watching us from the window."

No answer from either of the men.

"You were, weren't you? I know you were. That is so . . . Well, thank you." She didn't know whether to be amused, annoyed, or flattered. They'd been watching her—or Jon or Amanda—from the window.

"Why?"

Ted looked confused. "No reason."

They walked in silence back to the office. She hoped the witches weren't cause for alarm; they seemed like normal people. Though they had done that circle thing. But Liv knew the power of suggestion: The protester feared evil, equated them with evil, so was cowed when confronted.

"Simple psychology," she said, mainly to herself, as they walked up the steps to town hall.

"What is?" asked Ted.

"Oh, just that ranter and his fear of witchcraft."

"The women did seem rather sweet." Ted sounded relieved. He held the door open. "I would like to see their Samhain ritual."

"Are outsiders invited?"

"Don't even think about adding that as an event," A.K. said.

Ted and Liv both stared at him.

"They wouldn't like the commercialization, and there are more where that street corner howler comes from."

"Volatile situation," Liv said.

"Volatile."

Ted and A.K. followed Liv into her office. Liv sat and riffled through the folders on her desk for the one marked *Security*.

"Did you know they were friends?" A.K. asked.

"Amanda and Yolanda? No. I really only met Amanda recently and Yolanda briefly on Saturday."

"I think he means Jonathon Preston and Amanda." Ted looked particularly bland-faced.

"No, he never mentioned it. Why?"

Neither of the men spoke.

"What? You think we're on the grant list because of Amanda? That would be a case of overkill, wouldn't you say?

She already donated ten K to the winner. Though from what people say, she could finance the entire center if she wanted to." Liv paused.

"She could, but I can't imagine why she would want to," Ted said. "It's not like she's ever in town or shown an interest in what goes on here. Strange that she should come forward now. Perhaps this guy Preston suggested it."

Liv narrowed her eyes. "Because he isn't going to approve the grant request and he's trying to soften the blow?"

"It's a possibility."

Liv hadn't allowed herself to wonder what would happen if they didn't receive the grant money. She knew it was a crowded market, everyone working on shoestring budgets. And friends didn't get priority. Which was why she'd hired a professional grant writer to help her draft a proposal.

She pushed it out of her mind and opened the security folder. For the next few minutes they discussed the usual points in crowd safety.

"Bill has assigned extra patrol cars for the weekends, especially the actual Halloween weekend," A.K. said. "I'd like to add at least eight more operatives on foot. And four additional sets of two operatives at each major event location within the town limits."

"Do you have any specific locations in mind?" Liv knew it was a stupid question. Of course he did. He was a man in control. "What I mean is—"

"At the Lindquist site, at each quadrant of the park during the zombie parade, and outside the movie house before and after the play."

"You think there might be problems at the theater?"

"That play *Little Shop of Horrors* has a cult following, and any time you have passionate people, things are easily ignited." He looked seriously at Liv.

Over a man-eating plant? Still, Liv's mouth went a little dry. "Well, yes. I see how they could. And how much will this cost me?"

He reached in his briefcase. Handed hard copies to Ted and her. Kept one for himself.

It had a hefty price tag. But not nearly as hefty as the fallout from too little security might be. The town had insurance that they paid an exorbitant premium for. It was one of the few things the trustees all agreed on. No one wanted to get sued for negligence. Or anything else.

Liv pulled up the budget file on her laptop. They were getting to the top of their security budget and there was still Thanksgiving and Christmas to get through before the new budget would be considered. "Ted?"

"I think A.K. is right. We can cut down some for the next two holidays, mainly keep security on shops and parking lots."

Liv nodded. "Do you what you need to do."

A.K. nodded and put his papers back in the briefcase.

"But keep me posted on the hours and services. I don't want to have to go to the board and beg for more money."

The corner of A.K.'s mouth twitched.

She'd amused him. She smiled back at him and shrugged.

The phone rang and Ted went into his outer office to answer it, leaving A.K. and Liv half smiling at each other.

Ted was back a minute later. "They found Lucille Foster's car."

"Where?" Liv asked.

Ted sat down. "In the parking lot over behind the bakery and the other stores."

"And they're just finding it now?"

"Hidden in plain sight," A.K. said, his deep voice rumbling.

"Do you think that was it? Was whoever killed her trying to hide the car? Why not dump it in a back alley or off a deserted road?"

"I'm sure that's what the police thought. They were looking for an abandoned car." A.K. turned to Ted. "Did Bill say if they found any signs of struggle?"

"No, not on first inspection, but they're having it towed and will have a forensics team look over it."

"Did they find her shoes?" Liv asked.

Ted shook his head. "But he's still on site."

No one needed encouragement; the three stood simultaneously and headed for the door.

They retraced their steps past the Corner Café but turned into the alley before they reached Yolanda's store, the Mystic Eye.

"We were just here and didn't hear or see anything. Thank heaven," Liv added. "That's all we need Jon to see."

They hurried past the side of the Mystic Eye and went through the opening to one of the town's several parking lots. This one took up most of the interior of the block, stretching the length of the stores on the main square.

Lucille's Jaguar was already sitting on the bed of an Arlen Towing and Plowing flatbed truck. Several police cars were parked nearby, preventing anyone from entering the area, though they had attracted a fairly large crowd that huddled around the several pedestrian openings that led across the alley to the stores. The county crime scene van was just pulling away.

Bill saw them and walked over. He was moving slow.

Liv sent a quick prayer to the sciatica gods that he would make it through this investigation without pain.

Bill placed both hands in the small of his back and stretched. "You okay?"

"Yep."

"They're taking Lucille's car away already?" Liv asked.

"We've been here for a couple of hours."

A.K. lifted his eyebrows toward the sheriff.

As if he'd asked the question, Bill said, "Doesn't look like it was used. But we're taking it in for a thorough forensic look."

"What about her shoes?" Liv asked.

Bill shook his head. "We searched the vicinity, underneath cars, in the Dumpsters. Nothing. I'd better get back."

"Bill," Liv said quickly. "Is Ernie still in jail?"

"Had to let him out. There's nothing as yet to connect him to Lucille's death. He's still under suspicion of vandalism, but until we can prove it, we can't keep him. Not that I want to. What a dumb-ass thing to do."

"If he did it," Ted said.

"Who else would?" Liv asked.

Ted gave her a look. "You've been here a year. I bet if you set your mind to it, you could name a dozen possible candidates . . . without even thinking much."

"You think the vandalism might just be coincidental to Ernie lashing out about losing to Barry?"

Ted threw up both hands. "Don't look at me. I don't know anything."

And if Ted didn't know anything, it meant neither did anyone else. Because it didn't matter how hush-hush something was, how deep the secret, no matter how tight lips were over any bit of news, Ted always knew. He was Celebration Bay's Gossip Exchange Central. Yet Liv had hardly ever caught him actually gossiping. He just seemed to learn what was happening by some kind of osmosis.

"Well, let us know what and when you can," Ted said. "We have to get back to the office. Liv has a lunch date."

Bill eyebrows shot up. "A date or a meeting?"

"A meeting and luncheon with Amanda Marlton-Crosby and her husband and the representative of the grant foundation."

"Oh, well, have a nice lunch. I hope you get lots of money for the community center." Bill nodded to them and went back to work.

"Well, we'd better get you back if you going to primp for your luncheon date."

"Would you stop it? It's just business." Liv glanced at her watch. No time to walk home and get to the inn in time. They'd just have to put up with her work clothes. Besides, Amanda and Rod were pretty casually dressed.

Liv headed for the town hall ladies' room and freshened up as best she could with the scant makeup she carried with her, then headed to the inn.

Jon was sitting in the foyer reading a newspaper when Liv arrived promptly at one. He saw her, folded the paper, and put it on the table next to him. It was a copy of the *Celebration Bay Clarion*.

"Just catching up on the local news. You have a very active Four-H Club here."

Liv couldn't tell if he was being serious or sarcastic. "It's their busy season," she said, straight-faced.

He laughed, a friendly baritone sound that invited more laughter.

"You should see some of the pumpkins they've grown," Liv continued. "Not to mention the animals. Unfortunately you missed the county fair."

"Yes, most unfortunate." He leaned over and kissed her cheek. "Amanda and Rod will be here soon. She volunteered him to help move some boxes for Yolanda and company. She just called to say they were on their way and to get a table."

He guided her into the dining room, a bright windowed room that overlooked the lake. The tables were covered with white linen tablecloths and napkins.

Liv rarely ate here, preferring the bar across the foyer, which had a low-key, casual environment couched in dark wood wainscoting and tall-backed booths.

The hostess showed them to a table set at a diagonal to the windows, giving all four diners a bit of view. Jon held a chair for Liv, then sat in the chair to her left.

"So fill me in," Liv said as soon as the waitress had taken their drink orders, Liv's a seltzer with lime and Jon's a Pellegrino.

He smiled, his eyes crinkling in that same attractive way they had when they'd first met. She'd been coordinating a fund-raising weekend for several related charities. His smile had separated him from the other suits, though he was serious and questioned every line item on her budget.

In those days she didn't have to worry too much about tight budgets, thanks to well-heeled fathers of the bride, corporate executives with a seemingly unlimited entertainment business, or oil men visiting the city and inviting the crème de la crème of society for a weekend cruise.

One of Liv's great assets had been to recognize who would spend what and how far they were really willing or able to go.

"Are we talking business already?" Jon asked.

"No, well, not exactly. But last I heard you were in Bangkok or someplace until this coming weekend."

"True. Is this a problem?"

"Of course not. I'm just surprised."

"Well, I finished up early. The organization there has to have a total restructuring before we can funnel funds into it. Much too much waste. So I came back until they get it together. No one was pleased, not on our side or theirs. Nor me, I'm still jet-lagged.

"I meant to take a few days to get back on daylight savings time and catch up on some sleep before I came up here. But the best-laid plans and all that . . ."

"I didn't realize you knew Amanda."

"Oh, we're old chums. Though I haven't seen her for ages. Our fathers are on some of the same boards and the families belong to those clubs you always made fun of."

"I did not. It was just when you showed up to the Hart's meeting wearing that ridiculous-looking yachting outfit."

"And I'll tell you what I told you then."

"I remember." Liv lowered her voice and said primly, "'This is the official Yacht Club uniform.'" She bit back a laugh. "Though I have to admit you looked awfully cute."

Jon rolled his eyes. "If my father heard that, he'd have an apoplectic fit. And I, of course, would never say that you look just as cute as a fresh-faced country girl."

"Well, if I'd known you were going to show up out of the blue, I would have dressed accordingly."

"No, no, I love the way you look." He sighed heavily. "Actually I envy you the comfort factor."

"So you decided to pay Amanda a visit before your official visit?"

"Yes, a rather delicate subject, which . . ." He looked toward the entrance doors, smiled, and waved. "I'll tell you later. Though I must say you wear country with much more panache than poor Amanda."

He was right about "poor" Amanda, at least as far as her wardrobe. Standing beside Rod, she looked like she was dining alone. He'd made an entrance while she sort of drifted in beside him. Liv didn't understand their relationship unless she defaulted to the obvious: He married an heiress and she married a stud. Behind their smiles, neither of them looked very happy.

They crossed the room, Rod dutifully resting his hand on the back of Amanda's drab canvas jacket. Liv knew the jacket cost hundreds, but Amanda wore it like it came from the closest thrift store.

"Did we keep you waiting long?" Amanda asked as soon as Rod had pulled out her chair next to Jon.

"Not at all," he said. "Liv and I were just catching up."

"That's right. You've worked together before." Amanda gave Liv a warm and friendly smile.

"A few times," Jon said.

And several more when she had been working an event and he'd been a guest.

"How did you and Yolanda meet?" Liv asked.

Amanda smiled. "College. We both went to Middlebury."

"And did you know the others, there?"

"No. Yolanda didn't develop an interest in Wicca until after graduation. When we were in school, she was an avid skier, studied languages. She planned to become a translator for the UN, that is until she decided to go over to the 'light' side, as she calls it."

Liv laughed. "I take it you didn't join her."

"No, no, we haven't seen each other in years. We reconnected on Facebook and when she found it necessary to relocate her store—she was having some problems where she was before; small minds, you know—I suggested she visit Celebration Bay. She fell in love with it here. And the building was perfect for her, the way the last person had fixed it up to be all natural wood."

"Does she know its, um, history?"

"Yes. It's not a problem. She knows how to cast out bad spirits."

The waitress returned with menus and conversation ceased while they listened to the specials of the day. Liv's attention didn't make it past the appetizers. She was too busy wondering what had happened to Yolanda's former store, whether she had she brought those problems with her, and if one of them was the end-of-the-world predictor.

Chapter Eleven

··

It only took a few minutes for Liv to realize it was going to be a long lunch. There were undercurrents roiling around the other three. Jon hardly touched his food. He was as alert as a hunting dog, though the analogy wasn't really apt; more like an urban damage control consultant.

Rod began complaining in a too loud voice. "We were ready to close up and get the hell out of here, when Amanda decides to let her friend's coven rent out the fish camp for their woo-woo weekends. I just hope they don't trash the place."

Amanda gave Rod a look that was somewhere between patient affection and steel magnolia.

"You know they'll do no such thing." She patted his hand, which had been reaching for his Manhattan glass. "Yolanda has pedigree. You'll barely know they've been there. Just a little light cleanup and you'll be done."

Liv felt a frisson of chill run up her back. She didn't think she had mistaken Amanda's undercurrent of malice. She

remembered Chaz saying that Rod wanted to go to Miami
for the winter. Liv had just presumed he was a user, but
something told Liv that Amanda could hold her own in that
relationship. She just wondered whether any of it included
love.

Liv glanced at Jon, who was looking out the window
toward the lake. She wasn't sure how he fit into the Marlton-
Crosby equation and she really didn't have time to figure it
out. She just hoped that once he was staying at the inn, rather
than with the Malton-Crosbys, he'd be free to concentrate
solely on the grant. She needed his full attention so she could
convince him of the need and viability of the community
center.

"And besides," Amanda continued, "I wanted to be
around to award my donation personally. I think Barry
Lindquist did such an excellent job. Don't you, Liv?"

"Huh? Oh, yes. Excellent."

"That's the man whose haunted house was vandalized?"
Jon asked.

"Yes."

"What is going to happen to it?"

"If Barry can't get it back up and running, we'll default
to the runner-up."

"That would be a shame. The Museum of Yankee Horrors was quite good. Unique," Amanda said. "It was one of
the reasons I decided to donate the money outright. I mean,
who doesn't love a good haunted house." She sighed and
placed her napkin back on the table. "It's a pity someone
was malicious enough to wreck it, not just for Barry but for
everyone."

"We heard that they suspect the runner-up of trashing
the place," Rod said.

"Ernie Bolton."

"Pretty dumb thing to do. It's kind of obvious."

"Well, they took him in for questioning, but there doesn't
seem to be any evidence." Liv frowned. "Jon, don't get the

wrong idea. This is usually a very safe town, but we have a lot of visitors throughout the year."

"I'm not complaining. I thought I was going to be bored up here in the hinterlands, but I didn't even get half this much excitement in Bangkok."

"Yolanda was telling us about it," Amanda said. "How awful. Poor Lucille. Isn't that just awful, Rod?"

Rod looked up from his roast beef sandwich. "Uh-huh," he said and kept chewing.

Jon cast him a disgusted look. "Evidently Yolanda heard it from the woman who runs the fabric store, I forget her name."

"Miriam."

"Right, who heard it from the lady at the bakery."

"Dolly."

"Just one big happy family," Jon said.

"Usually," Liv said.

"You don't think someone wanted to kill her, do you?" Amanda asked.

Rod patted her hand. "She was probably just in the wrong place at the wrong time."

"Like she saw something she shouldn't have seen?" Amanda's eyes widened, then narrowed. "Maybe she recognized Ernie vandalizing the place and tried to stop him."

"They don't know for sure that Ernie did it," Liv said.

"Who else would have reason to destroy Barry's hard work?" Ron asked. "Or . . . With Barry's place trashed, wouldn't the ten thou go to the runner-up?"

"This Ernie was the runner-up, right?" Jon asked.

Liv nodded.

"Does he need money for any reason?"

"Who doesn't need money?" Rod said.

Something flashed in Jon's eyes. Liv thought it might be disgust. Yes, there were definitely undercurrents going on between those three. Liv just hoped it didn't take Jon's mind from the business of the grant.

"What are you thinking?" Jon asked, and his amused expression was back.

"Me?" Liv asked.

"Yes, you. I know that look. You're way ahead of the rest of us."

"Not really." Mainly she was just worried that they might lose the grant and Amanda's ten thousand dollars. "Just that the town is pitching in to help. The entire cast of *Little Shop of Horrors* plus the sewing group at A Stitch in Time are all helping to refurbish the museum. We have every hope that they'll be ready to open in time."

"But will the police be ready to release the area in time?" Jon asked.

"I'm sure they will." Liv was getting anxious for the check to come. Not only did she have to prepare for tonight's meeting, but she wasn't sure how much she should be talking about Lucille's murder with Amanda, Rod, and Jon. She didn't want the case to color her project with the foundation.

The waitress finally brought their check, and Jon reached for it. Rod didn't try to argue, just sat there like he knew someone else was going to pay. Liv was pretty sure somebody—Amanda—always did.

The four of them walked out to the foyer. The Marlton-Crosbys said their good-byes and headed toward their car.

Jon lingered behind for a minute. "Thanks for joining us, Liv. I know you're busy and I'm a few days early."

"I'm always busy, but I'll always be glad to see you."

He gave her a light hug. "I'll be moving into the inn on Wednesday. If you can arrange some time for me in between your busy schedule, I'd love for you to show me around town a bit."

"I'd love to."

"And maybe have dinner?"

"I would love to do that, too."

"Great. Until then." He jogged down the steps to the Range Rover and climbed in the back.

Liv watched them go. She was getting a funny feeling about all of this. Sort of like the fly probably felt when he first stepped into the spider's parlor.

Liv walked back to the office, wondering why Jon hadn't called or texted in advance to let her know he would be in town earlier than expected. And when exactly had he arrived? Had he said? Today? Yesterday? The day before? If he'd been here for the award ceremony, surely Amanda would have brought him with her. Or was he really here early to check things out by himself?

She considered stopping by the Buttercup for a shot of caffeine but decided to check with Ted first.

He was reading a thick, oversized soft-covered book. "Tax code," he said without looking up.

"Do we have a problem?"

"No, just checking, but we do have a mayoral emergency meeting of the judges committee this evening at seven that we'd better prepare for."

"How? It will just be ranting and screaming and nobody will be able to hear the other guy and nothing will get solved."

"Is this really Celebration Bay's most illustrious and successful event planner I'm hearing?" He followed her into her office.

She sat down at her desk. "Sorry. Sometimes I just feel like I'm always juggling odd objects."

"You are, my dear. The secret is not to let the ax fall on your head."

She snorted out a laugh. "Thanks. You really know how to make a girl feel better."

He bowed himself out of her office. It was true, but it was funny. *Lighten up, Liv,* she told herself. *It could be so much worse.*

They convened that night at seven. Since there were only the members of the judging panel, plus the mayor and

Ted and Liv, they were using the smaller meeting room at the east end of the building.

Since Liv knew Janine would be at the meeting, she changed into her meeting suit, which she kept hanging in the event office closet, and traded her loafers for a pair of three-inch heels.

A quick trip to the ladies' room, where she twisted her hair into a knot at the base of her head and reapplied lip gloss, and she was ready for all their questions.

Which made her laugh, since she didn't haven't any answers.

"Ah, I see you're wearing your power suit tonight," Ted said. "I hope that isn't Jonathon Preston's influence."

"Don't be silly."

"He's not going to try to lure you away, is he?"

"Of course not. I'm afraid you're stuck with me, though sometimes I do wonder what possessed me to sign a two-year contract."

Ted raised an eyebrow. "Ready?"

They joined Jeremiah Atkins, who was just coming in the door. Jeremiah was the president of the First Celebration Bank. He looked just how Liv imagined a small-town banker would look. White hair growing thin on top, just the beginning of a paunch above the belt of his suit pants. Tonight he'd traded his jacket and tie for a navy blue cardigan sweater.

They nodded to one another.

"Terrible business about Lucille," Jeremiah said.

"It truly is," Liv agreed.

"I don't suppose the police have any leads . . . besides Ernie, that is?"

"I don't know."

"Neither do I," Ted added.

"I don't suppose anyone has even considered Barry."

Ted and Liv shook their heads.

"I mean, he did have that altercation with Lucille's husband over the failed senior complex." Jeremiah shook his head. "I don't know why people don't ask the advice of their regular banker before they go off and commit their hard-earned savings to some get-rich-quick scheme."

Liv made appropriate noises as her mind connected the dots. Barry had lost money in one of Carson Foster's investment plans. Ernie gave away property to his ex-son-in-law, who later sold for a profit . . . to Carson Foster.

Could either of those have any connection to Lucille's murder?

The door to the meeting room was open and they walked in to see the other three members of the judges committee already seated. Roscoe Jackson was sitting next to Janine, who appeared to be trying to convince him of something. Probably to figure out how to pin the latest disaster on Liv, since that seemed to be Janine's primary reason for staying close to the business of town hall.

Rufus Cobb was already chewing on his mustache, a sure sign that he was agitated.

And the meeting hadn't even started yet.

Jeremiah sat down next to Rufus. Ted and Liv took a seat along the wall.

"Guess who's MIA," Liv said under her breath. She wasn't surprised. Chaz had inherited the trusteeship from his father and pretty much considered it a waste of time. Evidently there had been a Bristow on the board of trustees since the beginning of time, so he was stuck. "Do you think he'll come?"

"Anybody's guess."

As much as Chaz annoyed her, she knew he could be depended on—most of the time—to stand with her and Ted. Liv had a feeling that she could use him here tonight.

The mayor came in and the others stopped talking. He stopped at the head of the table and Liv was glad to see he'd left his gavel behind. He was a firm believer in "the louder you bang, the more they quiet down." They never did, but it didn't prevent him from liberally sprinkling every meeting with ear-splitting hammering.

He stood at his place, looked around the room, and sighed. "Ted and Liv, you might as well come sit at the table since it looks like we're all here."

Liv automatically looked toward the closed door. On cue, it opened. Chaz Bristow sauntered in, looked around the table like he was surprised to see them, then sat down opposite the mayor.

Liv looked down to hide a smile.

"Oh boy," Ted said under his breath. "He's in a mood tonight."

He and Liv moved to the table.

"I think you all know why I've called you here tonight," the mayor began.

Only Chaz shook his head.

"Because, Chaz, we have to find a replacement for Lucille on the judging committee."

"Why? The judging is over."

"Well, we all thought so, but there may be a need to choose another winner."

"You have a winner and two runners-up. Isn't that enough?"

"The winner was vandalized and the first runner-up is in jail. We cannot have the official town haunted house owned by a criminal."

"Now, Gilbert," Jeremiah said, his deep voice the voice of reason. "Nothing has been proved against Ernie. In fact, I hear they let him out and he's back at home."

"Maybe not. But they haven't figured out who did it. I think we should postpone inaugurating the haunted house until next October. Since I have the whole board of trustees here, I think we should vote."

"Wait," Liv said, half rising from her chair. "There hasn't been any discussion on this."

The mayor automatically reached for his gavel, realized it wasn't there, and stood. "Doesn't matter. Things are a mess."

"Again," Janine added.

Liv gritted her teeth. *One day,* she thought. *One day, Janine, you will see what a real Manhattan event planner is capable of.*

"We'll have to cancel."

"Gilbert." Ted's voice was sharp edged. Liv blinked. Even Chaz, who had been pretending to doze, turned to look. "You haven't stopped to look at the financial considerations. Much less the suits that will follow."

"Suits?" The mayor tugged at his collar. "What suits?"

"All the people asking for their money back, plus compensation for their work and supplies, and hours they put in on their entries because it was for a good cause, part of a fund-raiser to aid the town. Over one hundred people paid to enter the contest, knowing they wouldn't win, but just to support the event. That will be a big drain on the town's coffers.

Roscoe looked alarmed, Rufus chewed faster on his mustache, Jeremiah nodded wisely.

"And if Mrs. Marlton-Crosby rescinds her donation, then we'll be back to square one, with the addition of a lot of hard feelings and uncertainties about our ability to move forward on the community center. Plus, many others donated money to the fund-raiser itself. Who's going to tell the townspeople that their money won't be used for the community center but to pay for all those suits that will be lining up at your door?"

Liv was amazed. Chaz looked a little dazed.

"The representative of the VanderHauw Foundation has already arrived and met with Liv today," Ted said.

The mayor looked from Ted to Liv.

"He wasn't supposed to be here until this weekend," Janine said.

Ted shrugged. "He's a very busy man and he fit us in where he could. He's interested, but not if we throw in the towel. We'll become the bad risk among funding organizations. Is that the kind of reputation you want Celebration Bay to have?"

The mayor shook his head. He seemed to be stuck for words. He looked around the table and stopped at Liv.

"Liv, can you guarantee that Barry's museum will be up and running in time for the Halloween kickoff next week?"

Janine stood. "Of course she can't."

For a nanosecond Liv thought Janine might be sticking up for her.

"Liv's the reason we're in this mess to begin with. Whose idea was it to have this official haunted house? Hers."

"I suggested a fund-raiser for a new community center. The board came up with the idea of the haunted house contest."

"Not me," Chaz said.

"And what have you made? Twenty thousand dollars? Get real. That's not even a down payment on a building. This is just another one of her harebrained schemes to land us in trouble. She's obviously out of her expertise. She was a party planner before she came here."

Liv had had enough. She stood. Ted pulled her back down, and he stood instead.

"Janine, you're just spewing venom. We've all seen Liv's résumé, and we know what she's done for this town. You couldn't find a more experienced event planner. And I'm getting a little sick of your sour grapes."

"Ted," Liv said. She tugged at his sweater, telling him to sit down.

Janine rounded on him. "And you know less than she does! I don't know how you got this job."

Ted opened his mouth and started singing "I'm Still Here" from the Sondheim musical *Follies*.

The members of the board stared openmouthed.

Liv clamped her hand over her mouth. She'd never seen Ted so outrageous before.

Chaz wore an expression of unholy glee. He looked at Liv and mouthed, *Holy sh—*

Janine snapped her head toward the mayor. "He's out of order!"

"Be quiet, Janine," Roscoe said.

"Everyone just stay calm," urged Jeremiah.

Gilbert tried banging on the table with his palm to no avail.

Chaz held his sides, laughing.

Ted stopped singing; Liv took a deep breath. "Mr. Mayor. Barry is certainly doing everything he can to get the museum in shape for the opening. He has quite a few volunteers helping out. Let's give him a chance to restore the displays before we do something we can't undo."

The mayor looked from Liv to Janine, who shook her head, and to the other three board members, who nodded in unison.

Gilbert huffed. "Okay, but Liv, make sure it gets done. No more screw-ups and no more murders."

As if they were Liv's fault.

"Do you understand?"

"But—"

"We won. Let's go." Ted grabbed her by the elbow and dragged her out of the room. "Good night, all."

Liv pulled away. "I've had it with their petty, incendiary—"

"Party of the first part," said Chaz from behind her.

She turned on him. "Just be quiet. I don't need you making fun of me on top of everyone else." She yanked her arm away from Ted. "Great speech," she said, and stormed off down the hall.

Chapter Twelve

....

Ted and Chaz were still standing in the hall when Liv emerged from the events office a minute later, carrying the clothes she had changed out of to the ladies' room to change back into them. It had been stupid to change anyway. Janine would always be better dressed than Liv unless she pulled out her NYC wardrobe and those shoes she'd relegated to the back of the closet. And Liv wasn't willing to do that. For dinner with Jon maybe, but not to impress Janine.

Ignoring the two men, she slipped into the ladies' room, changed back into her day clothes, and pushed the door open.

Chaz was standing on the other side. "Better than a phone booth."

"Are you comparing me to Superman?" Liv snapped.

Chaz yawned. "No. I was comparing the bathroom to a phone booth."

"Aargh." Liv pushed past him and strode down the hall in her bare feet.

Shelley Freydont

She made it to the events office door before she realized she was holding her shoes in her hand.

Shoes. You took off your shoes and carried them when . . . it was raining or muddy, at the beach, when you were in hurry to get someplace—or to run away. Why had Lucille Foster taken off her shoes? Where had she left them? Where had she gone after the award ceremony?

They'd searched the vacant lot twice, looked around the outside of the museum. Even ventured into the neighbors' yards. It was the end of October. Cold. Wet. Not a time to be barefoot. *Where were Lucille's shoes?*

She stopped at the office door, dropped her own shoes to the floor, and shoved her feet into them. Ted's hand appeared before her and turned the doorknob. The door swung open and Liv went inside, followed by Ted and Chaz.

She went straight to her office and began hanging up her clothes.

"You must be tired," Ted said. "You don't normally let Janine get to you like that."

Liv turned on him. "I don't know how you stand it. We work our butts off with practically all volunteers. We've tripled festival attendance and pulled this contest out of a hat. And they're not even nice. No 'thanks, Liv and Ted, for letting us have a stupid idea and then making it work.' Hell, we could have raised money raffling off a car or something simple. But no, we had to oversee judging of a hundred houses, and what do we get?"

"Nice work? If you can get it?"

"Not funny." Liv leaned against her desk. "Sorry. But there's a lot riding on this next weekend and I don't need the mayor and his hench . . . woman stirring up panic.

"It's bad enough that Lucille Foster was murdered. I'm sorry about that. But Jon and Amanda already knew all about it. I could see that Jon is already waffling. He was asking all kinds of questions about the murder. If we blow this . . ." She bit her lip.

"Liv," Ted said. "What are you up to?"

"Nothing. I don't know. Something. I'll figure it out."

Chaz pulled away from the doorframe that had been holding him up. "Stay out of it, Liv."

"Out of what?"

"Don't be dense. You spend your energy charming your city boy and let Bill take care of the investigation."

Liv stared at him. "If I said what I'm thinking right now, Ted would be shocked."

"I doubt it," Chaz said. "But spare us. I can imagine. Stay out of it."

"Fine." Liv reached over the desk and closed her laptop, pushed away from the desk, and stood. "Good night." She lifted her coat and messenger bag off the coat rack and left the room.

Rufus, Jeremiah, and Roscoe were still standing at the end of the hall talking. They looked up as Liv came out of the office. She raised her hand and hurried toward the door to the street.

She knew she was reacting out of proportion. It was so unlike her. *Cool under pressure* was her middle name. But for some reason, tonight she'd just had enough.

For some reason? Liv thought she knew the reason, though she didn't want to admit it. Seeing Jon had been like a shot of excitement from her past life. She'd been tired of the constant stress of that life; that's why she took the job in Celebration Bay.

Normally she loved her job, but sitting at lunch today dressed in country corduroys with Jon in his designer suit made her wonder if she was losing her touch.

She crossed the street more slowly, the anger and the aggravation dissipating and leaving her feeling limp.

She cut through the park on her way home. She hardly ever brought her car to work. Walking was a surefire de-stresser, reinvigorator, helped to sever the work frustrations from her home life.

Tonight it wasn't working.

She slowed as she reached the middle of the park where all the paths converged. To her right, store lights were just beginning to go dark. To her left at the far end of the park, the band shell was lit by a Victorian streetlamp on each side and one security light on the stage.

What had happened between Friday night and Saturday morning? Instead of going toward home, Liv veered toward the band shell. Several benches were placed facing the band shell, though most people sat on the grass on lawn chairs brought from home. There was a narrow strip of pavement where folding chairs could be placed if needed.

Liv sat on one of the benches. Imagined the scene Friday night. Everyone had been there. Where had Lucille gone after she left the square? Why hadn't she just gone home with her husband?

An extra ten thousand dollars. It had seemed like manna from heaven. Now it might be snatched away. The whole effort to house a new community center could be killed by one slash of Jonathon Preston's pen.

"Ugh." She covered her face with her hands. She needed to fix this and she didn't have a clue how.

"Can anybody join this pity party or is it a private affair?" Chaz stood over her, hands in his pocket, looking serious.

Liv slowly looked up.

Chaz exhaled. "Whew. I was really afraid I'd caught you with red eyes and a runny nose."

"Ha. What would you have done?"

"I'd have had to loan you my sleeve because I don't carry a hanky." He sat down.

Liv sniffed. "And it isn't a pity party. I'm pissed."

"At Janine? At the mayor?"

"That somebody trashed all of Barry's hard work, jeopardized the community center's future, and murdered one of the judges."

"Oh, is that all."

"Grr." Liv started to stand up.

Chaz pulled her back down. Put his arm around her shoulders. "Don't worry. I'm not making a pass; I'm just making sure you stay put while we have a little chat."

"About what?"

"Are you sure that's all that's bothering you?"

"Do I need something else?"

"I thought maybe you were worried about your grant rep."

"I am. If we look like a bad investment, they'll bail. We'll become the pariah of the not-for-profit world." She slumped against him. "And I was sure I could get it."

Chaz smiled.

"What?"

"Ted said he came in early. You had lunch with him."

"And the Marlton-Crosbys. So?"

"And you're having dinner later this week?"

She gave him a look. "What are you, my social secretary?"

"Ted told me. Said he was very distingué."

"He is."

"Missing your old life just a little bit?"

Liv frowned at him.

He shrugged. "Thought so. It's only natural. But don't let him lure you back to the city."

"Everyone's lives would be a lot easier without me. Yours certainly would be."

"Yeah, but it would be so boring." He moved a little closer.

"Lure," Liv said distractedly. She turned abruptly to face him. Jumped back when she found herself nose to nose with him. "Do you think maybe someone lured Lucille to Barry's museum?"

Chaz sank back to his side of the bench and started laughing to himself. She knew he was laughing because his breath was making like puffs in the night air.

"Think about it," Liv said. "We all thought she went home with her husband, but he says he wasn't at the ceremony. So either he's lying or she didn't meet him. But maybe she met someone."

Chaz stood up, pulled Liv to her feet. "I give up. Let's go over what happened Friday night."

"We went up to congratulate the finalists and winners." Liv walked toward the stairs at the side of the band shell. Chaz followed her. "Everyone was gathered at the front, talking. I went to thank Amanda Marlton-Crosby and you went to flirt with Lucille Foster."

She cut him a look.

"Really, Liv, I did not lure her to her death."

"I wasn't thinking that."

"Were you jealous?"

"Annoyed."

"Then what happened?"

"Amanda met Rod. Exit stage left. And the mayor and I went over to Barry, Lucille, Janine, and the others."

"Maybe Janine lured Lucille to her death."

"Get serious."

"I am serious. And if we got rid of Janine, your life would be calmer; mine certainly would."

"I was standing about here with Ted. You were there between Lucille and Janine. Two really well-dressed women, though Lucille had it over Janine by a long shot. I would practically have killed her myself for those Louboutin heels."

"Definitely hot. I'm envisioning you in the four-inch red soles and nothing else but lipstick to match."

"Don't you ever get tired of giving me grief?"

Chaz's mouth twisted. "Alas, that's not what I was think-ing about giving you. "

"Friday night?"

"I was standing talking to Lucille and Janine."

"Looking like you just hopped off a freight train."

"I did not." He shrugged. "Then Ernie got testy and stormed off, knocking into Lucille—"

"And knocking off her shawl."

"Did he?"

"Yes, you guys were all so busy fawning over Lucille, and yelling at Ernie, nobody noticed it lying on the ground. It was beautiful, pashmina wool, really beautiful. I handed it back to her."

"I remember. She called you *hon*. I thought you were going to deck her."

"It was rather dismissive. But—wait a minute."

"What?"

"Shh." Liv thought back. "Saturday morning. I remember running to see why Marla Jean screamed. I could see a bit of Lucille's off-white trench coat and I knew it had to be her. Everyone moved back, and Ted knelt down to check her pulse. I didn't notice at the time that her shoes were missing. Other people were in the way. But I did see her face and shoulders. There was no shawl there."

"She might have been lying on it."

"Possibly. Or she left it in her car."

"Which was found on the other side of the square," Chaz said.

"But her shoes weren't in her car. And I'm sure Bill would have said something if they'd found the scarf. His words were, 'Nothing.'"

"But she was wearing it when she left?"

"Yes, she threw it over her shoulder and the mayor asked if she needed a ride and she said, 'No, there's Carlton.' She waved and hurried off that way." Liv pointed to the south side of the park.

"But Ted said— Where is Ted? Is he okay? I've never seen him lose it in a meeting before." Actually she'd only seen him lose it once before and it had been a frightening experience. "Is he still upset?"

"He went to the play rehearsal. Now, can you please focus?"

"Right. Ted pointed out that Lucille said, 'Oh there's Carson,' but we didn't actually see him. Did you see him?"

Chaz shook his head.

"You know . . ."

"Uh-oh."

"We've all been thinking that Lucille's murder was because of the vandalism. But what if it was something different altogether?"

"Like she wasn't meeting her husband, but rather a lover?"

"Ted said she had affairs but no one ever talked about it."

"Pretty much true. Either out of respect for Carson or because he holds the lien on the house or business of half the people in town and they're petrified of offending him."

"So *is* she having an affair with someone now?"

"How should I know?" He took her elbow and maneuvered her away from the band shell.

"What are you doing?"

"Preventing you from going off on another tangent without following through on the information you need."

"Which is?"

"Was the scarf at the crime scene or not?"

"Oh, right." She reached in her messenger bag and pulled out her cell. Called Bill. The call went to voice mail and she left a message for him to call her back.

Chaz took her arm. "Let's go."

"Where are we going?"

"I'm walking you home."

"You don't have to," Liv said.

"Fine. You can walk me home."

Chaz walked her home. They didn't talk much and Liv hoped it was because he had his investigative reporter brain on and not because he was thinking of provocative things to say to her once they came to her door.

Fortunately, she'd have to stop at the sisters' to pick up Whiskey and they would put the kibosh on any of Chaz's ulterior motives. Not that Liv didn't want someone to have ulterior motives on her, but she didn't know how she'd ever even go on a date around here, knowing the eyes of Celebration Bay were on her and second-guessing the outcome of the evening. She loved her new hometown, but it was hard to have a social life when the residents had their ears to the ground and their CB radios.

At least Jon was from out of town.

Miss Edna came to the door when Liv rang the bell. Chaz had followed her up the steps. She didn't understand why he was being so overbearing. It wasn't like she was in any danger. At least none that she knew of.

"Well, come on in," Edna said. "Ida," she called. "We have company." She opened the door and Whiskey came trotting out of the parlor to say hello. Liv stepped inside and turned to see if Chaz was coming in.

"You, too, Chaz," Edna said. "Ida made some of her apple spice raisin cookies this afternoon."

Chaz gave Edna an over-the-top smile. Clean-cut boy in a grubby newspaperman's body. The smile he turned on Liv as he passed her was very close to a smirk.

She followed behind him and said under her breath, "You are so annoying."

Miss Ida patted the wisps of hair that invariably floated around her face. "We weren't expecting company. But we're so glad you came," she added hastily. She pushed to her feet. Liv noticed she was wearing fuzzy bedroom slippers with her heather tweed sweater and skirt. "Would you like tea or coffee?"

"Chaz would like a beer and Liv will join us in a glass of wine," Edna said. "We'll be right back. Come along, Ida."

Whiskey followed the sisters to the kitchen and Chaz and Liv were left alone. They'd been alone at the park and then walking home, but sitting in the Zimmermans' parlor waiting for homemade cookies just felt awkward.

And Liv knew why. The Zimmerman sisters loved Chaz, even though Edna had been known to call him a demon and hell on wheels. She always said it fondly.

Liv knew both sisters thought she was just the woman to make him settle down and be a productive, model citizen of Celebration Bay.

Liv was afraid they were going to be disappointed.

The sisters never did anything by halves and they returned with a tray of cookies, plates, cut-glass wineglasses, a bottled beer, and an uncorked bottle of red wine. Ida had changed into her daytime shoes. It made Liv want to hug them both.

"Let me take that tray for you, Miss Ida." Chaz jumped up from the chair he'd been sprawled on and took the tray from Ida. He placed it carefully on the coffee table while Ida smiled at him. Edna looked amused but gratified.

They were indulgent with the energetic, inquisitive, and sometimes troublesome boy they remembered from their teaching days. He in turn seemed very attached to the two retired teachers.

He'd been through a lot since leaving Celebration Bay, seen things he'd probably like to forget as an investigative reporter in Los Angeles and if he chose to put on an air of blithe nonchalance, it seemed to work for most people. But Liv had seen some of his darker moments and knew there was a lot more to Chaz than the façade he showed to the world.

"What?" he said, frowning at Liv.

"Nothing," she said and reached for a cookie.

Edna poured the wine and beer and sat down next to Ida across from Liv and Chaz.

Whiskey, considering his best vantage point for snagging crumbs, posted himself by Chaz's chair.

"Now, how is the investigation going?" Edna asked.

Chaz groaned.

Liv shrugged. "I haven't seen Bill since . . ." Had it only been that morning? It seemed like days ago. "Since this morning. They found Lucille's car."

"So we heard," Ida said.

Chaz looked at the ceiling.

"They don't seem to have any suspects yet," Edna said.

"The first forty-eight hours has come and gone," Ida added.

Edna nodded seriously.

"I'm sure Bill is following all the leads," Chaz said.

"Oh, we're sure he is, but Bill is needed all over the county. I'm beginning to agree that it may be time for Celebration Bay to have its own police force right here in town rather than out on the highway that we have to share with the rest of the county."

"But Edna," Ida said. "We know Bill and we don't know what we might get if we had to hire someone from the outside." She put her fingers to her lips. "I don't mean you, Liv."

"It's okay, I've had my share of that this evening."

"Yes," Chaz said. "Our big tough forty-karat-word event planner is feeling a little fragile tonight."

"I am not."

Ida perched forward on the edge of her seat. "Oh my, what happened?"

"Janine," Chaz said, before Liv could repeat that it was nothing. "But Ted let her have it," he continued.

"I don't believe it," Edna said. "Ted never gets angry."

"Tonight he did."

"Unusual times," Edna said.

"It's this murder," Ida said. "Who do you think did it?"

"And why?" Edna added.

Chaz held up his hand. "Stop right there, ladies. If you're determined to pursue this—and for my sins, I know you are—you don't start with guessing. You taught me that if I ever wanted to be a good reporter I had to remember who, what, where, when, and how. I added the last one myself."

"We did teach you that."

"You were always so bright."

"Hmmm. Then start with what you know."

"What do we know?" Ida asked.

Liv's cell rang. "Excuse me." She went out to the hall to answer it. It was Bill Gunnison and he had no good news. They hadn't found Lucille's scarf with the body or in her car or in the vacant lot.

"So do you have any ideas about where it might be?" Liv asked only half expecting an answer.

"Unfortunately, no. Where are you?"

"At the Zimmermans'."

"Is Chaz there?"

"Yes. He walked me home."

"Well, if you guys come up with any brilliant ideas, let me know. I'll be at the station."

He hung up and Liv returned to the parlor. "That was Bill. No dice. No one has seen Lucille's shoes or the shawl she was wearing."

"Well." Edna poured more wine.

Chaz passed on the offer of another beer. "Have to keep my wits about me when I'm with you three."

"So we know *who* and *what*," Ida said encouragingly. "Lucille Foster's body."

"In the vacant lot without her shoes and shawl," Edna added. "Very strange."

"*When* is sometime after the award ceremony, where she was last seen alive and kicking. What are we missing?" Liv asked Chaz.

"What happened between the time she left the park and the time you found her body?"

"I didn't find her body. Marla Jean Higgins did."

"Marla Jean?" Ida looked at her sister. "Ernie's daughter?"

Liv nodded.

"What on earth was she doing there?"

"She was rehearsing the play across the street and Henry Gallantine brought the cast over to help round up the mannequins." Liv paused. "That's before we knew there was a real body there."

"I had her in class," Ida said. "Such a plain little thing, poor dear. She had to repeat fourth grade. It was kind of sad, really. She wanted to be a princess, remember, Edna?"

"Every Halloween. She'd wear her costume to school even after she was way past the age to dress up. I'm sorry to say the kids made fun of her."

Liv nodded. It seemed Marla Jean still hadn't outgrown her love of dressing in costume.

"She had a job at the drugstore, then she married that awful Eddie Higgins."

"Certainly not the prince she dreamed of, poor soul."

"Is this relevant to the discovery of Lucille's body?" Chaz asked.

The three women looked at each other.

"It might be," Liv said. "I mean Ernie is accused of vandalizing the museum and his daughter is there the next morning cleaning up? Holy cow. We've all been thinking that the vandalism happened first. But what if the vandalism came second in order to obscure the body?"

"Do you think that could be it?" Ida asked.

"Possibly," Chaz broke in. "But that's not the point. Does anyone know Lucille's movements after she left the park?"

The three women exchanged another look.

"Not even gossip," Ida said, disappointed.

"The mayor asked her if she needed a ride and she said her husband Carson was waiting for her," Liv said.

"We know that," Chaz said.

"But Bill said that when he talked to Carson Foster, he said that he hadn't seen her since lunch the day before."

"It doesn't make sense," Edna said.

Chaz opened his eyes. "Sure it does. We just have to figure out which one of them is lying."

Chapter Thirteen

....

Since they only had Carson Foster's word for it that he hadn't seen his wife, and Lucille was no longer around to tell her side of the story, the four of them tabled that aspect of the mystery for Bill to handle.

They finished off the wine and called it a night. Chaz insisted on walking Liv to her door.

"You realize you're not coming in," Liv said as they waited for Whiskey to make his security round of the garden and driveway.

"Even with Miss Ida and Miss Edna watching?"

"Especially with them watching."

Chaz cocked his head and Liv could understand why the sisters forgave him all his childhood exploits, but he was no longer a child. And Liv refused to be beguiled by it. She had a reputation to protect.

Chaz laughed. "You'll give in one day."

"Probably," Liv said. "But you will probably have lost interest by then."

"Probably," he agreed. He whistled for Whiskey, scratched him behind the ears, before sticking his hands in his jacket pocket and walking off the down the driveway. From the corner of her eye, Liv saw the curtains in the Zimmermans' dining room—the room with the best view of Liv's carriage house—close.

Liv opened the door; Whiskey shot inside. Liv sighed and went in behind him.

It was barely six a.m. when Liv bolted upright in bed. She needed to warn the folks at the community center that Jon Preston would be stopping in the following day, then stop by Barry's to make sure the refurbishment of the Museum of Yankee Horrors was far enough along to show to the grant representative.

She showered and changed into work clothes. But not her usual in the field cords and heavy sweater. She wanted to be prepared if Jon made another unscheduled appearance. Today she put on a pair of black slacks and a gray knit shirt with a cowl collar that she'd brought from the city and hardly ever wore.

She had a pair of high-heeled boots in a box somewhere but not even for the community center grant would she wear those while running around all morning. She opted for a pair of ankle boots with a wedge heel.

Understated, casual . . . too casual? She pulled the elastic from her ponytail and her hair spilled over her shoulders. She looked in the full-length mirror behind the door. One good wind and she'd be eating flying wisps. She pulled her hair back into a ponytail.

It would have to do. She had serious work to accomplish.

Whiskey was waiting by the front door when she came out shrugging into her fall jacket.

She clipped his leash and he happily trotted out the door.

But when she stopped at the sisters' Victorian house, he rebelled, pulled on the leash.

"Heel," she commanded.

He barked, shook his head, and turned toward town.

She'd kept him from work for two days and there had been no emergencies. It was pretty obvious he meant to go today. He was probably missing his friend Ted. Liv knew Ted was missing him.

Liv, however, was not missing the caterwauling the two of them called singing.

"Okay, but you're going to have to stay with Ted while I'm running around."

"Arf," said Whiskey, and trotted off happily.

Bill must not have made much progress in the case, since there was no new gossip at the bakery or the Buttercup Coffee Exchange. "Haven't heard a thing," said Dolly as she handed Liv a bag with two croissants and another with a witch's hat doggie biscuit. "But don't you look nice?"

"Nothing," BeBe said before the sound of the steamer drowned her out. She handed Liv a cardboard tray with coffee and tea in orange and black cups.

"You're sure this is my plain latte and you didn't try to slip me any Frankenfrapuccino?"

"I know better. You've trained me well. But I still have hopes that I can expand your java horizons."

"Not going to happen."

"Well, call me if you hear anything new. The tom-toms are silent."

"Will do."

"You got a hot date? Love that sweater."

Liv just waved and left. Whiskey seemed in a hurry to get to work. He only stopped once to claim the leg of a bench and to sniff a bag that had missed the trash receptacle. Liv picked it up and tossed it inside.

By the time Liv reached the door to the office, Whiskey

was jumping around like it was Doggie Christmas. Which reminded her that she needed to check with Dexter Kent's Landscaping and Nursery about housing the reindeer for the Santa parade. Liv was always living in several holidays at once. Luckily, she only got confused when she was really, really tired.

As soon as the door swung open, Whiskey dashed inside. He'd finally trained Liv to drop his leash before she opened the door.

"Whiskey!" greeted Ted and came around his desk.

Whiskey sat at his feet.

"Their house is a museum . . ." Ted crooned the lyrics to *The Addams Family* theme song.

"Arr-ar-aa-arr-ar-aroooo . . ."

Liv went in her office and shut the door.

She started on her latte without waiting for Ted. He could be out there yodeling away until her coffee grew cold.

She quickly looked through the day's agenda. She should be able to get to everything she needed to do before doing it all over again tomorrow with Jon. And she'd check for any more bodies along the way.

Not funny, Liv, she told herself. *Not funny at all.*

She added calling Bill Gunnison to her to-do list.

The boys finished their concertizing and came into the office. Ted dropped a stack of folders on the desk. Whiskey retired to his doggie bed to eat his witch's hat.

Liv added checking out Yolanda's store to her to-do list. She'd have to get going pretty soon if she was going to get everything done before the afternoon. Probably a case of overkill but she wasn't taking any chances.

A quick division of tasks between the two of them and Liv was out the door. She stuck her head back in. "Better have Dexter send over an invoice. I bet you dollars to donuts, the reindeer rental place is going to jack up their prices this year."

"Probably," Ted agreed. "The price of success. I'll get on it."

She started to leave, stopped once again. "Oh, and can you check on the status of the doomsday prophet removal?"

"Yes."

"And—"

"—don't feed the dawg," he said.

Whiskey barked.

Liv rolled her eyes. The sisters swore he understood what they said. Sometimes Liv believed them

"Get out of here, you're walking around the neighborhood, not going on a world tour. Chop chop. By the way, you look really nice."

This time Liv left.

She headed for the community center. There wouldn't be any kids there today, but she knew the bridge club met at ten three days a week, and there was a nutrition class geared to seniors every Wednesday.

She'd love to bring Jon by when both groups were there to show the center's multigenerational function.

She walked east along the park, nodding to the Garden Club members who volunteered to tend the town's planters. Today they were deadheading huge plantings of bronze, yellow, and burgundy mums.

Liv crossed the street and passed the cemetery, turned left at the First Presbyterian Church and turned right on Baxter Street where the community center and Ernie Bolton's Monster Mansion were both located. Maybe she'd just drop by and see how he was doing since he was out of jail.

She purposely didn't look toward the *Clarion* office as she passed by it. Chaz's constant bantering was exhausting and she felt herself giving in. In Manhattan she might have just gone out with him and they'd be over each other by now. But this wasn't Manhattan. Besides, there was also A.K., who definitely sparked her interest—except she never consorted with coworkers.

She stopped in the middle of the street.

Liv, what is wrong with you? You have a murder and a

semi-disaster lurking around the next corner and you're thinking about men? Focus!

She marched ahead, down the sidewalk, across the parking lot, where cars were already parked, and opened the pedestrian door to the community center.

There was a chill in the air. It had previously been an auto body shop, and it was poorly insulated. The church had donated space heaters, but Liv considered them inadequate and dangerous. She couldn't wait to move the center into a real building.

A handful of people were either playing bridge or working on a jigsaw puzzle. As she walked over to the puzzlers, Pastor Schorr came out of the back room, which was really the hallway to the one bathroom and also served as the "kitchen," which consisted of an old refrigerator, a hot plate, and a microwave oven lined up along one wall.

Liv mentally crossed her fingers that they soon would have a nice warm building with several bathrooms and a full kitchen. And separate rooms for when the seniors and kids were using the facility at the same time.

"Liv. How nice to see you." Pastor Schorr suddenly looked wary. "Right?"

"Yes, I just came to see how we're doing here. I'm bringing Jonathon Preston to visit tomorrow."

The pastor smiled, relieved. Dressed in slacks and V-neck sweater, he looked even younger than he did in his surplice. He was thin, though his freezer was never bare, since he was a single man and the ladies of his congregation made sure he had everything he needed. To excess.

"Hopefully it will be a little warmer by the time he comes through." Pastor Schorr's smile broadened. "Unless we should turn the heaters off and look bereft." He paused. "Of course you know I was just kidding."

"Of course. But do leave the heat on. The first rule of fund-raising: Look your best. People like to give money to projects that look like they'll succeed. It kind of works."

"We're all praying that it does."

Liv smiled. "Well, I'd better get going. I was going to stop over at Ernie's Monster Mansion. Have you seen him since . . ."

"No, but I know that Harriett and Marla Jean have been staying there at night to prevent anyone from breaking in."

"There haven't been any attempts, have there?"

"Not that I know of."

"I'll just check on them on my way to Barry's."

She waved good-bye to the seniors, most of whom were too intent on their games to notice her.

Pastor Schorr walked her to the door. "I don't suppose the sheriff is any closer to catching the person who killed Mrs. Foster."

"Not that he's said. But he'll get to the bottom of it," Liv said with more optimism than she was actually feeling. Her landladies were right. The first forty-eight hours were crucial, and it was long past that.

She cut diagonally across the parking lot to Ernie's Monster Mansion. The house had belonged to Ernie's in-laws. But they no longer lived there and the house had sat empty ever since. The Monster Mansion at least put it to good use for a few weeks.

As she started to cross the street, she noticed someone on the porch. A woman wearing a white dress with a blue sash tied in a big bow in back, like something Sleeping Beauty would wear in a Disney movie. Marla Jean. It had to be. She moved across the porch, turning in circles until she got to the far end, then turned back again. When she reached the opening to the steps, Marla Jean threw her arms out to the side, faced the street, and bowed to an imaginary audience.

Then she saw Liv and stopped. Froze like a deer caught in headlights. Then she turned and ran into the house.

That's when Liv saw the bottom of her shoes and the flash of red before Marla Jean bolted inside and closed the door. At first Liv just stood there computing what she had seen. She didn't want to make a scene if she was wrong.

But she wasn't wrong. The soles of Marla Jean's shoes were red. And red soles were the signature feature of the shoes Lucille Foster had been wearing the night she was killed.

Liv reached for her phone and keyed in Bill's number as she crossed the street. She paused in the yard to leave a message. "Bill. This may be a false alarm, but even if it isn't, you need to meet me at Ernie Bolton's haunted house immediately. I think I've found Lucille's shoes."

She disconnected and, hoping she hadn't called Bill out on a wild-goose chase, went up the steps to the porch.

As she reached the top, the coffin lid flew open and a skeleton popped out, laughing hideously.

Liv screeched before she caught herself. Marla Jean must have turned on the skeleton once she was inside.

Liv walked up to the door and knocked. The outside lights popped on. But since it was daylight, the effect wasn't as surprising.

She knocked again. Music began to blare out of the speakers.

Liv pounded on the door. "Marla Jean, open up. I just want to talk." When still no one answered, she tried the knob. The door opened.

Liv shook her head. A locked door would have been a better deterrent than scary music and a skeleton.

She opened the door and stepped inside. "Marla Jean?" Nothing.

She peered through the dark rooms. Saw strange silhouettes and shadows. Any of them could be hiding Marla Jean.

"Marla Jean. It's Liv Montgomery. You're not in trouble. Just come out and talk to me."

Between the piped-in music, the popping lights behind her, and the dark in front of her, Liv couldn't tell if she was alone in the house. Marla Jean might have run straight through and out the back door, for all she knew.

She called out again. She was sort of trespassing. If she could just find a light switch . . . She reached out and touched something slimy. Her instinct cried "run" at the same time her mind was saying "gel strings."

Still she snatched her hand back and rubbed it on her black pants.

She could see a bit of a light ahead. The back door? She groped her way forward. "Marla Jean. This really isn't funny."

The floorboard above her head creaked.

Liv froze. Waited. Another creak, and another. Someone was walking across the floor above her. Down the hall probably. "Marla Jean are you upstairs?"

One more creak.

Cat and mouse. "I know you're upstairs. I'll come up if you don't want to come down."

Liv felt her way across the wide, empty space. Her eyes were more accustomed to the dark now and she could make out shapes. The stairs were straight ahead.

She stepped forward.

The space in front of her wavered, creating a distorted image. She tried to move past it but it moved with her. Then she got it: carnival mirrors. And the moving image was herself. She felt her way past the mirrors, came to a heavy black curtain.

"Marla Jean, are you in there?"

Liv pushed the curtain aside, but there was nothing behind it but wall.

She found the stairs by stubbing her toe on the bottom tread. She groped for the banister and a strobe light began to pulse as horror masks appeared and disappeared, the strobe making them look as if they were moving closer.

If she hadn't seen them before, during the preview, she would probably have run for her life. Even so, it was pretty scary. And fun if you liked that kind of thing.

But she needed to talk to Marla Jean.

Liv started up the stairs. It was lighter on the second floor, which hadn't been converted to the haunted house and looked stark and empty in contrast.

"Marla Jean?" Liv said more quietly.

She heard a *whoosh*. The door to her right opened, and Ernie Bolton stepped out of the bathroom.

Liv screamed.

Ernie let out an expletive. But he recovered first.

"What the heck are you doing up here? The museum is closed. And anyway, the upstairs is off limits."

"Sorry. I didn't know you were here. I saw Marla Jean on the porch and came over to talk to her. She came inside. I called and called but she didn't answer."

"Maybe she didn't want to talk to you."

"Ernie, I know you're upset."

"Upset? Bill Gunnison threw me in jail like a common criminal."

She couldn't argue with him there. Except maybe he *was* a common criminal. "I'm sure he didn't want to, but you did seem the obvious choice."

Ernie stepped toward her. "I might have been mad about losing. It's always the same with the rich people in this town. They just get more and more and the little guy gets less and less."

"Barry isn't rich, is he?"

"Barry? Nah, but he has Lucille's ear. Her husband cheated Barry good but he knows where the bodies are buried. He probably blackmailed her into voting for him."

"There were five judges, Ernie."

"All of them with an agenda." He walked past her and started down the stairs.

Liv hurried to keep up. "What kind of agenda?"

"You should know, you're one of them."

"What? I wasn't a judge. I'm not one of anybody. I'm just the new person who everyone blames when something goes wrong."

Ernie hesitated, looked back at her. "Well, I guess that's true. Still doesn't give you a right to come in here."

"The door was open. Do you know where Marla Jean is?"

"Down here somewhere. All dolled up in one of her costumes. Sometimes I think that girl doesn't have a lick of sense. She lives in a dream world. Bad enough before Fast Eddie Higgins got to her. Then he turned out to be the skunk we all knew he was, and now she's worse than ever. And I'm out of a good parcel of land just to get rid of him."

"Did that have something to do with Lucille's husband, Carson?" Liv was fishing and she knew she was taking a chance. Never ask a question you don't know the answer to. Though if the gossip was true, she did know the answer.

"Carson bought it, didn't he? As soon as I turned it over to Higgins, he turned around and sold it to Foster for twice what it was worth."

"Didn't you ever try to sell it to Foster?"

"None of your business. But, what the heck. No, I didn't want to sell it at all. I don't want to sell any of my property. But I can't pay the dang taxes 'cause I don't have enough income. Now, with Marla Jean back and living with us . . ." He sighed heavily. "Don't know why I'm telling you all this."

"I won't gossip."

"Don't matter. But just so's you know. I didn't vandalize Ernie's house and I didn't kill Lucille, not that anyone believes me."

Liv didn't answer. She didn't want to agree with him. But it was sort of the truth.

They'd reached the kitchen and Ernie turned on the faucet and filled a glass of water. Guzzled it down. Yelled, "Marla Jean, you got company!"

He walked to the door to the hallway. "Marla Jean, get yourself out here right now."

And Liv suddenly realized what a precarious position she'd gotten herself into. She'd meant to confront Marla

Jean. But with her father suspected of murder and standing here four feet away from Liv and his daughter wearing the victim's shoes, Liv could be in a heap of trouble.

The door to the pantry opened and Marla Jean stepped out. She was still wearing her dress and socks. No shoes.

"What the hell are you doing in the dang pantry, girl?"

Marla Jean hung her head. "Looking for . . . some . . . cookies." She looked up, wary.

Liv knew she had to act fast.

"That's a nice dress, Marla Jean."

Marla Jean avoided looking at her, shrugged.

"Where are the shoes that go with it?"

She shrugged again.

Ernie looked from Liv to his daughter. "What's this all about? You came in here uninvited just to talk about shoes?"

"Actually, yes. Marla Jean, can I see the shoes you were wearing just a minute ago on the porch?"

Marla Jean looked at her, then looked toward the door as if she might bolt. Then something in her changed. Her lips tightened and she stepped back, barring the pantry. "No. You can't. They're mine."

Ernie shrugged. "She don't want to show you her shoes. Crazy females."

"I'm sorry, I can't leave until I see them."

Ernie's gaze slid to Marla Jean's socks. "We don't have any shoes here for you to see." He took a step toward Liv but she held her ground. As a threat, it fell wide of the mark. "You better leave now or—"

"Or we'll kill you," said Marla Jean.

Chapter Fourteen

....

Liv swallowed. Wished she had thought first and leapt later, but she'd been afraid Marla Jean would be able to get rid of the shoes if she waited for Bill. She should have waited, because along with the ghoulish laughter, the moaning cries, and bloodcurdling screams, there was not one sound of a siren coming to her rescue.

Ernie stared at his daughter. "Marla Jean. You're talking crazy. Nobody's going to kill anybody. What's the matter with you, girl? Where's your mother?"

"Don't know."

"Well, go turn off that infernal noise. You trying to get the cops to come after us?"

Marla Jean shook her head.

Liv was thinking, *Yes, please come. And hurry.*

"Can't move."

"Why not?"

Marla Jean scrunched up her face. "'Cause."

"'Cause why?"

She twisted her face the other way. "I just can't."

For the first time, Liv seriously wondered if Marla Jean could have killed Lucille. Threw her in the vacant lot with the dummy parts and stole her shoes—and scarf? It sounded plain crazy. But then Marla Jean seemed a little . . . well, she didn't exactly seem to be living in this world.

Ernie huffed out a sigh. "I never know why women are always carrying on about shoes."

Liv stepped toward Marla Jean.

Marla Jean shook her head violently.

"Just give her the gol-darned shoes, Marla Jean. You got plenty."

"But these are special. And I didn't know. They were so pretty and somebody had just thrown them away."

Ernie's face and voice softened.

"Well, it was probably just a misunderstanding, Marla Jean. You found them and thought they didn't belong to anybody. But if they're Liv's shoes, you have to return them. That's only right."

"They're not Liv's."

"Then whose are they?"

Marla Jean frowned at Liv, belligerent—and afraid, Liv realized. Not for herself, but because the shoes implicated Marla Jean's father for the murder. How dense could she have been not to see that until she was confronting the possible murderer and accomplice after the fact?

"Just stay there. Both of you," Ernie said, and left the room. A minute later the moans and screams and laughter ceased. Ernie came back. "A man can't hear himself think with that racket. Now Marla Jean, if Liv says those aren't your shoes, then you need to give them back. You can buy new shoes."

"Not like these."

"Marla Jean. Get the shoes."

Marla Jean shook her head, more like a recalcitrant two-year-old than the fortysomething woman she was.

"Dad . . ."

"Get them."

Marla Jean reluctantly went back into the pantry.

"I don't know what she's so stubborn about. She hasn't been the same since she married that deadbeat Eddie Higgins."

Liv suddenly hoped Marla Jean would take her time. Things might get dicey once she actually turned over the shoes. And there still was no sign of Bill.

Marla Jean returned with the shoes clasped to her chest. So much for trying to lift prints from them. Though perhaps it wasn't too late. Liv held out her hands to take them.

Marla Jean hesitated. Looked at her father, then handed them over.

Liv took them gingerly, balancing the back of the heels on her fingers.

They were Lucille Foster's shoes, all right. From the front they looked like a simple black shoe, studs covering the back of the heel. But it was impossible to miss the distinctive feature of the shoes: the red soles. Liv had seen them from across the street. Impossible not to recognize.

"Is there a place we can talk?" she asked.

Ernie frowned but pulled a chair from the kitchen table for Liv to sit.

She placed the shoes in front of her, vaguely remembering an old saying about shoes on a table bringing bad luck. But there was really no other place to put them. The superstition probably held for countertops, too. It was a good thing she didn't believe in superstitions. Not even at Halloween.

Marla Jean sat down to Liv's right, keeping her eyes on the shoes.

Ernie sat across from Marla.

Still no Bill.

"Well," Ernie said, "I don't mean to be impolite, but what do you want to talk about? I have work to do. And if you think Marla stole those shoes—"

"I don't," Liv said.

"I didn't," Marla said simultaneously.

"Then what's the fuss? Return them to whoever owns them with our apologies."

"I'm afraid it isn't quite that simple," Liv said.

"I didn't steal them," Marla cried. "I found them. I didn't know. Why don't you leave us alone?"

"Because," Liv said, choosing her words carefully. "They're important—"

Ernie shifted in his chair. "Didn't know what, Marla Jean?"

Marla Jean shook her head.

"Tell me, girl. Ms. Montgomery and I don't have all day."

"They're the dead lady's shoes." Marla Jean began to cry, accompanied by big gulping sobs and sniffs.

"Good Lord." Ernie stared at his daughter as if he were in a trance, then he snapped his head toward Liv. "I didn't kill Lucille and neither did Marla Jean, if that's what you're thinking. So just take your shoes and get out."

"Ernie . . ."

"Now!" He stood abruptly, sending his chair skittering along the old linoleum. He took a menacing step forward.

The doorbell rang. Liv breathed a sigh of relief. She hadn't been able to get out of the chair, much less grab the shoes and run.

A knock on the back door. Liv saw one of Bill's young officers through the window.

Ernie must have seen him, too, because he swerved around, started for the hallway door, then swung back to the kitchen when the officer yelled, "Open up, in the name of the law!"

Liv cringed, but the young police officer was alert and insistent. She just hoped he wasn't trigger happy.

"You better open the door, Ernie."

Ernie took a swift look at his daughter, whose head was buried in her folded arms, and went to let the policeman in.

Liv recognized him but couldn't remember his name. "No cause for alarm," she told him. *Yet,* she added to herself. "Is the sheriff with you?"

"Yes, ma'am. He's at the front."

"Why don't you go let him in?"

He stood his ground, unhooked his walkie-talkie, and told Bill he'd was holding the suspects in the kitchen.

Liv shot Ernie an apologetic look.

Ernie wasn't having any of it. He stood braced on both feet, his fists opening and closing at his sides.

"It's all right, Ernie," Liv said.

"The heck it is. Me and my family had nothing to do with all that stuff over at Barry's poor excuse for a museum. And if he says different, he's a liar. And I didn't kill nobody, and neither did Marla Jean. I'm not going to jail for something I didn't do." He glanced toward the back door.

The officer reached for his pistol. Fortunately Bill came through the back door. He was moving slow, but not bent over in pain like he had been the first time Liv had encountered him. Bless those yoga classes. They seemed to be working. At least he was mobile.

"Ernie, Liv, Marla Jean." Bill nodded to them, then nodded to his officer, who took a protective stance by the door. Liv could see A.K.'s influence. Until Bayside Security began working for the event office, Bill's patrol had been much less intimidating. They must have been watching and learning.

Bill glanced at the shoes on the table, then to Liv.

She nodded.

"Have a seat, Ernie, and let's talk a bit." Bill pulled up the fourth chair and sat down at the table across from Liv. "Now, someone tell me what you're doing with these shoes."

"I found them," Marla Jean wailed.

"Fine, good, Marla Jean. Can you tell me where you found them?"

She shook her head.

Liv wondered why she was so loath to tell. She glanced at Ernie, who was looking confused and scared.

"Marla Jean," Bill said a little more harshly.

"Outside."

"Where outside?"

She hung her head and mumbled something.

"Just tell the sheriff the truth, Marla Jean," Ernie said, though his eyes were flitting around the room as if he were already looking for a means to escape.

Marla Jean took a shuddering breath. "In the yard."

Liv heard Ernie gasp, but her attention was trained on Marla Jean.

"This yard?" Bill asked.

Marla Jean nodded. "Yes, sir, in the front yard. One was just lying next to the bottom step." She glanced at her father. "And the other one was in the bushes next to it."

Bill nodded. Looked at Ernie. "And do either of you know how the shoes got there?"

Marla Jean shook her head, but couldn't resist a glance at her father. Which just made him look guiltier than he already looked.

Bill turned to Ernie, but before he could ask, Ernie blurted out, "I don't know how they got there. I never saw them before. How do you even know they belonged to Lucille?"

"I recognize them," Liv said. "They're very distinctive. They have to be hers. I doubt if there are more than one pair of these in Celebration Bay. They cost upward of eight hundred dollars."

Bill whistled. Ernie stared. Marla's mouth dropped open and even the young officer craned his neck to get a better look.

"My daughter already said she didn't steal them, and I didn't even know about them until Ms. Montgomery came trespassing and demanding to see them."

Liv shrugged. She could tell Bill the whole story when he was finished with Ernie and Marla Jean.

Bill was silent for a minute. He was slow and methodical but he always got the job done. "So, Marla Jean. When did you find these shoes in the front yard?"

"Saturday morning."

"Before you went to play rehearsal?" Liv asked.

Bill cut her a look.

"Sorry."

"Before play practice?"

Marla Jean nodded.

"And you were there at Barry's Museum of Yankee Horrors when they discovered the body?"

"You know I was. I was the one who discovered the body." Marla's lower lip trembled, but she had managed to stop the sobbing. It was so odd, Bill in uniform questioning Sleeping Beauty—or maybe it was Snow White—around a kitchen table in upstate New York.

"And when Ms. Montgomery told everyone to look for the shoes, you didn't come forward to say that you had already found them?"

"I didn't know these was the ones they were looking for. What were they doing—" She broke off, but they all knew what she'd been about to say. *Why were the shoes in her front yard when the body was found at Barry's?*

"But you must have guessed that they were the same. Not many shoes have these red soles."

"I just wanted them. It's not like Mrs. Foster needed them anymore."

"Well, I'm afraid the police need them for the investigation."

Marla Jean looked longingly at the shoes, close enough for her to touch, but she didn't try. Just sighed unhappily. "I didn't think I did anything wrong."

"I know," Bill said sympathetically. "Ernie, do you know anything about how these shoes got in your front yard?"

"I didn't put them there, if that's what you mean. I told you I didn't have anything to do with breaking into Barry's or killing Lucille Foster, not that I expect you to believe me."

"Why is that?" Bill asked calmly and slowly.

"You already took me in once for no reason. Just a bunch of gossip and speculation. I've never said two words to that woman. Yeah, I was pissed that Barry won. Everybody knows I needed that prize money. As it is, I'm going to have to give this place over to the bank anyways. Don't want to. It belongs to Harriett's mother. Had to put her in a home. Kinda lost her marbles, ya know? Harriett wants to keep it in case she comes home. But she's ain't ever coming back. Still and all, there's always hope."

Dementia or Alzheimer's, Liv thought. That probably cost Ernie plenty. No wonder the man was having trouble paying his taxes. And still clinging to hope.   •

"And you don't know anything else about the shoes or what Lucille was doing over there in the middle of the night?"

"I already told you," Ernie said, his voice tight with exasperation. "And if you think my Marla Jean had anything to do with it, you're as bonkers as my mother-in-law."

Bill didn't even flinch. "Marla Jean?"

"I just found them. I knew I probably should've turned them in. But they were in our yard. Somebody put them there, to make it look bad for my dad. I knew you'd make me tell where I found them and then you'd arrest Dad again." Marla looked longingly at the shoes. "They were so pretty. What harm did it do?"

"It interfered with a murder investigation," Bill said. "If you know anything more—anything at all—I suggest you tell me now."

Marl Jean shook her head.

Bill looked at Ernie.

Ernie slowly shook his head, an echo of his daughter's gesture.

Liv wondered if Marla Jean was telling the whole truth.

Bill motioned to the officer by the door. "Dawson, see if you can find a large evidence bag in the trunk of my cruiser."

The officer nodded sharply and went out the back door. No one spoke while he was gone. As soon as he returned, Bill dropped the shoes in a paper evidence bag and sealed it, before handing it back to Dawson.

"Now, Marla Jean, if you'll accompany me to the front yard, you can show me exactly where you found these shoes."

Marla led them back through the dark house where odd shapes and figures languished in the corners.

Once they were all on the porch, Bill stopped.

"Everybody, stay on the porch or the walk, please," he said. "Marla?"

Liv noticed that two officers in a second police cruiser had come to stand on the sidewalk that ran in front of the houses on that side of the street.

Marla Jean went slowly down the steps, turned around. "One was there." She pointed to the ground near the right of the first porch step. "It was just sitting there."

"And the other one?"

"Well, I looked for it, didn't I? I mean, why would someone lose one shoe and not the other." Her face took on a wistful expression. Liv wondered if she were conjuring up an image of Cinderella.

Marla Jean was obviously not happy with her life.

"And you found it where?"

"Over there, right under that bush. It was sticking out a little bit."

Bill motioned to his men, and one trotted over carrying a camera. He took photos of the position of the first shoe and the second.

"Did you find anything else?"

Marla looked confused. "No. What else would there be?"

Bill glanced at Liv. "I don't know, just wondering. But I do need my men to search the grounds for any evidence. And, Ernie, we'll need to look around inside, too."

"Why? So Marla Jean picked up the shoes. She didn't know they were evidence. Somebody must've thrown them there." Then his expression changed. "Oh no, you're not going to pin this on me or mine. I was mad at Lucille and the others, but I didn't kill her or anybody else."

He lifted his hand abruptly. Liv tensed. Bill reached to

his hip. But Ernie just scratched his head. "Somebody's trying to frame me. It's that low-down Barry Lindquist. His place isn't even a haunted house. Just a bunch of dummies that don't do anything."

"We have probable cause. We can do this the easy way or I can get a search warrant," Bill said. "But if I get a warrant, the whole town will know."

"The whole town will know anyway. Ruth Benedict's driven by twice today already. She's got her nose everywhere, the old bag. Go ahead and search, things can't get a whole lot worse than they are now."

Liv thought they could get a lot worse. But she kept it to herself.

Bill nodded sympathetically. "We'll be quick and I'll swear my men to secrecy. This is an ongoing investigation."

Ernie barked out a derisive laugh. "Suit yourself."

"I don't need to tell you and your daughter to please stay in town and be available in case I need to talk to you again."

"I told you—"

"And I may need you to tell me again. So if you don't want me to haul you down to the station right this minute, you'll agree to cooperate."

"All right, all right. I'll stay put and I'll cooperate. Not like I have anyplace else to go."

"That goes for you, too, Marla. Understand?"

"Can I at least go to the play rehearsal?"

Bill slowly inhaled, the only nod he ever gave to exasperation. "Yes, but I would suggest you don't talk about this to anyone."

She nodded. "Can I have the shoes back after you're done with them?"

Bill shook his head, though Liv thought it was more in dismay than rejecting the girl's request.

"I'm going to send two of my officers to look around the yard, then have them come into the house."

"What are they gonna look for?" Ernie asked. "Maybe we can help."

"That's not necessary, but thanks for offering."

Ernie took Marla Jean's arm and started up the steps.

Bill nodded to Officer Dawson, who followed Ernie and Marla Jean into the house.

Bill called over the officers from the second car. Told them what he wanted them to do. Had Liv describe the scarf. "And anything else that looks suspicious."

"Everything around that place looks suspicious," one of them said. "It's full of Halloween stuff."

"Use your judgment. And be neat. Ernie needs to open his house to the public by this weekend. Don't aggravate him any more than necessary."

The two officers began moving around the foundation of the house, looking at the ground.

Liv didn't envy them. The yard was one thing. But there was a garage and toolshed that were probably filled to the ceiling. She knew Ernie had moved a lot of furniture out to make room for the spooks and goblins.

And looking for a scarf in that dark and scary setup could take them all day.

"Liv, are you finished here?" Bill asked.

"Yes." She stood.

"Where are you going now?" he asked. "Back to work?"

Liv glanced at the time on her phone. "I'm going to drop by Barry's and then go to the office. I have Jonathon Preston coming tomorrow and I want to make sure things are in good condition."

"Then hop in. I'll give you a ride."

Liv climbed into the front seat, and they drove the three and a half blocks to Barry Lindquist's Museum of Yankee Horrors. The original yellow caution tape had been removed from the entrance to the parking lot, but the new crime scene tape still cordoned off the vacant lot.

Liv gestured to the tape. "Any idea how long the tape will be up? I need to get those weeds mowed before the opening."

"Not quite yet. Until we're sure we have collected everything we need for the case, it stays as is."

Liv sighed. "I suppose we could hang some orange lights around it."

They parked next to a BMW coupe.

"Thanks for the ride," she said, and got out of the cruiser.

Bill got out, too. Smiled at her. "I was on my way here, too."

"More problems?"

"Not that I know of. But then I hadn't expected to see Carson Foster's BMW here."

Chapter Fifteen

....

"That's Carson Foster's car?" Liv picked up her pace.

Bill hurried to keep up. "Where are you going in such a lather?"

"Sorry. It's not my business. But what's he doing here? What else can go wrong?"

"Hopefully, nothing. But hold up for a minute. I want you to do something for me."

Liv stopped. "Sure."

"I need someone to go through the museum and look for that shawl." He looked around. "Someone who can recognize it and do it without causing alarm. It's bad enough that I have uniforms over at Ernie's. But the fact that we found the shoes will be all over town. I don't know how, but news gets out. Always has. And I expect it always will."

"You don't want people to know about the shawl? Surely if you announced it, someone might come forward if they'd taken it." Liv frowned. "Or the murderer would try to destroy it—if he hasn't already. You think the shawl may lead us to the killer?"

"It's worth a try. If he doesn't know about the shawl, he may let his guard down."

"His?"

"Or her. Between you and me, the coroner found a contusion on Lucille's head, but cause of death was strangulation. She's not—wasn't—a tiny fragile thing. She would have fought back if she could."

"Unless she was knocked out first."

"Exactly. Something's not adding up. Until we have a clearer picture, I don't want anybody to know about the shawl until the police have it in their possession."

"So if I find it, don't let on? Leave it in place?"

"Exactly. Can you do that?"

"Sure. I'll just have to call Ted. I want that proselytizer gone before I take Jon Preston on a tour of town tomorrow."

"Well, that's one thing I can help you with, at least. We took him to the edge of town and now he's gone."

"That's a relief. He can be someone else's problem. You don't think he'll come back?"

"I hope not, but if he shows his face here again, we'll arrest him. He's wanted on suspicion of theft and disrupting the peace in at least two other towns. And we'll gladly give him a ride."

"Theft? I guess he's not a real preacher?" Liv asked, thinking of Reverend Schorr, who was her idea of a good man.

"No. Just a grifter with a flair for drama and sticky fingers."

"Great."

"We'd better get a move on." Bill sounded tired. Liv was sure his sciatica was acting up again. Hopefully this murder investigation wasn't cutting into his yoga classes.

As they neared the house, the front door opened and one of the volunteers looked out. Liv could hear shouting coming through the open door.

The volunteer saw them and motioned for them to hurry.

Bill moved first but not fast. He was definitely in some pain.

"It's Mr. Foster," the volunteer said. "He's really mad."

Bill nodded. "You'd better let me go in first, Liv."

That was fine by her.

Bill stepped up to the door. "Barry, this is Sheriff Gunnison and Liv Montgomery."

"Sheriff, in here!"

Bill went in. Liv waited a second, then went in after him.

It looked like the rehearsal for a play. Barry and the man Liv guessed was Carson Foster stood in the middle of the parlor. Face to face.

They were about the same height, though Carson was definitely the more sophisticated of the two. His silver hair was cut in a style that screamed salon. His face was tanned in spite of it being October, and not from working outside, Liv guessed, but from sailing or some other outdoor sport.

Barry's face had turned nearly as red as his hair and beard. And his paint-splattered work clothes served as a sharp contrast to Carson's conservative business suit.

A group of volunteers clustered stage left, and another group of seamstresses looked out from the opening to the dining room, which had been commandeered as a sewing and costume room. And all around the room, the criminals of history watched it all with their blank mannequin eyes.

"What seems to be the problem here?" Bill said, striding into the room.

"I demand you arrest this man," Carson said.

"Why?"

"For murder, of course." He switched his concentration back to Barry. "You just never got over it did you? Had to pay me back."

"By wrecking my own place and killing your wife? Get real."

"To get back at me."

"What? How would trashing my place and losing ten thousand dollars be getting back at you?"

"To throw suspension off yourself."

"You're nuts."

"No, I'm fed up. What did Lucille ever do to you?" Carson's expression froze, then twisted in rage. "Why you—" He grabbed for Barry but Barry jumped aside.

"Carson, cut it out," Bill ordered.

"I never even looked at your wife," Barry yelled. "You're making a dang fool of yourself, and in front of all these people. Man. Get a grip."

Carson rubbed his hand across his mouth. Looked around like he was just becoming aware of his rather large audience.

"You're a lying, cheating son of a bitch," Barry said. "Trust me, if I wanted to get back at you for years of bad financial advice, I would have gone after you, not Lucille."

"Okay, that's enough. Both of you. Do you want me to have to call backup?"

Both men stepped away from the other.

"You can both make your accusations out at the station, if you feel it's necessary. If you were just blowing off steam, I think you should call it even. Carson, go home and let me do my job."

"He killed my wife."

"As yet, we have found no evidence that points to Barry."

"As yet?" Barry snapped, his face growing even redder. "You won't find any, unless someone put it there and is trying to frame me. And we all know who that would be, don't we?"

"That's it," Bill said. "I'm taking both of you in until you can cool off."

"Aw, Bill. I got work to do," Barry groused. "And I wasn't the one coming in here making all sorts of absurd accusations."

"Well, I'm certainly not going to be arrested for trying to bring a murderer to justice."

"Carson," Bill said, "you'd better watch what kind of things you say in public or you could find yourself smacked with a lawsuit. Now, get out of here and go to work, and if I find you on this property again, I *will* arrest you."

"Ha," Carson said, but he was already hurrying toward the door.

Bill pointed to Barry. "No more trouble."

"I didn't start it, and how dare he accuse me of those things. I don't even like his wife—but I don't dislike her enough to off her," he added hurriedly. "There are others though . . ."

Bill narrowed his eyes at him. "Do you have any actual knowledge of anyone who would have a reason to kill Lucille?"

"Besides her husband? Not really. But if my wife ran around on me like that—I wouldn't kill her, but I *would* divorce her. 'Course I am divorced, but not cause of that," he mumbled as an afterthought.

Bill gave Liv a significant look, which she took as her cue to ingratiate herself with Barry.

Bill cleared his throat. "Liv wants to take a look around before she brings the grant money rep around."

"Why? We're going great guns," Barry said looking around at the half-finished displays. "That theater group has been a godsend, then Miriam Krause over at A Stitch in Time sent some of her ladies over to help and donated some material for repairs."

His eyes misted over. "Sure makes you proud to be from Celebration Bay."

Liv nodded.

"Really. There's no need to worry."

"I'm not worried," Liv assured him. "It's just that I want to show the representative from the grant foundation around tomorrow, if that's okay. I'd like to familiarize myself with the different exhibits. That way if he has questions, I won't be caught not knowing the answer."

"Oh. You take all the time you want, just be careful you

don't trip over something. I'd take you around myself but I'm overseeing the construction out back."

"Just pretend I'm not here. I'll be fine."

Bill and Barry left and Liv stepped into the former parlor. All around the room Barry had transformed lifeless mannequins into realistic horrors. She read the plaque that described the first grisly scene. *Sarah Good, condemned as a witch, Salem, Mass., 1692*. It was one she hadn't noticed before, tucked behind the pocket door that led into the main room. Against the wainscoted wall a woman in a pilgrim dress and cap hung by her neck from a rope. Liv wondered if Sarah had been the headless mannequin the actor had danced with outside. Her last waltz before dancing at the end of a rope.

Yuck. She moved to the next display, also a scene of the witch trials. A plaque read *The Pressing of Jacob Kahn*.

A man lay on a slab of rock. Another slab had been placed on top of him and was slowly crushing him to death. His arms were stretched out, his fingers splayed. His face was distorted, eyes bulging, mouth opened in a silent scream—a latex mask fitted over the serene face of the mannequin. The stones were foam, Liv reminded herself, but it still looked like an awful way to die.

This wouldn't be a good venue for smaller children. Liv made a mental note to have Barry put out a sign directing parents with young children to Patty Wainwright's child-friendly spook house.

But now she had another job to do: Find Lucille Foster's shawl. She pulled her gaze away from that tortured face, and after making sure she was alone in the room, stood on tiptoe to look behind the slab. Moved closer and peered in the dark corners. No sign of gold and brown pashmina wool.

Liv continued around the room, studying each scene, while she looked for Lucille's shawl and kept one eye out for Barry. The room felt airless, the only sound the distant whirr of the sewing machines. It was eerie and unsettling—and spooky. With each new venue, each tragic scene, she half expected to come face-to-face with another murder victim.

But fortunately she didn't, just more reenacted horror. And by the time she finished searching the room, she was about to admit the futility of her search. This area had been totally cleaned out and restructured. If someone had found a shawl, it would either be in a pile of discards, appropriated for use in one of the scenes of horror, or tossed in the garbage.

She headed to the next room and encountered the Man in the Iron Mask, New England style. She methodically searched that room and the next until she'd made the complete rounds and was thoroughly sick of horror.

And she still hadn't found the scarf. She wandered upstairs to find most of the rooms padlocked shut. There was no way she could get in without asking Barry and blowing her cover.

She went back downstairs and into the sewing room, where several volunteers were bent over sewing machines. They were surrounded by stacks and stacks of material.

"What is all this for?" Liv asked, trying to sound enthusiastic.

"To replace what was not repairable. Miriam donated all of it. Isn't that wonderful?"

"I'll say."

"You can see what we had to discard, such a shame."

"It truly is," Liv said as she peered at the pile of dirty crushed fabric that lay in the corner. She didn't see one tiny patch of fabric that looked like Lucille's shawl.

If someone had taken the shawl home, no one would ever be the wiser. If the killer had gone to the trouble of throwing the shoes on Ernie's yard, what might he have done with the scarf? Liv wondered if Bill's men had been any more successful.

She had looked everywhere but outside. With a sigh, she

went out back to look through the trash. Fortunately for her, the trash had been separated with the fabric contained in plastic bags to be sent to be recycled.

It only took a few minutes to admit defeat. If the shawl was on the property, it had to be locked up or very well hidden.

Liv did a quick cleanup in the kitchen sink, thanked Barry, and left. If anyone thought it odd that she was poking around, they didn't say a word.

She walked past the theater, where a man on a ladder was putting up the marquees for *Little Shop of Horrors*. She cut diagonally across the park, and even though the Buttercup and a second latte beckoned, she didn't give in to temptation.

When she reached the far side of the park, Liv paused to look for the doom and gloom man, who was blessedly gone.

But she did see the Peterson Glass truck parked outside the Mystic Eye and two of their workers carrying a large piece of plate-glass toward the store.

Yolanda Nestor stood at the sidewalk, watching them. The men passed by her to the store, momentarily blocking Liv's view of Yolanda.

Then Yolanda turned and looked straight at Liv.

Liv detoured over to the Mystic Eye.

"What happened?" Liv asked, as she watched the men carefully fit the glass into the gaping hole where the window had been.

"Someone threw a rock through the window sometime last night."

"That's terrible. Did they take anything?"

"No," Yolanda said. "But that's hardly the point."

Liv totally understood. And she bet money that this wasn't the first time Yolanda had suffered from this kind of vandalism.

"I hope you called the sheriff?"

Yolanda shrugged. "I'd rather not call attention to the fact."

"Well, you should. Sheriff Gunnison will want to know.

We don't accept vandalism in Celebration Bay." Liv sighed. "Though we seem to be having a rash of bad behavior lately."

"So I've noticed."

"It's very unusual."

Yolanda nodded. "Will you come in? I can't really open the store until the window is fixed. And I could use a cup of tea."

Liv had lots of stuff to do, but she certainly didn't want Yolanda to feel that she was snubbing her. "I'd love to."

Yolanda gestured her inside. She turned the Open sign over, and reached for a round piece of cardboard that read *Be Back at* with a clock beneath. She moved the cardboard hands and hung it below the Closed sign.

Liv looked around the store. It was far different from Pyne Bough, which had been in the space until last winter. Then it had been filled with natural woods, hand-dyed colorful wools, wind chimes, hand-carved Christmas ornaments, and orange and cinnamon sachets.

This store was dark except where the missing window allowed weak shafts of light to penetrate the gloom. A large astrology chart painted on the remaining window blocked out any other daylight.

Several rows of shelves were filled with books. Liv walked over to read the titles. Mostly books about witchcraft, chanting, casting spells, a few fantasy novels, even a couple about meditation and Buddhism.

Posters hung on the wall, all dark colored with magical signs and depictions of imaginary creatures. Tiny bottles of oil, a row of clothing, a basket of diaphanous scarves. And behind the counter, unusual silver and wooden instruments, probably used in some kind of rituals, Liv guessed.

The smell of incense hung in the air. And another smell . . . sage. Something Yolanda and the previous owner had in common. The whole space seemed a bit overpowering and the smell was cloying.

Yolanda turned and smiled.

"It's very . . . interesting," Liv said.

"It is."

"And it doesn't look like the vandal even came in. You're sure nothing is missing?"

"Fairly certain. At first I was afraid Elemanzer had gotten out. Oh ye of little faith, isn't that right, El?"

Liv didn't think Yolanda was talking to her so she wasn't totally surprised when a huge black cat rose up from the counter and stretched. He jumped down to the floor, made a figure eight around Liv's feet, and padded over to Yolanda.

A black cat. *Of course*, Liv thought. Yolanda had gift for presentation. Everything in the store helped to create the otherworldly atmosphere. Including the cat. Smart. Liv bet she was a successful businesswoman. She also wondered what had happened to her last store that she had to move.

Yolanda smiled. "He says you'll do."

"Well," Liv said taken aback. "Thank you, Elemanzer . . . I think."

Elemanzer meowed.

Yolanda laughed, a large, throaty sound that seemed to fill the room. "You passed muster, and he's very particular."

Liv smiled. *Rein in your imagination,* she admonished herself. *Even Whiskey comes when he hears his name. She's just an ordinary woman with a marketing plan.*

"We're all ordinary women," Yolanda said. "Shall we go in back and have some tea?"

Wordlessly, Liv followed her past a curtain and down the short hall to a back storage room, bracing herself for whatever she might see there. The space had been transformed into a comfortable sitting room with two overstuffed chairs with a small antique table placed between them. The shipping area was shielded by a series of dark wooden trifold doors. Still, Liv couldn't suppress a shudder.

"Phantom emotion," Yolanda said quietly.

"What?"

"That's why you shivered, you felt it. Much sadness here."

Yolanda shook her head. "Happiness floats out into the world to be shared by all. Dark emotions are tenacious, they linger. It takes some work to dissipate them. Won't you sit down?"

Liv sat in one of the chairs and watched as Yolanda went about making the tea. She moved gracefully, and her hands as she reached for the tea tin, poured water from an electric tea kettle, were mesmerizing to watch.

When the tea was steeped, Yolanda handed Liv a cup. Not a heavy mug but a delicate red china teacup. Liv breathed in the steam, a heady mixture of herbs and honey.

"My own blend," Yolanda said. She placed her own cup on the table between them and sat opposite Liv. When she reached for tea, Liv noticed that the nail of one of Yolanda's long, supple fingers had a Band-Aid around it.

Yolanda looked at it. "Split. Between the weather and some stubborn cardboard boxes. I should really cut them short but I have so much fun with them." She held out her hands. Her nails were long and curled under slightly. Each was painted a deep purple and dotted with little stars and moons.

Liv smiled, but she was thinking about what Bill had said. If Lucille had been unconscious, a woman would have the strength to strangle her.

Yolanda might be strong enough, but what motive could she possibly have? She'd just moved here. Besides, nails that long would have left marks, and Bill had only said bruising, not cuts and bruising.

"How are you liking Celebration Bay so far?"

"It's a lovely town, and perfect for the Mystic Eye. Almost everyone I've met has been welcoming."

"There are always a few of the others," Liv said.

"Amanda said you've only been here a year."

"Yes."

"But you seem to be respected by everyone."

"I try, but it takes time."

"Amanda says you're the person everyone goes to when there's a problem."

Liv sat up. "Are you having trouble? Besides the window, I mean?"

Yolanda shook her head. Looked into her cup and back at Liv.

And Liv was struck at the change in her face. That slightly mysterious and eternal look had gone and Liv saw a much younger-looking woman, at least ten years younger. And worried.

"As you might have guessed, I didn't choose the location of my old store well. I was met with resistance from the close-minded uptight citizens of the neighborhood and some of the more backward-thinking 'spiritual' leaders. Amanda invited me for a visit last year. She thought Celebration Bay would be perfect and would be near to her.

"Amanda and I go way back, boarding school, college. We went through a lot of things together. And I'm worried about her."

"Worried about her health? Her safety?" Liv asked.

"Both. She isn't happy. I could tell that right away. And I think it's because of that husband of hers."

Liv felt slightly uncomfortable with this kind of gossip, but she had a feeling Yolanda wasn't just gossiping.

"She doesn't say so, but I can tell. Even if I didn't know her, I could tell. His aura." Yolanda shuddered. "A mass of cloudy miasma. And now with Jonathon here . . . there is much conflict. That much I can see."

"You can actually read people's auras?" Liv didn't know how much of this to believe.

"I can *see* them. But they're not as simple as you might think and I can't always tell what they mean. Do you want to know what yours is?"

"No . . . thank you."

That throaty laugh again. "Afraid? Don't be. Yours is clear as a bell."

"I hope that's a good thing."

"Yes. You've found happiness here."

Really? Up to her eyeballs in murder and vandalism, Liv didn't think this was one of her better days.

She smiled. "Well, thank you for the tea." Liv stood. She had the strange feeling that Yolanda's reason for telling her about the Marlton-Crosbys was more than just idle gossip, but Liv wasn't sure what those reasons were. She'd have to talk to Yolanda again later. Right now she wanted to get back to work.

There was something more important pulling at her brain. She needed to talk to Bill about one more thing.

Fingernails.

Chapter Sixteen

....

Liv left the Mystic Eye a few minutes later, her mind spinning. Two vandalisms. Were they related? She'd have to tell Bill even if Yolanda didn't want to involve him.

It was obvious Yolanda didn't trust the police to look after her interests. And all that stuff about auras, and the dissension between Jon Preston and Rod Crosby. Heck, Liv had seen that herself and she didn't need an aura to tell her. It was pretty clear that Rod married Amanda for money. Maybe Yolanda, too, wanted to reconnect with her old friend and her old friend's money.

Sad, Liv told herself, but the situation really did nothing to bring them closer to finding out who vandalized Barry's museum or who killed Lucille Foster.

Ted looked up from his desk when she walked into the office.

"Fingernails," Liv said.

"As in the catfight variety? Don't tell me you and Janine have been at it again."

Janine? Liv paused. *Who had said Janine and Lucille had a fight at the manicurists the week before?*

"Uh-oh, I know that look," Ted said. "I'll just grab my notebook."

Liv hung up her jacket and went into her office. Whiskey got up from his corner, which, Liv noticed, had more crumbs on it than when she'd left that morning. She knelt down and scratched his ears.

"I guess I don't have to feel guilty for neglecting you, since I'm sure Ted has been taking very good care of you."

Ted, who had just stepped into the room, frowned at Whiskey. "Have you been telling on me?"

"Aarf."

"I didn't think so." He leaned over and said in a stage whisper, "She's smart like that."

Whiskey let out an *"Aar-roo-roo-roo."*

"I know," Ted said, and sat down, pen poised above a legal pad.

"You guys are weird," Liv said, and sat down on her side of the desk.

"So what have you been up to?" Ted asked. "What's all this about fingernails?"

"Where to start?"

"How about when you left the office, before anything else happened."

Liv told him about visiting the community center, seeing Marla Jean wearing Lucille's shoes. "I called Bill, of course . . ."

"Of course."

"Once we made Marla Jean hand over the shoes, Bill had his men search the property for the scarf, too. Then he drove me over to Barry's. I just wanted to check out the state of the museum for the tour tomorrow, but while we were there, Bill asked me to search for the scarf—without letting anyone know what I was doing.

"I came up empty-handed. But when we arrived, Carson

Foster was having it out with Barry. Accusing him of murdering his wife."

"The mind boggles," Ted said.

"He thought it was Barry's way of getting back at him for bad investment advice."

"Like I said . . ."

"And then when I was on my way back here, Yolanda flagged me down. Someone threw a rock through her window."

"Was Bill there?"

Liv shook her head. "She seems less than enthusiastic about informing the police."

"Probably had run-ins with them before."

"Because of her store or because she's a witch?"

"Both, I imagine."

"Once you take them out of Halloween or the Salem business district, witches do have a way of pushing some people's buttons."

"Is that what drew that street-corner provocateur here? The thought crossed my mind that maybe he was the one who'd broken the window. She and her friends were pretty aggressive toward him."

"It's possible."

"Just an isolated case of hooliganism, or part of plan? Could he have trashed the museum, too?"

"And killed Lucille?"

"It does seem a bit farfetched, but certainly better than finding out it was one of us." Liv leaned back in her desk chair, then sat up. "I don't suppose Doomsday Man would have any reason to kill Lucille?"

Ted shrugged. "Convenient, but not a shred of evidence."

"Well, there's lots of evidence," Liv said. "Just none of it pieces together."

"True." Ted stuck his pen behind his ear. "If it's any consolation, the mayor pulled old Doom and Gloom's permit. It turns out the guy's name and check were both bogus. Helen down at Permits and Licenses said she warned Gilbert, but he was blinded by a few measly dollars."

"He'd make a good suspect," Liv said. "Except the police escorted him to the town line and he's gone."

"I heard. But I also heard that Bill put out a 'something-something-something' on him—I forget the police code, you'll have to ask Edna and Ida. Anyway, it warned other communities to be on the lookout for bad checks.

"Turns out he's already wanted in several towns up the road. So hopefully if Bill doesn't nab him, somebody else will."

"Well, that's a relief."

"And how does all this lead to fingernails?"

"Oh. Well, Yolanda is very . . . compelling, I guess is the word. And I was watching her make tea and thinking how it looked like conjuring. Her nails were polished purple with little moons and stars. I noticed a Band-Aid around one of them. She said she'd split her nail opening a cardboard box." Liv frowned.

"And?"

"Well, suddenly I remembered Bill saying that Lucille might have been unconscious when she was strangled."

"Ah. Making a woman a more viable suspect than if Lucille was able to fight back."

"There was no sign of a struggle."

Ted nodded. "And as far as we know, no nail marks."

"But would it be possible . . . Sit back." Liv got up from her desk and went around to stand in front of Ted.

Ted looked dubious but leaned back in his chair.

"If she was lying on her back, and I . . ." Liv put her fingers around his neck and thumbs resting over his Adam's apple. "If I put my whole body weight behind it . . ."

Ted moved her hands away. "So are we adding Yolanda to the list of suspects?"

"Seems like we have too many suspects already."

"It seems to *me*," Ted said, "that if we could just figure out where Lucille went that night, the case would solve itself."

"Sure, but everyone thought she went with her husband. Except for her husband. He says he didn't pick her up, didn't even notice she was gone until the next morning."

"A quandary, to be sure. But considering her car was found downtown, she must've gone off in someone else's car."

"Or someplace within walking distance," Liv said.

They looked at each other. "Like the Museum of Yankee Horrors."

Liv moved back to her side of the desk and sat down. "Maybe we should be asking where Barry was all night."

"I'm sure Bill has. And I'm sure he'll apprehend the murderer sooner or later."

"Me, too," Liv said. "Preferably sooner."

But Bill hadn't found either the murderer or the doomsday man by the next morning. There were too many loose ends, questions, unsolved crimes. And into this mess, Liv had to lead Jon Preston. No wonder she was feeling a little stressed by the time she climbed the steps to town hall the next morning.

It hadn't helped that as she was reaching for the door, a hand opened it for her, and Chaz Bristow said, "After you."

Chaz was never up this early, unless he was coming home from an overnight fishing trip—or some other dalliance. And he avoided town hall like the plague.

He smiled at her and ran ahead to open her office door.

Ted's expression was so bland, Liv immediately suspected a plot.

She eyed both men suspiciously.

Ted stood. "Where's my favorite dawg today?"

"I'm giving Jonathon Preston a tour of town today, as I'm sure you know. I wasn't sure what you had on the agenda today, so I thought it would be better to leave him with Ida and Edna."

"Hmmm." Ted took their morning drinks and pastries from Liv.

Liv hung her jacket up.

"Well, don't you look nice this morning," he said.

Liv gritted her teeth. She was wearing black slacks and a soft gray nubby silk jacket that would fit right in on the streets of Manhattan, but that was perhaps a tad overdressed for the sidewalks of Celebration Bay. She'd even traded her ponytail for a messy bun and added a little extra to her makeup.

Well, of course she'd made a special effort; their grant money depended on it. Besides, she didn't want Jon to think she'd let herself go just because she'd moved to the . . . the . . . boonies? The country? *To one of the most popular destination towns on the east coast. And I'd better not forget it.* "Thank you. I try."

Ted grinned.

Chaz just frowned at her.

"What? You never saw a business suit before?" she said at her driest. "What a silly question. You don't do business."

"Ouch," Chaz said, and he followed uninvited into Liv's office.

Ted set the breakfast tray on Liv's desk, and sat in his usual chair.

Chaz pulled up one of the extra chairs they kept for visitors. He sat down next to Ted. "Do you guys eat like this every morning?"

"Would you like some cinnamon swirl bread?" Ted asked.

"God, no. I've only had two cups of coffee this morning. Totally not ready for food."

"Well, I'm not sharing my latte," Liv said.

"I never drink those girly drinks."

Liv looked at the ceiling and flipped the top of her latte, before booting up her computer. "Okay, what's up?"

"Nothing," Chaz said. "Anything up with you, Ted?"

"Not with me." Ted bit into a thick slice of cinnamon bread.

Liv looked from one man to the other. Obviously they were either waiting for her to leave so they could talk about something they didn't want her to know about, or she was imagining things, which was possible since she was short on sleep. Trying to come up with scenarios that would miraculously catch a killer and put him away before Jon picked her up at ten was exhausting.

She opened the file on the zombie parade.

"Have you cleared the parade route with Fred and the traffic committee?" she asked Ted, ignoring Chaz.

"Yes. All vehicular traffic will be rerouted away from the square from five to approximately nine o'clock. The zombies will gather at the post office and walk around the park to gather at the band shell for costume judging."

"Trampling the grass and flower beds and creating job security for the public works department," Chaz said.

Liv cut him a look.

He raised his eyebrows.

"Are you going to march in the parade?" she asked conversationally.

"Nah, this zombie's hired someone to cover it for me and take a few choice photos so a certain event coordinator won't read my beads until next week over something else."

"Oh, I'm sure if pressed she could think of something," Liv said sweetly and turned her attention back to work.

They were still sitting around her desk when Jon came in forty-five minutes later and understanding dawned.

Chaz popped out of his chair with more enthusiasm than Liv had ever seen from him. "Chaz Bristow, editor of the *Celebration Bay Clarion*." He pumped Jon's hand.

"This is Jonathon Preston of the VanderHauw Foundation," Liv said.

Jon withdrew his hand. Nodded to Ted and looked at Liv. "Shall we go?" he asked, barely suppressing a laugh.

Liv blushed. What the heck was going on? She was missing a whole lot of subtext. Which was probably just as well. Right now she just wanted to get Jon out of the office as quickly as possible.

"Yes." She reached for her messenger bag and slipped her iPad mini inside.

"Never without her electronics," Chaz said.

Liv cut him a look that could have sliced bread. Jon turned toward the door. *Thank goodness it's Jon*, Liv thought. *He had a sense of humor.* Some other representatives would not look kindly on Chaz's attitude.

Jon held the office door for her and she went through without looking back.

They were on the sidewalk before Jon said, "Should I look up and see if they're watching from the window?"

"Don't egg them on," Liv said.

"I'm really having trouble picturing you living and working here. I mean, it's a lovely town . . ." He stopped by a silver Mercedes and beeped it open, then held the passenger door for Liv. She hesitated, as a thought crossed her mind. She let it pass. Silver Mercedes were pretty common during the town's busy seasons.

"I'm sure no one else in Celebration Bay locks their car, but I confess to being an uptight New Yorker."

"That's perfectly fine," Liv said. "It took me months before I stopped locking my car, and it isn't nearly as nice as this."

She got in; Jon closed the door and went around to get in the driver's side.

"Now I hardly ever use my car."

Jon sighed. "Sounds bucolic." He started the engine and backed out of the parking space. "Where to first?"

"Well, I thought we'd take a look at the current community center. There's a retirement planning course for seniors this morning. But make a left at the corner and I'll give you the Cook's tour of downtown Celebration Bay on our way."

Jon drove slowly as Liv pointed out the Corner Café: "Delicious home-style Italian." A Stitch in Time: "The sewing circle stayed up all night to sew a replacement Santa suit for last year's Santa parade."

"Newlands Gifts just reopened this past year. An old Celebration Bay family who have been in business for years." She refrained from telling him they'd almost lost their store the year before.

Bay-Berry Candles, the Bookworm. Buttercup Coffee Exchange.

"Quaint."

"As good a cup of coffee as you'll find on the Upper East Side, and run by my best friend in town."

"Ah," said Jon, slowing down and glancing at BeBe's storefront. "I'll have to make sure to visit it before I leave."

She didn't like to hear him talk about leaving; they had just gotten started. Liv warned herself not to start reading signs in everything that was said.

"The Apple of My Eye Bakery. I know, also quaint, and I guess Dolly Hunnicutt, the proprietress, is quaint, too. People here take their holidays seriously. And Dolly's pastries could compete anywhere."

"They certainly have an excellent advocate." Jon leaned over and looked at the brightly colored bakery. The door opened and Dolly held it while Ruth Benedict carried a stack of pastries out to the sidewalk.

"They must be good," Jon said.

"Garden Club brunch this morning," Liv said distractedly.

Ruth saw Liv, but instead of nodding or smiling, her face went slack and she stared as the Mercedes passed on and made the next turn.

"Are we creating a scandal?" Jon asked.

"Good heavens, no. You just witnessed the town's biggest gossip. Fortunately nobody listens to her." *Much,* Liv added to herself.

They continued on their circuit around the square with Liv pointing out the various businesses and churches, while wondering why Ruth had looked so shocked to see her and Jon. The whole town was expecting him; maybe they just hadn't expected him to be so good-looking, or urbane. Even Ruth would be hard put to conjure a scandal out of a daytime tour of the town.

They left the square and two minutes later were turning into the parking lot of the community center. Liv had wanted to have an organized day at the community for his drop in, all clean and filled with activity. But they didn't have the funds for that much programming, and besides he would have seen through any subterfuge.

She and Jon were both savvy in the ways of business and entertainment. In the end it wouldn't matter. If he thought they were a good prospect for the grant money, it would be based on criteria he'd been trained to recognize, not on manipulation by a country event planner, no matter how good her chops were.

"Your community center is in an old body shop?" he asked.

"Yes," Liv said. "With inadequate heating, no insulation to speak of, and one bathroom that wasn't great when it was put in. The kids don't mind so much, but it's hard on the seniors.

"And unfortunately it's being sold. Besides, it's too small to service our entire community. This will be a perfect time to establish a center that caters to the needs of all our citizens."

Jon pulled to a stop near the pedestrian door of the building. Switched off the ignition and looked at her.

Liv grimaced. "Sorry. Didn't mean to give you the pitch."

"Occupational hazard," Jon said. "I do it myself. Let's try to avoid it today. You just tell me what you need, and I'll take it to my people and see if they're interested."

With a recommendation—or not, Liv added. But she just nodded and they both got out of the car.

They'd both still be pitching, all right, just with more finesse. When you were negotiating, you could be honest—should be honest—but there was still a certain amount of positioning that went on.

They were both veterans of the game and had just advanced to level two; there would still be positioning, but using more subtle techniques.

A thrill of excitement caught Liv off guard. She'd missed this, and she was enjoying it.

Of course, Jon was good, a challenge, and at one level that would make for a lot of fun. But the outcome was deadly serious. Had already become deadly serious. Someone had died over this fund-raiser.

The whole town was counting on her to make it right.

Jon had turned to look out over the neglected parking lot and whistled. "You'd think a town this successful would have a decent place for seniors and students. Or maybe they didn't think they needed one?"

"On the contrary. Celebration Bay was a depressed town for several decades. It pulled itself up by its own bootstraps and started this tourist business. But they're just now getting out of the woods."

"Thanks to you, I bet. If anybody could pull a whole town up by its bootstraps, as you so quaintly put it, it's you."

"Thanks," Liv said, feeling disproportionately gratified. She'd worked her butt off. "We're getting there." And everybody depended on her for their continued success. "It's a pretty big responsibility."

"Shall we?" he asked, and opened the door. They stood just inside while Jon slowly took in the circumference of the space. Liv tried to see it through his eyes. It was pretty bleak.

Pastor Schorr had promised to meet them at the center, and as they entered, he came out of the tiny kitchen area with a smile on his face. He immediately took over, guiding Jon through the scratched tables, mismatched folding chairs, and sagging furniture. They paused at the old pool table while the pastor told Jon of his plans for the center.

"A place for all ages, but especially teens and seniors, with programs for young families and accompanying day care while they're in class."

Jon nodded as he listened.

They stopped in the back corner of the room, where a space heater cut the chill in the air, and a dozen or so senior citizens were listening to a volunteer CPA guiding them through a PowerPoint explanation of estate planning.

Not that any of these seniors had much in the way of an estate. But they each had something they wanted to leave behind.

After a minute, the three of them moved back to the other side of the room.

"Do you have any questions?" Pastor Schorr asked.

"Not at this time," Jon said. "You have a very good advocate in Ms. Montgomery."

"Oh yes, Liv is indefatigable in her work for the people of Celebration Bay."

Embarrassed, Liv pretended not to hear him. Fortunately the class broke up at that moment, and several of the participants came over to put in their "two cents."

They spent a few minutes chatting with the seniors. Jon was his charming self. Even though Liv knew this was part of his job, and he'd honed his persona over years of meetings, galas, and openings, she still admired the way he seemed to really take an interest in the people he talked to.

A few minutes later they were back outside.

"Well, Mother Teresa, where to next?"

"I'm not. Pastor Schorr is just very complimentary to everyone."

"Uh-huh."

They walked across the street to look at the exterior of Ernie's Monster Mansion, then got back in the car and drove to Barry's museum.

A few minutes later they were pulling into the parking area. "This is the winner of the contest, the Museum of Yankee Horrors, and the recipient of Amanda's ten-thousand-dollar donation. In addition, this year's proceeds will go toward the community center fund. Actually, several business have promised a portion of their Halloween take."

"How altruistic," Jon said. "Insurance?" he asked, stopping at the bottom of the steps to the museum's porch.

"Town wide, plus individual. That was one of the stipulations of the contest."

Barry met them on the porch and Liv relaxed a bit as he gave a tour of the museum. Liv was pleased to see that most of the exhibits had been finished and many of the others were close enough to fire the imagination.

Jon seemed interested and in no hurry to end the tour.

"You live in perpetual holiday mode here?"

"Pretty much." *Except when dealing with murder,* Liv added to herself.

"I would think that would get cloying pretty quickly."

"We're always planning something new or reworking something old. We're having our First Annual Zombie Parade tomorrow."

"This I have to see. But why midweek? You could get a lot more people on a weekend."

"But I'm not sure what kind of people we would get, and how many. My security budget is stretched to the max."

"The guy with the shaved head, right?"

"Yep. A.K. Pierce. Bayside Security. All of his staff have military experience or I'll eat my hunting hat."

"Please tell me you don't really have a hunting hat."

"Well, I do. But I drew the line at actual hunting."

"Thank God for that."

"Anything else you'd like to see? There's the abandoned cannery, which will be another project for some day in the future. Great bones, but big."

"I think I've gotten a good overview. What do you say I take another look over your prospectus this afternoon and we discuss this further over dinner at the inn? Say eight?"

Liv quickly ran through her schedule. "Sounds like a plan."

They chatted on their way back to town hall, where Jon let Liv off. All in all a delightful time; now if he could just get his organization to come up with the grant money, life would be good.

Ted was at his desk when she came into the office.

"How did it go?"

"Good, I think."

"It didn't last very long."

Liv glanced at her watch. "Two hours. We covered the major sights. We're going to discuss it further over dinner."

"Ah," Ted said, cryptically.

"What do you mean, ah? Ah, you see, or ah, it's what you expected?"

"Both." He followed her into her office. But instead of sitting down, he stood on the other side of the desk. Placed his hands on the desktop and leaned toward her.

"How well do you know Jonathon Preston?" he asked.

Liv blinked. "Well enough, I suppose. We've worked on a couple of fund-raisers together. Well, not exactly together. He was on the money end and I was on the 'get them all partied up so they'll feel like donating' side."

"So you don't really know him . . . personally."

"Not terribly well. We met for drinks a couple of times, mainly work related. I mean fund-raisers can be twenty-four/ seven kinds of affairs. You get to know people pretty well. Hang out together." She hesitated. "Stuff like that. Why?"

Ted shrugged. "No reason." Then he grinned. "Just want to make sure his intentions are honorable."

Liv snorted out a laugh. "No, you don't. You just want to be first on the gossip mill. Well, there will be nothing to gossip about tonight. I have a position in the community to consider."

Ted gave her a look. "You're the only woman in town who seems to be concerned about her reputation."

"It's not my reputation so much as how relationships complicate things and invariably screw up your work, especially work that's carried on in the public eye."

"Surely you can make room for both."

"I can have my share of fun. Just not where it interferes with my position as event coordinator. Are you asking me if I plan to yuk it up with the foundation rep?"

"No, not at all."

"Then what's troubling you, Ted?"

Ted pulled up his chair and sat down. Steepled his fingers.

Liv waited, but she felt a cold chill creep up her back.

"Ruth saw you and Jon drive by Dolly's today."

Liv rolled her eyes and relaxed. "Yes, so what scurrilous tale is Ruth conjuring now?"

"She says that Jon's Mercedes is the same car she saw driving back and forth to the fish camp Friday night."

"How can she be sure? You know how many Mercedes, BMWs, Lincolns, and other upscale cars we get during an event. Besides, Jon didn't arrive until Monday."

"Are you sure he wasn't here earlier? Amanda got into a silver Mercedes Friday night."

"Possibly. Does it matter?" Of course it did, what was she thinking. "I'll ask him tonight at dinner if it will make you feel better."

But Ted didn't look satisfied. "There's one more thing."

"What?"

"Lola Bang's cat got out Friday night. It woke her up fighting around two thirty a.m. She lives next door to the movie house, and when she looked out her window trying to coax the cat back in, she saw a silver Mercedes parked outside of Barry's."

Liv stood. "This has to be Ruth's doing. Did she coerce Lola into giving a statement?"

"I wouldn't put it past her. But Lola would never agree to say something that wasn't true."

"How certain can she be? It was dark, could she really tell if it was silver and not gray or white? All the time while she was looking for her cat? Frankly, I couldn't tell the difference between a Mercedes, a BMW, or a Ford at three o'clock in the morning. I doubt if a nearsighted librarian could."

"Hey, don't shoot the messenger."

"Sorry, but this just reeks of Ruth's meddling. So help me, if she wrecks our chances of getting that grant because of malicious gossip, I'll—I'll probably do something that will land me in jail."

Chapter Seventeen

....

Liv was still upset as she dressed for dinner with Jon. Upset and angry—and if she was honest, there was a little niggle of doubt. But she tried to convince herself that the doubt was based on things Jon hadn't said, not any lies . . . if the rumor was even true.

He hadn't told her in advance that he knew Amanda Marlton-Crosby. But then why would he? Just because Celebration Bay was a small town was no reason to infer dastardly underpinnings to his omission.

Liv twisted her hair up, changed her mind, brushed it out until it hung shiny below her shoulders, pulled up one side with a clip, then twisted it to the top of her head again.

She was suddenly indecisive about how to look. She had never second-guessed herself in Manhattan, rarely second-guessed herself in Celebration Bay, but ever since her two lives began to overlap, she had been playing a guessing game.

And it all centered around her appearance.

"You're nuts, Liv," she told her reflection. "Totally nuts."

She reached for her mascara. Leaned into the mirror to get a better view. She'd perfected putting on mascara without moving her mouth since an old boyfriend told her that models didn't look like a cow chewing cud when they were applying makeup.

Well, Liv wasn't a model, and he didn't stay her boyfriend for long. Still, she took his statement to heart.

She blew out a long breath. She was acting like this was something more than a business dinner. She'd sat through hundreds of them, some more challenging than this.

It must be Lucille Foster's murder that had her on edge. Things just seemed out of hand. Bill didn't appear to be doing anything, though she knew he had to be.

She'd already decided to just ask Jon if he'd arrived in Celebration Bay before he appeared at her office on Monday morning. There was no harm in that. Maybe he just wanted to spend a few days with a friend without being accosted by people who wanted money. Maybe he just needed a rest. Maybe he came to see the town for himself without an escort who had an ulterior motive. He probably did that in a lot of situations.

She wasn't offended. But she'd better not catch Ruth Benedict gossiping and starting up speculation that Jon, a stranger in town, was involved in Lucille's death. Because she knew that would be the next step. Ruth saw his car, or had seen a similar car over the weekend. Lola Bangs also claimed to have seen a silver Mercedes, maybe, parked at the museum on the night of the murder. Therefore, the outsider must be the guilty party.

And on top of that, secondary situations were taking up her brain capacity. The Doomsday Man and the witches, plus Amanda and her trophy husband, and somehow the two separate situations were weaving into one.

She screwed the top back on her mascara. *Enough already.*

The last decision besides what to eat for dinner would be which shoes to wear.

Ankle boots with conservative heels? Or should she go all out and spring for stilettos?

Shoes, she thought as she reached in the back of her closet for a pair of heels. How did Lucille's body end up in one place and her shoes in another? If she was killed at the museum, why would the killer have carried her shoes to dump in Ernie's yard? Assuming Marla Jean could be believed and she'd actually found them in the yard and not in the vacant lot with the body. But why?

Liv slipped her feet into her own shoes. They were tighter than she remembered. Probably because her feet had spread from wearing sensible shoes for a year.

Maybe Lucille's shoes had fallen off in the struggle—if there had been a struggle. Liv hadn't even thought to ask Bill because she'd been so caught up with her grant proposal.

And if they had fallen off, then that meant Lucille could have been killed at Ernie's, though what she would be doing there was a mystery.

Had she gone over to make up with Ernie? That seemed unlikely. Though why did Ernie think she'd promised him he would win? When had the two of them even crossed paths except during the judging? The entrants hadn't even been allowed in the building while the judges were discussing them.

Liv smoothed down the skirt of her little black dress, something else she'd hardly worn since moving to Celebration Bay. She usually left the overdressing to Janine and Lucille and their guild friends.

But not tonight.

She clicked down the hall to the living room and sat down at the computer. She had a few minutes before she needed to leave for the inn to meet Jon. She pulled up her spreadsheet of possible suspects and motives.

Janine—Rumors that Lucille caused her divorce. Implication being Lucille was having an affair with Janine's ex. The coroner had found death by strangulation, but he'd also found a bruise on Lucille's forehead. Strangling would have taken a good bit of strength, and Janine wasn't particularly strong. But if whatever caused the bruise had knocked her out, strangulation could have been accomplished with more ease.

Liv added *Fingernails—real or tips*. Not that she really thought Janine capable or murder—just being a pain in the butt. It probably was totally useless, but at this point, she didn't intend to leave any stone unturned, no matter how likely.

Ernie needed the prize money, but killing Lucille wouldn't have gotten him the money. Had Lucille witnessed him vandalizing Barry's Museum of Yankee Horrors, confronted him, and he killed her? Or had he made some arrangement that Lucille reneged on, and Ernie killed her in a moment of rage?

Carson Foster had accused Barry of killing Lucille because he blamed Carson for his failed finances. Which seemed convoluted. Liv would have been inclined to kill Carson if he'd screwed her out of a lot of money—not his wife. Not that Liv was inclined toward killing anyone.

And what about Carson? Didn't detectives always suspect the spouse first? There hadn't been much talk about Carson Foster. Bill hadn't seemed to consider him a viable suspect at all. He was well-respected in the community. Someone had called him likeable, but Liv wondered how many others besides Barry had suffered from one of his bad investment schemes.

And maybe it had nothing to do with investments. Even Ted had said that Lucille had a roving eye and more. Maybe Carson just got sick of her playing around on him. Maybe he caught her playing around and killed her.

With Barry? Was that why her body was found on Barry's property? Then why were her shoes found at Ernie's?

Liv huffed out a sigh. There was something missing here.

Someone. Some reason. There was a part of this puzzle that they hadn't discovered.

And now this thing about the silver Mercedes.

Liv looked at the spreadsheet. Typed in Jon's name. But Jon didn't even know Lucille.

He knew Amanda, a little voice whispered.

"That's different." But was it, really? Well, she wasn't going to jump to that conclusion until she asked Jon point blank. She deleted his name. Pressed save and went to get her coat.

Liv drove to the inn and parked in the lot. It was fairly crowded. Weekday evenings were still hard to fill but the inn's reputation was growing and it was beginning to attract diners from surrounding towns even when the tourists were scarce.

Jon was waiting for her in the lobby. He was wearing slacks and a black pullover under a tweed deconstructed jacket. He looked like a million bucks.

He smiled when she came in, kissed her on the cheek, and took her coat, which he handed off to the coat check girl.

They went into the dining room. Corinne Anderson, who owned the inn and restaurant with her husband, had a knack for design. She managed to make the dining room seem cheery in the morning, streamlined but charming for lunch, and elegant in the evenings. All with lighting, linens, and table settings.

The hostess led Jon and Liv to a table for two by the windows that looked out over the lake. A candle was lit in the glass hurricane lamp on the table. And lights embellished the small pier and shrubs, created an inviting ambiance.

Jon seated Liv, then sat across from her, smiling. She smiled back and it was just like the old days.

They discussed a choice of wine, ordered, then settled

into a comfortable conversation. Nothing about business. It was the way things worked. And Liv was determined not to bring up the subject of the Mercedes until at least dessert.

She did want to talk to Jon. Actually, maybe she wanted to warn him. She didn't think for a moment that he killed Lucille. It wasn't fair that just because he was an outsider, everyone seemed so eager to accuse him.

The waiter brought the bottle of wine and opened it for them. Poured a tasting for Jon, who nodded, then poured Liv's and then filled Jon's.

Liv realized how much her life had changed. Most dinners that she ate out, and there weren't all that many, were usually at Buddy's or maybe the inn's bar. There was pizza and Chinese and the deli; and the Corner Café that stayed opened for dinner on the weekends and evenings during the height of tourist season.

But she'd only dined at the inn's restaurant a handful of times with BeBe or Ted.

She was beginning to enjoy herself, was leaning in to hear something Jon said, when her eye caught a party of diners entering the restaurant.

She straightened up.

"What is it?" Jon asked.

"Don't look now, but my colleagues have just come in."

"Oh." Jon frowned. "Should we invite them to join us?"

"God, no. If anything we should tell them to butt out."

"Oh," Jon said. "Are they protecting your virtue?"

Liv gave him a look.

"Well, nothing would surprise me. After learning that you have a hunting hat, I figured anything goes. But Liv, you have to admit, it's awfully quaint."

He didn't know the half of it. And when he found out he was the object of speculation not only for his relationship to Liv, but as a possible murder suspect, he'd probably drive his Mercedes right out of town, never to return.

"Dare I turn and look?"

"No. I could kill them."

"How many are there?"

"Three. Ted, Chaz—the newspaper editor you met—and A.K., my security guy."

"I don't guess it could be coincidental?"

"Not likely. I've only seen Chaz in a suit once at a funeral, and I've never seen A.K. in a suit at all." Not that he was actually wearing a suit. A black turtleneck and a gray jacket that looked like it had been found at the last minute. He looked uncomfortable and out of place.

Well, good, he should be. She could imagine something like this from Ted and Chaz, but not A.K. He and Chaz didn't even like each other. She was going to let them have it so bad the next time she saw them.

Fortunately Jon was a master at keeping a person at their ease, charming and entertaining, with just the right amount of warmth that made a person relax, lean a little closer, listen a little more attentively.

And soon Liv had managed to successfully put the trio of chaperones out of her mind. She and Jon reminisced and laughed and dessert came without either of them mentioning the grant or the murder. Liv just hoped the spies were having a terrible time.

Jon suggested a brandy in the bar. "That way maybe we can ditch them," he said.

"Or stick them with our bill," Liv suggested.

Jon chuckled, "You are something else. But a bit extreme."

"Right now, I don't really care."

They left the table and walked toward the door, neither of them looking in the direction of the other table. Jon's arm slipped around Liv's waist and she leaned into him. It was more enticing than she'd considered and she almost forgot that it was just for show.

They sat at a table at the far end of the bar, out of sight from the door.

When the trio didn't follow, Liv relaxed. She shouldn't have.

A few minutes later, Bill Gunnison walked through the door, looked around the bar, and headed their way.

Liv felt the brandy burn a hole in her stomach.

Bill walked straight up to their table.

"Evening, Liv."

Liv didn't say anything.

"Mr. Preston?"

"Yes?"

"I'm Sheriff Gunnison. Is that your silver Mercedes parked outside?"

Jon glanced at Liv. "I have a silver Mercedes parked outside."

Liv glared at Bill. He ignored her.

"We have information that a car fitting that description was seen at a crime scene on Friday evening. Could you tell me where you were on Friday night?"

"Bill!" Liv exclaimed.

"I was visiting friends."

"All night?"

"Yes."

"Would you mind if we search your car?"

"Bill."

"Sorry, Liv. Sir, do you mind?"

"No. Go ahead." Jon reached in his pants pocket and handed Bill a set of keys.

"If you'd come with us to sign the requisite papers."

Jon sighed, looked at Liv, and followed Bill out of the bar.

Liv followed after them.

Jon signed the paper and stood on the porch while Bill and his officers began a search of his car.

Ted, Chaz, and A.K. stood on the far side of the parking lot, hunched together like the traitors they were.

Liv stood next to Jon, in case anyone wondered where her loyalties lay.

"Did you know about this?" he asked.

"Of course not."

"What crime am I supposed to have committed?"

"Somebody said they saw a silver Mercedes at the Museum of Yankee Horrors on the night Lucille Foster was killed."

"Murder. That's serious. I suppose I should call my lawyer."

"Jon, I'm so sorry. It's stupid, just a stupid mistake, and they—" She was interrupted by a flurry of activity around the trunk of Jon's car.

After a few minutes Bill walked back toward the porch. Several people had gathered on the porch to watch, among them innkeeper Corinne Anderson.

"What's going on?" she asked Liv.

"They think someone might have stolen Jon's car, you know, for a joyride or something."

"Oh, that's too bad. Not from our parking lot?" Corinne looked worried.

"No, while I was staying at friends on the outskirts of town."

Liv shot a glance at Jon. So he had been in town for the weekend.

"Oh, that's just awful. We do have a few kids hot-wiring cars for joyriding."

"Hmm," Jon said. He was watching Bill walk back toward the porch. He didn't look happy.

"Is there someplace we could talk, Mr. Preston?" Bill said. "I need to ask you a few questions."

"You can use my office," Corinne said.

"Thanks." Bill gestured Jon toward the office. Liv glared at Bill and linked her arm in Jon's. She heard Bill's sigh as he followed them into the inn's office.

Bill sat at Corinne's desk with Jon and Liv on a settee across from him.

"I'd just like to ask you a few questions."

Jon nodded.

Liv couldn't believe how calm Jon was. She knew where

this was heading and she bet Jon did, too. He would never forgive her for getting him in this mess. And she knew already that they could kiss the grant money good-bye. And all because of that busybody Ruth Benedict.

"How long have you been in Celebration Bay?"

"Well, I checked into the inn last night."

"And before that?"

Jon cast a quick look at Liv. "I was staying with friends nearby."

"And the names of these friends?"

"Amanda Marlton." He hesitated. "And her husband, Rod Crosby."

"For how long?"

"Since last Thursday night."

The brandy began to burn in Liv's stomach.

"Now, sir, can you tell me your whereabouts on Friday night?"

"As I said, I was staying with friends."

"And these friends are able to vouch for you?"

"Yes. Am I being charged with something?"

"No, but a car matching your description was seen parked at the site where the body of Lucille Foster was found."

"I see."

"Did you use your car on Friday night?"

"The night of your award ceremony?"

Bill nodded.

"Actually, I did." Jon shot an apologetic look at Liv. "I picked Amanda up when it was over. I drove her back to her house, where we stayed for the remainder of the night."

Liv stared at her hands while a hundred questions raced through her mind. Why hadn't he told her he was in town? Why hadn't he come to the ceremony if he was in town? And what was his relationship with Amanda Marlton-Crosby?

"Is it possible that someone else used your car?"

"Someone must have, if it was seen, since I didn't."

"So you didn't leave the house after that. About what time was that?"

"Probably seven thirty. I picked Amanda up from the award ceremony; her husband stayed in town. We went back to the house, had a glass of wine, and talked for a bit until I fell asleep in the chair. I'd just returned from Bangkok and was seriously jet-lagged. Later, when I woke up, I went upstairs to bed."

"And did you notice whether your car was still outside?"

"No. It didn't occur to me that someone might have taken it. You can't even see the house from the road. And you can't see the cars from the house, they're parked on a lower level."

"But would it be possible?"

"Sure. Mercedes are a favorite among thieves. Though they don't generally bring them back."

"True." Bill scratched his head. "I'm afraid we need to impound your car."

"For what?"

"For further investigation. We'll be as quick as we can." He heaved himself out of the chair. Winced.

Liv felt no sympathy.

"And Mr. Preston, please don't leave town."

Jon lifted an eyebrow. "How can I? You have my car."

Bill nodded and left the room. Liv held up a finger for Jon to wait, then she hurried after Bill.

He hadn't made it far. She caught up to him before he got to the front door.

"Bill!"

Bill stopped, slowly turned around. Waited for Liv to get closer. "Liv, you know—"

"No. You listen. I've known Jon for years, he's here to evaluate the community center for a huge grant. Anyone could have taken his car. You and the three stooges out there are going to blow this for us all."

"It's the law, Liv."

"Yeah? Well, you know what Dickens said about the law."

"No, what?"

"You don't want to know." Liv turned on her heel—her very high heels—and stormed back into the inn and right into Jon.

"Well, this is a first. So I guess your colleagues weren't here to protect your virtue but to make sure I didn't escape?"

"That's not funny."

"I'm not laughing."

"It's that stupid Ruth Benedict. She saw your car going back and forth from Amanda's house on Friday. She's the worst gossip in town. I know she turned you in. Then someone else said they saw a car like yours at the museum the night of the murder. It's Celebration Bay; gossip runs unrestrained here.

"I told them it wasn't yours, but I guess I was wrong. Why didn't you tell me you got here so much earlier?"

"Do you have time for a nightcap? I could use one at this point. And I'll explain."

"Can I take off my shoes?"

Jon smiled. "Absolutely."

Liv glanced out the window. She could see Bill and the stooges standing in the parking lot. "How about we have that nightcap in your room?"

Jon barked out a laugh. "Are you propositioning me?

"No, but they won't know that."

"The city and I have missed you and your convoluted mind. If your sheriff hadn't just accused me of murdering some poor woman I've never set eyes on, I'd be enjoying myself immensely. But Liv, what possessed you to move to someplace like Celebration Bay?"

Chapter Eighteen

....

Jon asked Corinne to send coffee and a bottle of Courvoisier up to his room. "You do have to drive home tonight,"
he reminded Liv as they walked up the stairs. "Unless . . ."

"Since when did you start mixing business with pleasure?" Liv asked.

"I haven't . . . yet. Have you?"

Liv shook her head.

"Alas, for us. Here we are." He unlocked the door and ush-
ered her into a large sitting room. A chintz love seat and chair
in a striped and floral pattern were positioned in front of a
small painted fireplace. A double window was flanked by
cream-colored draperies. Liv crossed to the window and
looked out. It was pretty dark, but she could make out the lake
in the spill of the parking lot lights off to the left. But she
couldn't tell the true colors or makes of the cars parked there.

She wondered if Bill and the stooges were still standing
out there confabbing. What a nasty thing for them to do. It
made her look ridiculous, had to be embarrassing for Jon,

and probably put paid to any chance of him recommending them for the grant money.

"Have a seat, Liv. Take off those killer shoes and relax."

Liv sat on the couch and pushed her feet out of her shoes. Got a flash of Lucille. Is that what she'd done? Purposely took off her shoes so that she could . . . what? Run after the vandal, run away from her killer? Or had she already taken them off and didn't have time to put them back on?

The knock at the door made her jump.

Jon went to answer it and stood aside while a waiter deposited a tray on the table. When he was gone, Jon poured a cup for Liv.

"How do you take you your coffee? I'm afraid I can't make you a latte."

"Black is fine."

He handed her a cup, poured a Courvoisier for himself, and sat in the chair facing the couch.

"I'm really sorry about all this, Jon."

"Not your fault. But it is weird."

Liv put her cup on the coffee table in front of her. "Now tell me. Why didn't you let me know you'd been here since Thursday?"

"I didn't want you to think I sneaked in to spy on you."

"But that's what you did."

"No, it isn't. It's a long story."

"There's a whole pot of coffee. Unless it isn't my business, though since you suddenly seem to be the prime suspect for murder, it might be to your advantage to tell me."

Jon leaned back and let out a sigh. "I wasn't spying on you. I was spying on Amanda and Rod." He paused. "I don't have to tell you that this isn't the kind of information the Marltons would like to get out. I can just imagine what your Ruth Benedict could do with this."

"It doesn't have anything to do with the murder, does it?"

"No, of course not. We go way back, Amanda and I. We were, uh, close for a while when we were much younger. The families had great expectations, Amanda's father and my father, you know, the old boy's club. Just didn't happen for either of us. She couldn't settle down. Or maybe she was too settled. I moved on and she ended up running off with Rod Crosby.

"Things went well in Bangkok and I returned earlier than I expected. Amanda's father asked me to come check on her. Lately, he's been hearing rumblings about erratic behavior, huge credit card bills, strange investments. Evidently she lost a bundle in a bad investment. Very unlike Amanda. He's afraid that her husband is playing fast and loose with her money. That he's the one racking up the bills and making bad investments."

"Did you ask Amanda about it?"

"Not outright. Her father did, before I came, and she told him that it was none of his business and accused him of spying on her."

"So instead you came to spy on her?"

Jon shrugged. "She's my friend. I want to help her out of a bad situation if I can.

"It's always been oil and water with her father and her. Since she ran off with Rod, it's gotten worse. It's clear she's unhappy, but she won't do anything to fix it. Marltons are known for being stubborn. Amanda is no exception.

"That's why I came up early. To try to convince Amanda to come home, not to kill some total stranger."

"And did you find out anything more? Because Lucille Foster's husband is the big investment banker around here."

"Who's Lucille Foster?"

"The woman who was murdered."

"I see."

"Hmm," Liv said, crossing her arms and leaning back on the couch. "What do you know about Yolanda?"

"The witch? She's a school friend of Amanda's, I met her a couple of times when they were in college. Marched to a different drummer. Why?"

"She's also worried about Amanda. Someone busted a

window in her shop last night. I went over to see and got an earful. She doesn't like Rod at all."

"I don't like the guy, either. I never did. He's a user and I'm sure he married Amanda for her money. Which would be fine if she was getting something in return. But I don't think she is. So that's why I was here early and why I didn't let you know. I don't want this whole thing to get out. I don't want Amanda to be hurt any more than necessary. It will be humiliating enough without it going public. The gossip rags will have a field day."

Liv shook her head. "So you come to do a good deed—"

"And now I'm apparently suspected of murder."

Liv stood, walked to the window and back. "So if your car was used in the murder—which seems unlikely, but just saying it was—who would have most likely taken it? No one knew you were here except Amanda and Rod, right?"

"Right." Jon frowned. "And I've hardly gotten to talk to Amanda alone. Rod seems to know what I'm up here for and he sticks to her like a cocklebur."

"Except," Liv added, "on Friday night, when he stayed in town after the ceremony to drink with his friends."

"That's right, but how did you know that?"

"We were walking past and saw him put Amanda in what turns out to be your car. You must have been driving."

"I was. What a coincidence."

"True, but I wonder where Rod went after that."

"Out drinking, he said. Why?"

"What time did he get home?"

"No idea. I didn't hear him come in."

"And you didn't hear Amanda go out?"

"Amanda? What are you getting at?"

"Seems like one of them had easiest access to your car. Or both . . ."

Jon popped out of his chair. "That's crazy. Amanda?"

"Bill said Lucille was hit on the head, then strangled. It

wouldn't take that much strength to strangle an unconscious woman."

"No way."

"I'm not saying that's what happened. Just that maybe you should be a little careful if you go back out to their house."

Liv glanced at her watch and slipped her heels back on. "It's after eleven. I'd better get home. I want to look my best for the zombie parade." She'd need her energy if she were going to clear Jon's name, catch a killer, *and* herd a bunch of zombies to the band shell.

Jon walked her back to the lobby where Corinne Anderson was still sitting behind the counter, waiting to see if Liv came downstairs again?

Liv hesitated at the door.

Jon peered outside. "Shall I see if the coast is clear?"

"No," Liv said. "If they're still out there, I'll kill them."

Jon took her elbow. "I'll walk you to your car."

"Are you going to be okay?"

"Yes, though I will call my lawyer first thing in the morning."

"Jon, I'm so sorry."

"Not your fault." He waited for her to get in her car, then leaned in and kissed her briefly on the mouth. "Drive safely."

She nodded and drove away without looking back.

The warm buzz from Jon's kiss lasted about a block. Then it turned to anger. How dare someone in town point to Jon as the murderer? Was this town just so addicted to gossip that they were willing to give false tips to the police? Or had someone really driven Jon's car to murder Lucille Foster?

She didn't see any cars following her, so she decided the guys had given up their vigil, which just made her angrier. Jon had been right, she realized. They weren't jealous or concerned for her safety. They wanted to make sure Jon couldn't get away before Bill impounded his car.

They'd wrecked the chance of the community center

getting the grant—or any other grant. The foundation community was very insular. Get a bad name, you kept a bad name, and Celebration Bay would be the newest bad risk. And they'd probably wrecked her relationship with Jon.

She could kill them.

Whiskey was waiting for her just inside her door. He must have sensed her mood, because he didn't jump or race down the hall to the kitchen for a treat, but followed her into the living room, where she threw herself on the couch.

He moved away and then ran and took a flying leap onto the couch, something he'd learned in the last few months. He snuggled up against her and she put her arm around him.

"You're the only man I'm not angry at right now."

Whiskey whined and rolled over to lick her face.

"Thanks," she said, and held him closer.

Liv didn't sleep much during the night. Her mind catapulted from lost hope to anger to trying to figure out a way to limit the damage. By five o'clock she fell into a fitful sleep. At seven the alarm went off. She got up, reached for her phone, and called the office. Ted wouldn't be in yet, but he checked messages first thing.

She waited for the beep. "This is Liv. I'll be working away from the office this morning." She hung up. So what if it sounded like she was pouting; she was pissed.

She fell back to sleep.

Her cell rang at nine. It was Ted. She knew it would be. She let it ring until it went to voice mail.

But she couldn't get back to sleep. All her anger at their thoughtlessness rolled back on her. She got up, made coffee. And sat at the kitchen table, wondering how long she could hold out.

It wasn't just because she wanted to punish them. She knew they cared about her. But they had to learn that she could take care of herself. And she certainly didn't want them getting into her personal life. Once she got one. If she ever got one. Which so far was looking questionable.

For a split second Liv imagined what life back in Manhattan would be like now that she'd tasted the country waters. She dismissed it. Usually she was happy here, she had friends here.

Her cell rang. She glance at caller ID. BeBe. *Wondering where I am?*

Liv picked up. "Hello."

"You're not going to work?"

"I'm working at home, then I'm going over to the zombie parade."

"Ted wants you to call him."

"He'll have to learn to take the consequences of poor decision making."

"You sound like someone's mother. He told me what happened. He says he only went along because he couldn't talk the other two out of going."

"Hmm," Liv said.

"Are you okay?"

"Peachy."

"It's just because they care about you."

"It's just because they're buttinskies. And they've wrecked my chances with Jon."

"Is that Jon the man or Jon—"

"The grant person. Wrecked our chances of getting the grant."

"Are you going to call him?"

"Only if there is an emergency."

"Are you coming in for coffee?"

"Probably."

"When?"

"See you later, BeBe." Liv hung up.

She checked her email, already feeling edgy because she was away from her office computer and the office phone and . . . and the office. But they needed to learn a lesson.

She showered and dressed and let Whiskey out for a quick trip around the shrubbery. She hadn't planned to take him with her today, since the zombie parade would be crazy. She'd meant to leave him with the Zimmermans, but now she was afraid Ted had called them, too, and she didn't want to have to explain.

She left one unhappy dog behind the door and set off on her own for the Museum of Yankee Horrors.

Miss Ida was sweeping leaves off the sidewalk out front.

"Morning, Liv. Where's Whiskey?"

"In the carriage house."

"Liv, before you go . . ." She hesitated.

"What? Did Ted call you, too?"

"Well, yes he did. He feels very sorry about what they did."

"Well, he should."

"Yes, well. You should accept his apology."

"I might, when I'm not so mad at him. Now, I really have to go."

"We'll take care of Whiskey."

"Thanks. I'll see you later."

"Liv, angry people are not always wise."

Liv nodded and kept walking.

When she reached the museum, she stopped to catch her breath. *Angry people don't remember to breathe,* she thought, paraphrasing Ida's aphorism.

She walked up the steps to the porch. A new sign hung over the entranceway. A good omen. She knocked, then stepped inside.

The place was already busy. She wandered through, taking it all in, thankful for Amanda Marlton-Crosby's donation and hoping she wouldn't rescind it in a fit of pique.

The actors were back, along with half the quilting club and a few others Liv recognized from around town. Barry was rushing from one room to the other, but he stopped when he saw Liv.

"Almost there," he said. There were bags under his eyes and his face looked thinner.

"Are you getting enough sleep?" she asked.

Barry waved the question away. "I can sleep in November."

She laughed. She would be getting ready for the Pilgrim Dinner for Thanksgiving, the scene of way too many people last year. They'd had to move it to the basement of two downtown churches. Then there was Christmas . . .

"We're on track to open Saturday."

"That's great." One less thing for her to worry about. "Are you going to take time to go to the zombie parade?"

"Wouldn't miss it. I'll be the zombie wearing a sandwich board that announces the grand opening of the Museum of Yankee Horrors."

Liv gave him a thumbs-up, waved at the seamstresses, said hi to a couple of the actors, and started to leave. Just as she reached the door, a hand grabbed her arm.

She turned around.

Marla Jean Higgins, dressed in a bloody wedding dress, her face made nearly white with makeup and deep red lips, pouted at Liv.

"Wow, Marla Jean. You look great."

"You got me in trouble," Marla Jean said. Her voice was flat and Liv wondered if she was in her zombie persona or if maybe she was actually clinically disturbed.

"I'm sorry. Over the shoes?"

Marla Jean nodded.

"How were you to know?" Liv asked. "You found them in your yard, didn't you?"

Marla Jean nodded again. "The sheriff came back later and asked me a bunch of questions."

"And could you help him out with your information?" Liv edged toward the door.

Marla Jean frowned. "I dunno. I guess so. Dad was upset."

"Well, he's had a rough week. Why don't you cut him some slack?"

"I guess."

Liv smiled and headed for the door.

On her way toward town, she called Fred Hunnicutt for an update on traffic.

"It's fine," he said. "I just told Ted the same thing."

"Oh."

"Are the two of you going to do two of everything today?"

"Did he tell you what happened?" Liv stopped at the corner then crossed the street.

"Yes." Fred chuckled. "I sure would have liked to have been there. I bet you were mad as a wet hen."

"I was," she agreed. "I still am."

"Well, I hope you two make up soon. Doing double the work will get old fast."

Liv knew he was right. But she really didn't want to see any of the culprits.

She could avoid Chaz with no problem. She should call A.K. to double-check that the extra security people were in place along the parade route. But she still couldn't believe A.K. had been a part of the nonsense last night.

Besides, Ted would call him. Ted was totally reliable. *He* wouldn't be walking around town holding a grudge.

Then again, Liv would never have spied on him on a date. She didn't even know if he ever dated.

Still, she was being irresponsible. She turned toward town. Called Jon at the hotel only to be told he was out. Hopefully, not on his way to jail.

She bypassed the bakery and the Coffee Exchange and went straight to town hall. Better to get it over with.

She walked into the office. Ted looked up from his desk. He didn't say anything, just lifted one eyebrow in question.

"You're not forgiven." Liv walked into her office and shut the door.

She booted up her computer, checked her voice mails. She heard the outer door close. Ted must have left.

She pulled up the zombie parade plans.

Twenty minutes later, the outer door opened. Footsteps sounded across the floor, and Liv braced herself. A knock, and her door opened. Ted walked in with a bakery bag and tea and coffee in cardboard cartons.

Without a word he sat down, placed a latte in front of her, and handed her a jack-o'-lantern cookie on a napkin.

She took the cookie.

Both of Ted's eyebrows lifted.

"I'm thawing," Liv said. "But it will take a while."

He nodded and bit into his cookie.

Chapter Nineteen

By midafternoon, Liv had forgotten her anger. She had her hands full. The parade was due to start at five, giving them at least a half hour before dark to walk to the band shell. The post office parking lot, where the parade was to begin, was overflowing with the undead, a good half hour before the parade. They had to put latecomers in the back parking lot of town hall.

There were three large tents at the back of the lot: one for snacks and beverages to keep the waiting ghouls hydrated and hunger-free, a medic station, and a makeup tent, where less creative zombies could pay a couple of dollars to get goreyed up, all proceeds going to the community center fund.

Liv radioed to A.K. to request more operatives in the holding area.

He didn't apologize or sound contrite. Just said, "Copy that." And signed off. *Back to normal,* she thought. She still couldn't believe that he had stooped to the antics of last night. She figured Chaz had been the instigator. It was just like something he would pull, just for the fun of it.

As the time for the parade drew near, businesses either closed early or ran on a skeleton crew, in some cases literally since the merchants had been dressing in costume since the last zucchini in the Harvest Festival was carted away. Even the ones who stayed open left their counters to watch the parade.

Yolanda had closed her store, though whether in protest of the zombies or to be able to enjoy the parade, Liv couldn't begin to guess. Did witches have a sense of humor about Halloween?

The sidewalks were filled with spectators, and everyone seemed to be in a festive mood. Everyone but Liv. And maybe the witches.

Halloween was not Liv's favorite holiday. Too many possibilities for tricks rather than treats. And tricks could easily turn fun into chaos. So today she was on a high state of alert, on the lookout for any problems. She thought she must be like a movie director or a novelist who could never look at other movies or novels without their internal editor clicking on.

Liv didn't think she would ever be able to enjoy a holiday without automatically powering up to orange alert.

She would be keeping both eyes open, though from the looks of things so far, the parade would be a great success. And thankfully it was a short walk from the post office and around the square to the band shell, where costumes would be judged.

But Chaz had been right about the grass. The paved area in front of the band shell would never accommodate the crowd.

A trumpet blast alerted everyone to the beginning of the parade. Then a discordant non-tuning of instruments followed as the Celebration Bay Zombie Marching Band tuned up and staggered into position.

The undead crowded behind them. Pirates with gashes on their faces and hooks for hands; a cheerleader with rubber hatchets—Liv had checked to be sure—rising from each pompom like a flower. There were zombie rock stars, zombie dentists—Liv shivered at that one—zombie firemen, several army zombies. Liv wondered if any of them were A.K.'s men.

Liv saw Barry as a zombie clown, complete with the sandwich board advertising the museum. Behind him Marla Jean was looking particularly undead in her wedding dress and black veil. At least Liv guessed it was Marla Jean beneath the thick netting. The spookiest participants though were the zombie children, each accompanied by a zombie adult. All of them seemed to be having great fun.

And the band screeched and clanked as its members limped and dragged their way toward the starting point.

Liv was contemplating earplugs when the undead drum major blew his whistle and the musicians straightened up; the drummers finally hit a discernible rhythm, and the band marched ahead to the beat of "Thriller," much to Liv's relief. The zombies surged forward and the parade "marched" into the street.

They made it a half block before the band erupted into chaos again, until at the whistle they regrouped and continued on to "Ghostbusters."

Ted radioed to Liv that the last of the town hall undead contingent had joined the end of the parade. Behind them a fire engine sounded its siren and took up the rear, all of its zombie firemen waving and throwing candy to the crowds.

Liv followed along on the far side of the street to make sure they all made it to the band shell.

At that point, the zombie band would take its place on the stage and play a few Halloween-themed tunes while the judges picked the winners.

Fortunately tonight no money was involved and there would be plenty of winners.

As the fire engine passed, kids ran into the street to pick

up the extra candy, until they were gathered up and the spectators turned toward the park. It was a mass migration as
everyone crowded toward the band shell, pressing forward.

The band broke into an incongruous "When the Saints
Go Marching In." Someone started singing "when the zombies go marching in." Pretty soon the whole crowd was singing along. Liv wondered if any of the churches would take
umbrage at the new words. *All for a good cause,* she thought.

She looked around and didn't see any uniformed police
or recognize any of A.K.'s people, but she knew Bill and
A.K. must be somewhere nearby. Fred Hunnicutt's traffic
volunteers were out in full regalia, with Day-Glo vests worn
over their zombie costumes.

Liv had to hand it to her town. They knew how to throw
a party and they were generous with their time and their
money. And even though she was still angry at three of them,
she felt a swell of pride.

She looked around to see if Jon was anywhere in the
crowd. She'd hoped he would enter into the spirit of things,
witness firsthand the town's enthusiasm. But maybe he was
sick to death of Celebration Bay. Maybe he was just waiting
for his car to be returned before he left town.

The seven zombie judges with red sashes tied across their
chests squeezed through the crowd, picking out winners to
stand in front of the band on the stage. Liv looked for Ernie
and Barry. She found Barry right away, his sandwich board
wedging him into the crowd. Marla Jean and others from the
theater group were standing around him.

But she didn't see Ernie.

A figure moving through the crowd caught her eye, dressed
all in black. Something seemed familiar about him. And then
she recognized him. The Doomsday Man, participating in the
zombie parade? What was he doing here? He should be in jail.

Liv watched him weave through the crowd, lost him for
a minute, then saw him emerge from the edge of the crowd.
He was moving fairly fast.

A hundred disasters ran through her head. He'd planted a bomb in one of the trash cans. Or maybe just shoved a bunch of pamphlets at people.

But it definitely looked like he was leaving in a hurry. Keeping her eye on the man, she pulled out her radio.

"Bill, come in." She started after the Doomsday Man.

Static, then, "Bill here. Over."

"I've sighted the Doomsday Man moving east out of the crowd. It looks like he's heading toward the river. No. He's going past the cemetery. Tell A.K. to look out for anything suspicious he may have left behind."

Liv began to run.

"Liv, where are you?"

"I'm in pursuit."

"Stay put."

"No way. I'm sick of this guy. He just turned at the corner."

"Which way?"

"Left. Gotta go."

"Liv. Cease and desist. I'm putting some men on it."

She reached the corner and saw the man turn again. He must be headed toward Ernie's. *Planning to do a little vandalizing while everyone else is in the square, you jerk?* "He's headed toward Ernie's."

Liv shoved the radio in her messenger bag and turned on the speed.

Sure enough, when she got to the next corner she saw him standing in Ernie's yard, fumbling with something in his pocket.

Liv sprinted toward him.

He ran up the steps and lifted his arm.

She was close enough to hear the shatter of glass. And then flames lick out of the window. *Damn, what if one of the Boltons was in there?*

He reached in his bag again.

"Stop! Fire!!" Liv yelled at the top of her lungs, but she didn't stop running.

He was trying to light the second device when she reached the yard.

"Stop!"

He didn't stop and Liv bounded up the steps. He threw the device at her, but she managed to duck aside. He lunged past her, knocking her down the steps and onto the sidewalk.

Everything went black for a moment.

"Liv! Liv?"

Liv opened her eyes and Barry Lindquist's face came into view.

"Barry?"

"Are you all right?"

"That's it, Mack." Barry was lifted to his feet. A.K. had him by both arms and looked like he was tempted to break them.

Liv tried to get up. "It wasn't Barry. It was the Doomsday Guy. You're letting him get away!"

A.K. dropped Barry and reached for his belt, spoke into a cell phone, shoved it back on his belt. "He won't get far. Are you okay?"

Liv had made it to a sitting position as several people rushed past her and up the stairs. "I think so."

Sirens filled the air. And to think she had questioned letting the firemen be in the parade.

"See if you can stand." A.K. offered his hand and stood hovering until she was on both feet.

"Right as rain," she said. Her knees were wobbly but she was pretty sure it was from adrenaline.

The fire engine arrived and the firemen moved everyone out of the way as they pulled a hose up to the porch and began to extinguish the fires.

The front door opened and Ernie came out. He was carrying a fire extinguisher and his face and clothes were covered in soot.

One of the firemen helped him down the stairs to the street.

His face was blank, then it twisted in anger. "You son of

a—" Ernie dropped the fire extinguisher and threw himself at Barry, who staggered back. But he was the larger man and he kept his feet until two of the bystanders pulled them apart.

"You crazy idiot. It wasn't me."

"You thought you'd get back at me, did ya? Well, I didn't wreck your place."

"And I didn't torch yours. I saw Liv take off like a bat outta hell and thought I better go after her. Then I saw this guy on the porch, then the fire, so I came to help."

Ernie scowled at him.

"That's the God's honest truth."

"Leave it, Ernie. I think we know who did the vandalizing," Ted said.

Liv looked around. "Ted. When did you get here?"

Actually Ted, A.K., Chaz, and Fred Hunnicutt were all standing in a line watching her. For a second she was completely taken aback. A.K. was the only one not in zombie gear, and to tell the truth, he was frightening enough without the blood and gore.

Ted was wearing a tuxedo and top hat with bandages wrapped around his head and a butcher knife sticking out of his back. Fred was a zombie farmer with a red kerchief and overalls showing beneath his orange traffic vest. Even Chaz had risen to the occasion, looking a bit like surfer zombie in his normal clothes but with some well-placed splatters of blood, compliments of the makeup tent in the parking lot.

"What are you all doing here? Who's looking after the zombies?"

Chaz broke into a grin. "That's our girl. All business."

"Well, someone has to be. Why are you dressed as a zombie? You said the parade was a stupid idea."

"I went undercover."

She heard Ted snicker, but when she turned on him, he shook his head and put up his hand.

"She's right," Ted said, gasping for breath between suppressed laughter. "You may have found your calling."

Liv rolled her eyes, picked up her bag, and started back up the street, just as the sheriff's cruiser pulled to the curb and Bill got out.

"Hey? Where are you going?"

"Well, somebody has to make sure they're not rioting in the street."

"A.K. and my people have it under control," Bill said. "Can you answer a few questions?"

Liv frowned. "Depends."

Bill's eyebrows quirked.

"On whether the questions are along the line of 'What the heck did you think you were doing?' or 'Could you give us an account of what happened?'"

"Ah." Bill looked around the group. "The latter." He fought a smile but gave in. "And a little of the former."

"What happened? I'll tell you what happened," Ernie snapped. "Someone tried to torch my haunted house." He took a threatening step toward Barry.

"Cut it out, Ernie. It wasn't me," Barry said. "Bill, when we were all at the band shell, I stepped out of the crowd to get rid of this dang sandwich board and I see Liv here start running down the street. Then I get that she's chasing someone."

"Did you see who it was?" Bill asked.

Barry shook his head. "I didn't, but I figured she might need some help so I started after them." He stopped to glare at Ernie. "To help, not to burn down your stupid haunted house."

"What are you calling stupid?" Ernie snapped.

"I take it back. It's not the haunted house that's stupid, it's—"

"That's enough," Bill said. "Go on, Barry."

"When I got to the corner, I saw Liv running up the steps. I thought maybe she was running after Ernie here."

"Why, of all the—"

"Quiet," Bill ordered.

Ernie slinked back and watched the firemen, who were moving their equipment back to the truck.

Bill pointed at Barry. "Hold that thought." He turned to talk to the fire chief.

"We caught it in time." The chief looked over to Ernie. "Just got the front part of the living room and the window. Nothing you can't fix up. We made a bit of a mess. But better safe than sorry."

Ernie's mouth twisted. Liv was afraid he might burst into tears. And who could blame him. He'd had a very disappointing week.

"Will he be able to get up and running for Halloween?" Liv asked.

"I'll keep someone here for a while to make sure we closed it down. Have to send in the inspector, but only because it was a case of arson. He'll have to make sure none of the electrical wires were compromised and check for structural damage just to be on the safe side. But we caught it before it spread, thanks to some quick thinking. Who called it in?"

"I did," Barry said. He glared at Ernie. Ernie glared back at him.

"Well," Liv said. "I'm sure there will be plenty of people to help you once you've been cleared, Ernie."

"Yeah," Barry said. "They got my place up again."

"I didn't wreck your place," Ernie said.

"Well, I'm thinking that the same person is responsible for both crimes."

Bill lifted his radio from his utility belt. "Liv, did you recognize him?"

Liv thought about it. "I saw the Doomsday Guy in the crowd. At least it looked like him. He was dressed in the same kind of clothes he was wearing last time we saw him. I tried to get closer to make sure it was him, but I lost him for a second. Then I saw him leave the crowd and start off down the street. He looked furtive and in a hurry. That's when I called you."

"Barry?"

"I didn't get a good look at the guy. He knocked Liv out of the way and took off down the street. I thought about running after him, but I was afraid Liv was hurt."

Bill nodded, pressed the transmit button, and waited. "Meese. Send a unit over to Miss Patty's Haunted House. Be discreet, but keep your eyes open for suspicious characters. Someone just tried to torch Ernie's. If he's preying on the haunted house finalists, he might go there next."

He signed off and turned to Liv. "You never got a good look at him?"

"No, I was trying to keep him from starting a second fire. He had some kind of incendiary device."

"I love it when she uses big words," Chaz said under his breath but loud enough for Liv to hear.

"That's enough from you," Bill told him.

"Rag in a glass bottle filled with gasoline," the fire chief said. "Thanks to Liv, we found the second device in the yard. If there were more, they are still on the arsonist's person."

Bill made another transmission to put out an APB on the Doomsday Guy. "Whose name, by the way, is Stanley Riggs, a two-bit con man, wanted in several towns for vagrancy and petty theft. And now arson."

"Why does he stand on corners spouting hellfire and damnation?"

Bill shrugged. "Just nuts, I guess."

"And dangerous," A.K. added.

His voice was so deep and serious that Liv jumped. He was looking straight at Liv. "In case you were wondering."

"Well, at least we know it wasn't Jon. You guys must be so disappointed."

"Hey!" Chaz said.

Ignoring him, Liv turned to Bill. "Do you think Lucille witnessed him wrecking Barry's and he killed her?"

Bill didn't answer, just said, "Why don't you get in the

cruiser? I'll drive you back to the office, where you'll be more comfortable. I can take the rest of your statement there."

"Your work here is done," Chaz said in a low radio voice. Then he grinned. "But you're not out of the woods yet."

Liv made a face at him and gladly climbed into the front seat of Bill's cruiser.

As soon as they reached the end of the block, Liv turned to look back on the scene.

Ted, A.K., Chaz, and Fred had all turned to watch them drive away. And she felt a surge of emotion, not anger exactly, sort of anger mixed with exasperation mixed with . . . affection? Nah, mainly exasperation.

"They mean well," Bill said.

Her moment of affection burst. "They're obnoxious, interfering numbskulls."

"That, too. But it's because they care about you."

"If you say so. Now tell me, do you think this Stanley Riggs killed Lucille?"

Bill kept his eyes on the street, but slowly shook his head.

"Then who?"

"We're still investigating."

Dread curved slowly through her stomach. "Have you finished with Jon's car?"

"Not yet."

"Why? How long does it take to search a car?"

"As long as it takes."

"You sent off DNA samples, didn't you?" No answer. "Didn't you?"

"Liv, you know I'm not at liberty to discuss the details of an investigation."

Liv thought it was a little late to split hairs, but she didn't mention that. She bet he would discuss it with Ted. Exasperation with her band of protectors changed back to anger.

"Well, Jon didn't kill anyone. If you found anything, someone must have stolen his car."

"And brought it back without him knowing about it?"

"It was parked at the Marlton-Crosbys. The house is surrounded by woods. The cars aren't visible from inside the house. It's totally possible that someone could have taken it after he'd gone to sleep. You heard Jon. He was jet-lagged and went to bed early. He didn't hear a thing all night."

"Liv, how close are you to Jonathon Preston?"

Liv narrowed her eyes at Bill, but since he was looking straight ahead, he didn't notice. "I've known him for years. He travels the world giving money away. Not killing women in fancy high heels. Which reminds me, did you ever find Lucille's scarf?"

No answer.

"You didn't find it in Jon's car? Bill, dammit. If you did, you know it was a setup. Trust me. Jon Preston is a brilliant man. If he did want to commit murder—which he didn't— but if he did, he would have covered his tracks much better than leaving a piece of evidence in his car."

She waited.

"We didn't find it."

She let out her breath. Surprised herself at how tense she'd become. It was ludicrous, the idea of Jon killing anyone. He was a philanthropist. He worked for one of the most prestigious charitable foundations. He was a good guy.

"Then I guess we'll have to keep looking."

"You stay out of it. Do you realize how close you came to being seriously injured, maybe worse, today?"

"I hadn't until you put it like that. It's because I was reacting instead of acting. But when I saw him light that—what's it called—Molotov cocktail? I kind of lost my head."

"You almost lost more than your head."

"Won't happen again, boss."

Bill chuckled. "You're incorrigible."

"I'm determined. Bill?"

"Yeah?"

"Do you think the murder and the vandalisms are connected or just a weird coincidence?"

"I'm not discounting anything at this time."

"Spoken like a true policeman." Liv's cell rang.

She reached in her messenger bag, took it out. *Jon*. She deliberated answering, thought what the heck, and swiped it open. "Hey."

"Hi. I looked for you at the zombie parade, but it was a madhouse."

"I was pretty busy. Listen, can I call you back?"

"Sure. Just wanted to let you know that I'm going to stay with Amanda until your sheriff releases my car. She's picking me up in a few minutes."

"Oh, okay. Bye." She hung up.

"Everything alright?" Bill asked.

"Yep," Liv said and wondered if he had been able to hear Jon's voice in the background. And why Jon had suddenly decided to leave the inn.

Chapter Twenty

....

By the time Bill had finished with his questions, the zombies had dispersed to bars, restaurants, and home, and Ted had returned to the office. They still weren't really speaking, but Liv was beginning to feel less angry.

When Bill left, she went into the front office.

"Why did you let them talk you into pulling that stunt last night? Do you know how stupid it made me look?"

"Would you rather have had the two of them there without me?"

Liv sighed. "I guess it could have been a lot worse."

"It certainly could have been."

"BeBe said you tried to talk them out of it."

"I did. To no avail. Sorry."

"Thanks. Though it doesn't matter really. With Bill impounding Jon's car and practically accusing him of murder, I'm guessing we can kiss the chance of getting any funds good-bye."

"It wasn't your fault."

Liv shrugged. "Maybe not my fault, but my responsibility."

"Are you having dinner with him tonight?"

"No. He's going to stay with Amanda and Rod. I think he's had enough of Celebration Bay for this lifetime."

"Why don't you go on home, Liv? Get some rest. I'll close up."

She nodded. She was suddenly tired. Tired and sick that they'd blown the future of the community center. At least for the time being.

She dreaded having to face Pastor Schorr and the kids and the seniors. They'd been so enthusiastic. So optimistic.

Well, they'd just have to make do with one of the church basements until they could raise enough money to rent or buy another place.

She packed up, said good night to Ted, and started across the park toward home. She hardly noticed the lights strung from the porch eaves, the blow-up ghouls in the yards, the hay stacks and coffins.

Barry was good to go. Hopefully Ernie could get up to speed. Halloween would arrive. The merchants would hand out candy and the next day all the ghosts and jack-o'-lanterns would disappear, to be replaced by cornstalks and gourds and merchants wearing pilgrim hats. And they'd prepare for the Turkey Trot and the Pilgrim dinner and then . . .

Then maybe after Christmas Liv would take a vacation, somewhere far away where it was warm with sun and beaches and drinks with little umbrellas in them, and no holidays.

"When pigs fly," she said out loud and kicked at a pile of leaves that someone had raked to the curb.

When she got home there was a note on the door: *We have Whiskey with us and chicken potpie, come over if you feel like it.*

She smiled at the thoughtfulness of her landladies, but she didn't feel like company and she knew if she joined them, they would want to know all about the fire at Ernie's and how the investigation was going, and Liv just didn't have the energy to go through it again.

And she was scared. Scared that they wouldn't be able to find funds for the new center. Afraid that Jon would somehow get implicated in the murder and be sent off to jail. And she would have that on her.

Or would she? She hung up her jacket and went into the living room. Jon said that he had also come to check out the situation between Amanda and Rod. Two birds with one stone, so to speak. Coincidence? Maybe he'd never intended to give them the grant at all, just used it as an excuse to visit the Marlton-Crosbys.

That thought made her even more depressed. Maybe she would visit her landladies after all, because sitting alone was just making her feel worse.

Whiskey was ecstatic to see her. Liv could hear him barking and jumping before Edna even opened the door. He bounded out without his usual running in circles. He went right to her and rose on his hind legs, his front paws balancing on her knees, and lifted his head to be petted.

She leaned over and scrubbed behind his ears. "Did you miss me?"

He barked.

Above them Edna shook her head. "That one is learning to talk. I swear he understands exactly what you're saying."

And feeling, thought Liv, giving Whiskey an extra pat.

The three of them went straight down the hall to the kitchen, where Ida was just taking a plate out of the oven.

"We kept it warm for you, Liv. You just can't microwave pie crust. I don't care what they say." Ida set the plate on the table and lifted off the aluminum foil.

"Thank you." Liv sat down. "It looks incredible."

"Would you like some decaf?"

"Just water, please."

Edna brought the water, while Ida poured two cups of coffee. The sisters sat down. Whiskey curled up under Liv's feet.

"We thought you might be having dinner with that nice young man from New York City."

"He had another engagement."

Edna put down her cup. "What engagements could he possibly have that don't include you? Please tell me he's not meeting with Mayor Worley without you."

"No. But he's an old friend of Amanda Marlton-Crosby's."

"Ah, that explains it," Ida said cryptically.

"Explains what?" Liv asked, and gingerly took a bite of the steaming pie.

"Why Ruth Benedict claims she saw his car parked at the fish camp."

Liv stopped the next bite of pie inches from her mouth. "The fish camp? Why would he park down there? That would be a hike through the meadow to the main house."

"Well, that's what she said. And she said she was going to tell the sheriff."

"She did. Now they've impounded his car and told him not to leave town."

"No! We hadn't heard," Ida said.

"Well, it's ludicrous and I'd appreciate it if you didn't say anything. I'm sure it's just a big mistake."

When neither Ida nor Edna agreed, Liv looked up.

Both sisters were looking at her sympathetically.

"He didn't do it."

"No, of course not," Ida said. "Would you like some more potpie?"

Liv shook her head.

"Well, don't you worry about it. Bill will figure it all out."

"With Liv's help, of course," Edna added. "Now finish your pie. You look like you could use some sleep."

Liv decided to take Whiskey to work with her the next morning. Actually it was Whiskey who decided. He was waiting by the front door when she put on her jacket, and sat patiently while she put on his leash. But when she started up the front walk to leave him with the sisters, he planted his feet and stiff-legged, and refused to go another step.

All the cajoling and promise of treats had no effect. As soon as she slackened the leash, he pulled toward the street. Ida came to the door and called him.

He was clearly torn but he stood his ground. And Liv caved. "I'll take him with me. He obviously has plans with Ted," she said, only half joking.

So the two of them started off for town, Whiskey spry and feeling his oats, clearly the winner of that early morning battle of wills.

"But you'd better behave. I may be really busy today."

Whiskey pulled away to sniff at a tree trunk.

They stopped at the bakery and for coffee, but neither Dolly nor BeBe seemed to have heard about Jon's car being impounded, and Liv didn't enlighten them. They might be able to get out of this unscathed if they just kept their heads together and their mouths shut.

She was surprised to find Bill sitting in Ted's office when she got to work

"Any breaks in the cases?" she asked warily as she handed Ted his tea and the bag of apple muffins. "Whiskey's treat is in the bag."

Whiskey pranced over to Ted. Ted looked in the bag and pulled out a dog biscuit in the shape of a pitchfork. Raised both eyebrows at Liv and said, "Grossly inappropriate." He turned it over. "Or apropos?"

Liv turned to Bill.

He didn't looked happy and Liv steeled herself for whatever he was about to say.

"Let's go into your office," Bill said. He pushed himself slowly and painfully to his feet.

"I thought yoga was helping your sciatica," Liv said over her shoulder as Bill and Ted followed her into her office.

"It was. But I haven't been able to go with this new murder investigation."

"Well, I think yoga should be your first priority. So you're in good enough shape to investigate."

She sat behind her desk and lifted the tab of her coffee. "Okay. Are you going to give me an update?"

"It's not looking good. We've sent samples out to the lab. It will be a while until they get back, but we did find hairs, matching the color of Lucille Foster's. And he's checked out of the inn without notifying the police."

Liv swiveled her head toward Bill. "You told him to stay in town. Amanda's house is in town."

"Strictly speaking."

Liv gave him an exasperated look.

"He should have notified the police that he was moving."

"It was no secret. He notified me."

"Liv," Ted began.

She cut him off with a look. "So you went hightailing off to the Marlton-Crosbys to make sure he hadn't bolted."

Bill's lips tightened. "Will you stop treating me like the enemy?"

"All right, but I still think you're on the wrong track."

"I hope I am, but the fact remains, it's looking like his car was involved somehow."

"So that's that. You just have to find who stole it."

Bill exchanged looks with Ted. "Not exactly."

Liv lifted her chin, determined to listen but not be swayed by whatever came next.

"Rod Crosby said he heard Preston's car drive away from the house late Friday night."

Liv leaned forward, her anger threatening to erupt. "Jon picked up Amanda from the award ceremony. Rod was with them. He put Amanda in the car and said he was going out drinking with friends. We saw him."

"Much later than that. After Mr. Crosby had returned

home and gone to bed. He said, he figured Mr. Preston was still suffering from jet lag and went out for a drive."

"Because someone is obviously trying to implicate Jon. Have you made an arrest?"

"No. Not yet. But Liv, you might want to prepare yourself."

She sprang out of her desk chair. "For what? For when you make a false arrest?"

"Liv, calm down. I won't make any move until we have enough evidence to hold him."

"Well, you'll have a long wait. I'm going out." She grabbed Whiskey's leash off the coat rack. "Come on boy."

"Where are you going?"

"Out." She didn't wait for a response but walked quickly down the hall and out of the building. She didn't know where she was going, she just knew she needed a place to think. About what? She didn't have a clue, but there had to be something they were missing, some reason for Jon's car being involved without it involving Jon.

She didn't really want to talk to anyone, either. She steered away from the park, avoided the bakery and Coffee Exchange, and had just decided to walk down by the river, when someone called her name.

She turned around. Yolanda was standing in the door of the Mystic Eye, waving her over. Today she was dressed in yoga pants and a long tunic of soft material that glinted in the sun. A scarf was tied around her hair and trailed down the front of her shoulder.

Liv sighed. She really didn't want to talk about Amanda Crosby right now. On the other hand . . . who better to borrow Jon's car without him knowing about it than Amanda or Rod—or possibly even Yolanda?

So maybe she was grasping at straws. Shocked at the turn her mind had taken, Liv hesitated, and as she stood there Yolanda started running toward her, looking frantic.

"I was just going to call you," Yolanda huffed out between breaths. The witch was seriously out of shape. "Liv, we need your help. It's happened again."

"What's wrong? Who needs my help? Has there been more vandalism?"

"Carol Sue called just a few minutes ago. She's one of our group doing the retreat up at Amanda's fish camp. They were out for their sunrise meditation and incantations, and when they got back to the cabins, they had been ransacked and—" Her voice wobbled out of control and she let out a cry. "All our books and instruments were ruined. What is wrong with people? We're not bothering anyone."

"Maybe you should call the sheriff."

"No! I called him like you suggested when the store was vandalized. And he didn't seem very sympathetic then. Slow-witted, if you ask me."

"It's just that he's slow and methodical, but he gets there."

"Not fast enough to help us. I won't be bothering him again. Witches have enough trouble without having to involve the police. It seems if you're not selling candles and love potions in Salem, people don't want you around."

"That isn't true," Liv said, not really knowing if it was true or not. She knew her first response on hearing about Yolanda's shop was that she hoped they didn't cause trouble.

Yolanda must have read something in her face, because she said, "I'm sorry I bothered you. But Amanda, Miriam, everybody said you were the person to go to when there was a problem, and I thought— But never mind, sorry to have bothered you."

Yolanda turned to go.

"Wait."

Yolanda stopped, slowly turned.

"Some people in town may be like that. In fact I know they are, and it's not just toward witches. It's toward anyone who's a little different, or just a stranger. Trust me. I've been on the receiving end of that myself. But most of us aren't that way." *Well, a lot of us aren't like that.* "Okay, I'll help. Tell Carol Sue not to touch anything until we get there. Rats. I don't have my car."

"Mine's parked out back," Yolanda said.

"What about Whiskey?"

"He's welcome. We're all animal lovers. How are his bloodhound skills?"

"If it involves food, he's pretty good."

Yolanda smiled halfheartedly.

Still Liv hesitated. She should call Bill. But she was still upset with him about Jon. It would better to take a look and then call in the police.

She followed Yolanda back to her store where Yolanda turned over the Closed sign, grabbed her purse from under the counter, and went through the store to the back door.

Her car, a late-model Honda, was parked in the alley.

Liv couldn't repress a smile.

"What?" Yolanda asked. "You were expecting maybe a broomstick?"

"Maybe." Liv opened the back door and lifted Whiskey in. "Stay." Then she got in the front.

Yolanda backed the Honda out, made a two-point turn, and soon they were driving east to the lake. At Lakeside Road, they drove south, past the inn, past the Cape Cods of downtown. Past the Gallantine House, where Henry lived, and where he allowed the town to conduct their Independence Day battle reenactment. Past the larger homes that followed the shoreline, and from where Ruth Benedict watched from her window.

As the road curved away from the lake, the land on the west side of the road turned to rolling hills. The land that hugged the lake became more wooded, only allowing glimpses of the lake through the final blaze of autumn.

Just before they got to the town limits, the road curved in again, running along the shoreline. They passed the old Marlton house that could just be seen through the trees. It stood at the top of a knoll and looked over a meadow and the lake . . . and farther along, the fish camp, though the trees probably hid it from view.

"Turn here," Liv said. The sign was so faded that it would be easy to miss the fish camp if you didn't know where you were going. Liv had been fishing there the summer before.

Once had been enough. Fishing and the fish camp did not hold very fond memories for her.

Yolanda pulled in to the parking lot. The camp had been closed for the season. The wooden office and bait and tackle shop was boarded over. There were only a handful of fishing boats moored at the pier. Most would be in dry dock by now. Or in driveways or at larger landings where they could fish all year.

Yolanda turned down a narrow path that led to a dozen small cabins interspersed in the woods. Not a place where Liv would choose to go on retreat. Martinique came to mind, or a five-star hotel, but to each his own.

The witches were all standing outside the first cabin. They waited quietly until Yolanda came to a stop and Liv retrieved Whiskey from the backseat. As soon as he hit the ground, he took off.

"Whiskey, come back!"

He gave her a look, but good dog that he could sometimes be, he came back and began snuffling at the group of new friends and potential treat dispensers.

A woman came up to greet them, and Yolanda introduced her to Liv as Carol Sue. She was in her thirties, wearing jeans and a Greenpeace sweatshirt under her open down jacket.

"It's . . . It's just awful."

"Maybe we should see," Yolanda said.

Carol Sue nodded and went to the first cabin, opened the door, and stepped aside.

Liv and Yolanda peered in. Clothes had been tossed on the floor, bedding pulled from the bunk beds, the curtains slashed, lamps and books thrown to the floor. Food was tossed out of the coolers and ice was making puddles on the floor.

The vandal had taken the time to pull pages from the books and they littered the floor, some of them soaking up the melted ice.

"They're all like this?"

Carol Sue nodded.

"Is anything missing?"

"Yes, whatever cash or jewlery we left in the cabins. Stephanie's iPod. And that's not the worst."

Liv braced herself. She felt Yolanda do the same.

"The lock to the ark was broken and everything was pulled out and either broken, torn, or dirtied. It looked like they stepped on everything."

They followed her on a short walk through the woods to the second cabin. It was just as bad as the first one. Same for the third and fourth cabins. But it was when they came to the fifth cabin that Yolanda let out an earthy moan.

A wooden cask lay splintered on the floor. Glass vials had been smashed and the smell of exotic oils clung in the air. It stung Liv's eyes and clogged her nostrils.

The violence of it made Liv feel sick. She could only imagine what the others were feeling. Their possessions and living spaces had been defiled. Their religion literally stomped on. It was awful.

"Is this all of them?" Liv asked when they were back outside and breathing fresh air again.

"Yes," Carol Sue said. "The others are empty this time of year, though . . ."

"Though what?" Liv encouraged.

"Several times one or the other of us has thought there was someone else staying here. In one of the other cabins."

"Did you see anyone?"

"No." Carol Sue turned to the women, who had followed them quietly from cabin to cabin. "Did any of you actually see anyone in any of the other cabins?"

None of them had.

"What about cars? Have any cars shown up while you've been here? I have to tell you that this place evidently has the reputation of being a trysting spot."

"You mean like a cheap hotel?" asked one of the women.

Liv shrugged. "It's just a rumor I've heard."

"No, but we weren't always here," said Carol Sue. "We've been hiking and we go out to dinner at night. One night we even went to the movies," she said guiltily. "Well, it's the only time most of us can get away. Most of our families don't know what the retreat is actually about."

The other women nodded.

"My husband thinks it's a ladies thing. But it *is* a ladies thing."

"Mine thinks I'm at the spa being pampered. Well, a person needs to pamper their spiritual side."

"I had to take all my vacation time to get off from work."

"And now it's ruined."

"No, it isn't," Yolanda said. "We will carry on. And with Liv's help maybe we can catch the culprit."

"Who else knew you were staying out here?" Liv asked.

"Miriam and the women in the quilting group," Yolanda sighed. "I guess that means just about everybody."

"Possibly," said Liv. "Let's start with our immediate surroundings. See if we can find evidence of your mystery visitor."

They followed her to the first of the other cabins. Liv tried the lock, tested the closed shutters to see if she could see inside. They didn't budge. She walked around the entire cabin looking for any sign that someone had been there recently.

They did the same with the next cabin, and the next. Then at the cabin closest to the lake and deepest into the wood, they found a loose shutter. Liv tried the window. "Unlocked."

She raised it and peered inside. It was too dark to see. She fished her cell phone out of her pocket, pressed the flashlight app, and climbed halfway inside to shine it around the small room.

"Eureka," she whispered, and climbed all the way inside. Yolanda and several other faces appeared at the open window.

"Liv, be careful."

Liv nodded. She didn't think anyone was still living here, but someone clearly had been. There were no clothes, and the trash basket was filled with fast-food bags, but nothing that qualified as a clue.

She got down on her hands and knees and looked beneath the two bunk beds. Nothing. Liv stood up, brushed off her hands.

Liv went into the tiny bathroom, nothing but a dried shriveled bar of soap. Whoever was squatting wasn't much into bathing. She looked for a trash can. There wasn't one, but in the corner of the old wooden floor was a stack of trifold pamphlets, presumably doing double duty as toilet paper.

She knelt down and focused the flashlight on them, trying to make out the writing. She didn't want to pick anything up in case it turned out to be useful to the police, but she managed to read the words, "End of the World."

No wonder the police could never find the Doomsday Guy, aka Stanley Riggs. He wasn't hitchhiking in and out of town; he was lying low right under their noses.

Well, she would clue Bill in, but not quite yet.

She backed into the single room, took a last look around, and climbed back out the window.

"Did you find anything?" Yolanda asked.

"Some hamburger bags, and a stack of pamphlets that I'm thinking might lead to Stanley Riggs."

"Who?"

"The guy standing on the corner screaming about devil worshipping."

"Eww," Carol Sue said and stamped her foot. "We should have finished him off the first time we encountered him."

Liv's eyes bugged.

"She didn't mean that in the literal sense," Yolanda assured her. "She meant in the spell sense."

"Good to know," Liv said. She stood in the clearing. "Where's Whiskey?"

Whiskey poked his head out of a bush.

"Come on, you. We don't want to have any close encounters with skunks or other beasties."

He came out, looked at her, and trotted off down a path.

"Whiskey. Come. Where are you going? Come back here."

"He probably smells our lunch. We've been picnicking in the meadow."

"It was where we were going to celebrate Samhain," one of the ladies said. "Now, what will we do?"

"We'll think of something," Yolanda assured her.

But Liv wasn't really listening. As she started up the path after Whiskey, she realized it not only led to the meadow, but also gave her a clear view of the Marlton house.

The witches had crowded in behind her. "What if we have to pay damages?"

"I don't think Amanda will blame you," Liv said.

"But that husband of hers wasn't very nice."

"Because he already had closed up for the winter when she sprang this on him. He thought he was going to Miami instead of spending the fall in Celebration Bay. None of this is your fault. I doubt if he can exact forfeiture from you."

"Besides," Yolanda added. "Amanda would never let him."

Liv walked up the path, thankful she'd worn sensible shoes. The leaves were matted and slick from last week's rain. And she had to be cautious to avoid slipping. She didn't stop when she reached the meadow, but kept walking until she could see the cars parked at Amanda's house.

The jeep and another four-door were parked slightly downhill from the house. Anyone—Stanley Riggs, for one—could have easily walked straight through the meadow to the cars and driven away.

Liv led the others back toward the camp. She knew she

should call the sheriff. Even though she didn't want to, and she knew Yolanda really didn't want her to. She was afraid this would make things worse. But she couldn't knowingly hide evidence, and this seemed like evidence.

Ahead of them, Whiskey scampered from bush to bush, having a field day with his freedom. Liv made a mental note to take him out in nature more often . . . after winter was over.

He darted past her feet and came back, darted away and ran toward the camp. Stopped, and cautiously began sniffing the ground.

"Do not eat anything nasty!" Liv yelled.

Carol Sue laughed. "I have a Maltese and he's a real garbage mouth."

Whiskey had stopped with his head down. Normally his play position, but today his hair was standing up along the ridge of his back, and a low growl rumbled from deep inside him.

"Whiskey come back here," Liv said, imagining snakes and rabid raccoons.

He pounced forward, muzzled his way beneath the limbs of the shrub, and after a quick wrestle, dragged something out of the bushes.

"Drop it!" Liv yelled.

Whiskey obeyed, reacting to the shrill note in her voice.

He dropped it, but he stood guarding his prey. A brown pashmina shawl, with shots of gold thread.

Chapter Twenty-one

....

Liv's world came crashing down. It had to be Lucille's scarf, but it didn't make sense. How did it get here? Had Lucille dropped it here? Or did someone hide it here?

Had she come to the camp to meet someone? Run into Riggs instead, and he killed her? Or someone killed her and Riggs found the scarf? Or he somehow lured her to the camp . . .

None of it was making sense. Anyone in town could have met her here and killed her.

Mechanically, she pulled the leash out of her jacket pocket and snapped it on Whiskey's collar.

"What is it?" Carol Sue asked.

"I'm pretty sure it's the shawl Lucille Foster was wearing when she was murdered last week."

Carol Sue leaned in closer.

"Don't touch it," Liv warned her. She turned to Yolanda. "We really need to call the sheriff now. He's old-fashioned but he's a good man."

Yolanda nodded.

Liv called Bill.

By the time he arrived, Liv had moved everyone to a safe distance away, though they were all focused on the dirtied piece of fabric. It had been rained on and was caked with mud. It might be impossible to find any DNA evidence, but at least it could prove that Lucille had been here that night. And possibly killed here.

Liv looked up the path to the meadow and beyond to the house. Then back at the camp.

"Were any of you here last Friday night?"

The entire group jumped like they had been goosed.

Carol Sue answered. "No, we all met at my house outside Albany on Sunday and drove up the next morning. We'd just arrived when we saw you in town."

"Think back," Liv said. "Did any of the cabins that you are using look like someone had been staying there?" The women looked at each other. "Even for a short time? Say a couple of hours?"

The consensus was no.

"And the other cabins have all been locked the whole time we've been here," Carol Sue said.

Liv was nodding but her mind wasn't concentrating on their answers. It was way down the road—or more to the point, across the meadow at the Marlton house.

Anyone down at the camp could see up to the house. Even in the dark; surely there would be some kind of security lights. Or else the killer knew there would be cars at the house because . . . they had seen it in the daylight or . . . She didn't want to contemplate further than that.

What would a jet-lagged charitable foundation representative be doing meeting a woman he didn't know down at the rustic camp? Liv couldn't see Jon having a torrid encounter in a tiny cabin on mattresses that looked at least twenty years old. *Ugh.* She couldn't even see Rod stooping that low. Of course, the other cabins were locked. One of them could be fitted out like the Kasbah, for all she knew. She'd tell Bill to have them searched—

Liv stopped herself. Bill knew what to do. She had to stop organizing everyone's job and lives and stick to her own job and life. Two things that she wasn't doing so well with this week.

She saw a flash of white through the trees. "The sheriff's here," she announced, and felt the entire group stiffen. She looked over the group. "Just be yourselves. He'll listen to you."

He'd called for backup. Two county cars stopped at the car path that wound through the woods past the cabins.

Bill got out of the cruiser and slowly walked toward them.

"Sciatica," Yolanda said. "I offered to give him a remedy, free of charge, when he investigated the rock-throwing incident, but he turned me down."

"Well, he has been doing yoga."

"Really?"

"So I figure there may be just a few short steps from yoga to spiritual oils."

Yolanda. "I'll get him on a rainy cold day."

Liv smiled in spite of herself.

"What do you have?" Bill asked Liv.

Officer Meese and another officer stood behind the sheriff, staring at the women. Liv wondered if Bill had told them about the witches. Were they disappointed that the women weren't dressed in black and wearing pointy hats?

"Where is it?"

"This way." Liv handed Whiskey off to Carol Sue and walked Bill up the path to the bush that half hid the shawl.

"Well, I'll be." Bill cautiously bent over the shawl. "You're sure this belonged to Lucille Foster?"

"Unless two women in town are missing the identical shawl. It's pretty expensive."

Bill straightened. "Meese, cordon off the area and get some photos."

Meese nodded and ran off to the patrol car.

"Not that I expect him to find anything," Bill said. "I assume this area has been trampled over several times since last Friday night."

Liv nodded. "The group arrived Monday morning, but they go on hikes and use the meadow for some of their activities."

Bill raised both eyebrows.

Liv pursed her lips. "Keep an open mind. They seem very nice."

"I always keep an open mind."

Liv decided it would be better not to argue.

"So they've probably wrecked any additional evidence?"

"Worse." She grimaced. "They've been vandalized."

Bill looked around. "And I suppose they called you instead of the police."

"They weren't sure you'd be sympathetic."

"I investigated their window incident, didn't I?"

"Evidently you didn't showcase your Yankee charm."

"Well, that woman is enough to . . ." He trailed off.

"Yolanda? I like her."

"You would." He looked over to where Meese was still taking photos and the other officer was holding a ruler for scale. Then he looked past them. His expression tightened. He turned to Liv.

Cutting him off before he spoke, she said, "It could be a coincidence. The murderer was looking for a handy way to move the body and chose the closest car. Mercedes are notoriously easy to hot-wire."

Bill gave her a look that said she was trying his patience. "So you think someone killed Lucille, walked all the way up to the house, hot-wired the Mercedes, then drove it down here, threw her body in the trunk—"

"You found evidence in the trunk?"

His mouth hardened. "Yes."

"So he put it—her—in the trunk and drove to town. That makes sense," Liv said.

"Then dumps her body off in Barry's vacant lot, drops the shoes off at Ernie's, and for some unknown reason returns the Mercedes and goes on his merry way? We didn't find a thank-you note."

"Don't be sarcastic, Bill. This is serious."

"It is," he agreed. "And you had better be careful not to obstruct justice."

Liv stared at him, openmouthed. "You actually think—"

"No, not intentionally. But you do have an emotional stake in this case."

Liv let out a controlled breath.

"Don't get huffy. Tell me about this vandalism."

"I'll show you."

Liv waited for Bill to order the women to stay put and stay out of the way, then she took him on a tour of the cabins.

When they were done, Bill called over to his officers. "Meese, if you two are finished there, come get some photos of these interiors."

Meese and the other officer trotted over.

"Wow, looks like a tornado hit," Meese said.

"It looks like an act of anger," Bill said.

Liv nodded. "Yes, it does, and I think we might guess who did it."

"You have a theory all ready?"

"Yes, actually. Come see." She led him around to the boarded-up cabin with the broken window.

Bill stuck his head through the opening, pulled out again. "Looks like someone's being squatting here, alright."

"I found a bunch of pamphlets in the bathroom. I bet they came from the doomsday guy's—Riggs—stash."

"You think he was staying here?"

"No one ever caught him. Everyone assumed he'd made a run for the highway. But it's possible he came here. That's why he could keep popping up and disappearing again."

"Hmm. I'll buy that. Unless it was some drifter that picked the pamphlets to use in the bathroom."

"A good use for them."

"So where is he now?"

"Are you asking me?" Liv said, bewildered.

"It was more rhetorical, but do you have any ideas?"

"Well, my guess is he's vandalized the two main entries in the contest—"

"And I got Ted to okay additional men from Bayside Security to watch on Miss Patty's."

"Good. Then there was the rock throwing at the Mystic Eye."

Bill rolled his eyes.

Liv ignored him. "And now this. It happened while they were out earlier this morning. He trashed the place and cleaned them out of all the money and valuables he could find. If I were him . . . I would get out of 'Dodge' pronto."

"I'll buy that, but it still doesn't explain what he had to do with Lucille, or what she was doing up here late Friday night."

Liv huffed a sigh. "Well, the camp is known for its, um, dalliances. Maybe she was dallying someone."

"Here?"

"We thought the same thing, but the four other cabins are locked and sealed up. Who knows what lies behind those doors?"

"Maybe I should ask Rod Crosby to open them."

Liv looked beyond him to the house and drive. The jeep was gone, but a second later it pulled up beside the police cars. Rod Crosby jumped out.

"Damn," Bill said. "I was hoping to keep this all quiet."

"Just tell him about the vandalism. I'll go tell the ladies to keep mum about the shawl." Liv ran off to warn the witches to let Bill do the talking.

"Got that, ladies?" Yolanda looked over the group. None of them said a thing, but Yolanda nodded as if they had. "We're a close-knit group and we keep to ourselves. No problem here."

"Great." Liv walked back to Bill just as Rod got there.

"What's up, Sheriff?"

"The cabins these ladies have been staying in have been vandalized," Bill said. "They called it in."

"Vandalized? Damn. Which ones?"

A look from Bill kept Liv in her place. Bill took Rod to see the cabins.

"Man. That sucks," Rod said as they came out of the last one. "And I was already closed for the season. I knew we should have left it that way." He lowered his voice. "If you ask me, they brought it on themselves."

"How do you figure that?"

"They're witches, man. People are bound to get upset when they're around. You were there, Liv, when they came to town, and that nutcase on the corner yelled at them."

Liv nodded.

"And Amanda and I heard someone threw a rock at the store window. They're just asking for trouble." Ron hesitated. "Not that I have anything against them. They're Amanda's friends, so . . ." He shrugged in a what-can-you-do gesture.

Rod seemed a lot more laid-back today than when Liv had met him the other day. She wondered if that was because he was talking to the sheriff or because Amanda wasn't there. She wondered if they brought out the worst in each other. Liv imagined that the woman could be a little demanding; she could appear meek and still wear the pants at home. But after what Jon had told her about the conditions of the marriage, Liv wouldn't blame Amanda one bit if she put it to her husband.

"Do you have insurance?" Liv asked. "They're worried about having to pay damages."

"Not up to me, but I doubt if Amanda will charge them."

"Good," Liv said. "Yolanda, why don't you have Rod drive you up to the house and ask Amanda what you should do? If it's okay with the sheriff, the group can clean up their possessions." She looked at Bill.

He nodded, but looked annoyed.

"Good. And since they're going home tomorrow, perhaps they should stay at the inn tonight. I can call the Andersons and see if they have rooms."

"Thank you," Yolanda said. "They could stay with me, but my apartment is very small and I think they will be more comfortable at the inn."

She went away with Rod, who was moving laconically and none too happily toward his jeep. They'd probably interrupted his plans for the afternoon. Well, tough.

The other ladies set about cleanup. Whiskey gladly accompanied them, probably in hopes of finding something yummy, or disgusting, to sniff.

Liv called the inn and reserved four rooms.

"I suppose there's a reason you got rid of everybody so expeditiously," Bill said.

"I was afraid somebody would say something about finding the shawl, and if that got out . . ." She frowned.

"Uh-oh. Liv, what are you thinking?"

"Just that . . . you said to keep it secret, but what if it does leak out? A controlled leak. Not that the shawl's been found, but that we—I mean you, the police—think they know where to find it and are going to search for it at first light. Then whoever comes back to look for it will be the murderer. Is that entrapment?"

"Not if the police don't start the rumor."

"I knew there was a reason Ruth Benedict was put on this earth. What would you say to me dropping a word in Ted's ear, then he can let it slip to Ida and Edna, who in turn will let it slip to Dolly and whoever else is in the bakery? And Dolly will tell Ruth Benedict and Ruth will tell everyone else. If we go back to the office now, that will give us all afternoon for the rumor to spread."

"Then I'll post men to wait undercover until the killer takes the bait."

"It's worth a try, isn't it?"

"I suppose as long as no one, including the Marlton-Crosbys, are in on the plan."

"Not even the Marlton-Crosbys."

"And if the killer turns out to be your friend Jon?"

"It won't," Liv said firmly. She wouldn't believe it until she saw him searching for the shawl.

"We'll have to find a substitute scarf. I don't want to take the chance of messing up the chain of custody."

"I'm sure I can find one," Liv said. "Yolanda might have one that's similar enough in her store, and if she doesn't, the dress store on Fourth Street will."

"I'll need to let A.K. in on the plan. I don't have enough men to stake out for a whole day and night. And we'll have to get them in place before the rumors start." Bill puffed out his cheeks. "But if it doesn't work, we will have played our best card."

"But if it works," Liv said, "we'll have our murderer before the tourists pour in this weekend and we can get back to the business of Halloween. If not," she shrugged, "there's still DNA."

Yolanda returned on foot about twenty minutes later. She stopped for a second to get her breath back, while the group stopped whatever they were doing to surround her.

"Where's Rod?" Liv asked.

Yolanda made a sour face. "He dropped me off by the side of the road. He said he was late for an appointment." She snorted. "Late for a rendezvous with a pool cue. Gotta get more exercise." She sucked in a couple of breaths. "Amanda doesn't hold us responsible at all," she said. "In fact, she offered to pay for our hotel rooms and dinner tonight. And she'll have Rod clean up everything so we can still have our Samhain here in two weeks."

Murmurs of relief and excitement passed around the group.

"That's great news. I made the reservations already, so they're expecting you at the inn," Liv said, and began to gently nudge the women into packing their cars up and driving away.

Then she and Bill just looked at each other.

"You know, Liv, this is not your job."

"Having second thoughts?"

"No. Thinking about lunch."

"Then let's get back to the office and order in while we fill Ted in on what he has to do."

Chapter Twenty-two

······································

Bill and Liv informed Ted of their plan over soup and sandwiches delivered from Buddy's diner. A.K. arrived just as they were finishing.

Liv listened as he and Bill discussed the number of men needed and the logistics of getting them in place while not alerting the public as to what they were doing. Both men's heads—one curly and graying, the other shaved to a shine— were bent over the rough map that Bill had drawn of the camp and meadow.

"Camouflage wear," A.K. said. "We all have night-vision goggles."

Liv stared. Bill's shook his head. "Obviously the private security business is booming. I'm lucky if I can get the extra hours approved."

"We'll fill in where you need us. Just say the word."

"Um, now that we've started this," Liv said, "how much is this going to cost the event office? Since Bayside Security is paid out of our budget."

A.K. looked at Liv. One side of his mouth twitched, barely a tic. But Liv had come to recognize it as A.K.'s version of a smile.

"We won't need that many men. Three or four max. We're used to long shifts."

Liv imagined that was true. As far as she had learned, A.K. and his crew all had served actively in the Marines or some other form of the armed services. They were very efficient.

"So, Sheriff, I suggest you position your men along the road in unmarked cars, close but where they won't be seen from the road."

Bill nodded. "There are drives and turnouts all along that area of road."

"But how will you get men in place at the camp?" Liv asked. "Anyone driving by might see you." She held up a hand. "Wait. I know. You have your ways."

"Actually," A.K. said. "I thought we might do a little fishing. I'm sure Chaz would be glad of a hire." He frowned slightly. "If he'll promise to stay out of the way."

Ted caught Liv's attention and half winked. She wasn't oblivious to the slight competition between the two men.

Ted claimed it was over her. Liv was sure they did it just to drive her crazy. As far as she knew, they'd never spent time together before the night they came spying on her and Jon. Well, good—this would give all three of them a chance to redeem themselves.

"Call him," Bill said.

Liv pushed the landline phone toward him, but A.K. had already stood, retrieved his cell phone, and was walking into the outer office.

Liv raised an eyebrow to Ted. "Do you think he doesn't want us to hear?"

"I think secrecy is just an occupational habit," Ted said.

Bill nodded in agreement.

A.K. came back into the room. "Chaz can have the boat

ready in half an hour. We'll meet him at Cove Marina and he'll take us close enough to shore to wade into position."

"Amazing," Liv said. "How did you get him to move so fast? He never wants to help out."

"Trade secret." A.K. turned to Bill. "Let's get the rest of the details ironed out."

It took less than twenty minutes to get the plan rolling.

"Ted, we'll call you as soon as everyone is in place and you can start the rumor mill."

Bill and A.K. both stood to go.

Liv realized that they weren't including her in their plans. Which was reasonable, but it was her idea, and besides, she'd just thought of something.

"Wait!"

All three men turned to look at her.

"I have an idea."

Bill automatically shook his head. "If it includes you coming with us, the answer is no."

"Not me, necessarily. But . . ."

Bill groaned and eased himself back into the chair. A.K. just stood where he was, using every intimidating inch of himself to let her know that he wasn't going to let her come.

"First of all, you great big planners forgot to get the duplicate scarf."

She could tell by their lack of expression that she'd caught them. Only Ted was smiling. And he was trying to hide it.

"Before you shut me down, just tell me what you think." Not getting a verbal no, she went on. "If whoever the killer is does come out, and he picks up the replacement scarf and it isn't even the right scarf—there's got to be a technicality there."

Bill sighed.

"We'll just get him to confess," A.K. said.

Even Bill looked alarmed at that.

"You might frighten him—or her—into confessing. But you might not."

"No," said Bill.

"No, what?" asked Liv.

"No to whatever you're planning that places you in jeopardy."

"Trust me, I don't want to be in jeopardy. But maybe we've got a better chance at confession if the killer is goaded by a helpless female."

Someone made a rude noise. Liv was sure it was A.K., but when she looked around his face was perfectly masked.

"She's right, though I hate to admit it," Ted said. "Are you sure there will be DNA that will stand up as evidence on the original scarf? Maybe the scarf fell off in the struggle."

"Or when Ernie bumped into her on the awards night," Liv added. "Or maybe her husband helped her on with her coat. No telling how many people's DNA is on that scarf; I hadn't thought about that."

"If we can get evidence off the body, then we won't need the scarf. She wasn't strangled with the scarf."

"Fine and dandy," Liv said. "You try keeping everyone in place while the state gets around to testing your DNA samples. Hmm, let's see . . . weeks? Months?"

"True, I doubt we're a high priority." Bill sighed. "Ted, give us twenty minutes until we can get the fake scarf in place, then make the calls."

Ted looked from Bill to A. K. to Liv. "Then what?"

"Then," Bill said reluctantly.

"*We're* going on a stake out," Liv said. "After you, gentlemen."

It was only five o'clock but already dark. Liv shifted in the makeshift bunker she was sharing with two of A.K.'s men. The replacement scarf had been surreptitiously placed back under the bush where Liv—or Whiskey, to be exact—had found it. And they were sitting about twenty feet away behind a wall of tangled bushes.

For once, Liv really hoped the town gossip mill worked quickly. She was bored, cold, and though she didn't want to admit it, a little nervous. She didn't really think anything would happen to her. There were enough men covering the area to subdue a small army.

And hopefully this would be only one man—or woman— if the killer took the bait. With the way things had been going, this would be the one day the murderer decided to go to Albany shopping and missed the rumors until it was too late.

She sighed. The minutes ticked by and Liv was beginning to think the trap wasn't going to work. Then one of the men suddenly put his fingers to his lips and moved silently to get a better view of the path to the meadow.

Liv hadn't heard a car, so the person must be on foot. Or had parked back at the fish camp and was walking the rest of the way.

That's when she saw the round beam of a flashlight swing across the meadow, getting closer. As it got closer, she felt the men around her tense with readiness.

Even Liv felt a little ripple of energy, but she was pretty sure it wasn't anticipation of a good fight, just plain old fear.

The light stopped; swung away. Liv saw someone go up the steps to one of the cabins, fumble with the lock, then the door swung open. The person shined the light around, but didn't go in. The light moved on. Slower now, and right past where Liv and the others were waiting.

It was a man, Liv could tell that much, but the flashlight pushed his features into deeper shadows.

He bent over, looking along the edges of the path, then straightened, and before he could move on, Liv recognized Rod Crosby.

One of her companions nudged her. She nodded. It was now or never. Liv stood. Was surprised at how stiff her legs were. Damn, she hoped the circulation returned before she had to run for her life.

Rod slowed again, shining the light along the ground. He was almost to the bush where the scarf was hidden.

Come on, come on, Liv thought. *Just look under the bush.*

The light moved over it and continued on.

He'd missed it. He took another step. Liv wanted to scream. Then Rod hesitated, turned the flashlight back to the ground. And stopped.

Eureka.

Liv's companion touched her shoulder, her cue to go as quickly and as silently as possible. She didn't know where the police or the rest of A.K.'s men were, but she knew they were close by and ready to come save her bacon.

She stepped out into the clearing. Rod had dropped the flashlight on the ground and was pulling at the scarf, which Liv had intentionally tangled around the branches to slow down his escape.

She reached him just as he pulled it free.

"Find what you're looking for?"

Rod let out a yelp and jumped to his feet. Tried to hide the shawl behind his back, but realized the futility of it.

He glanced down at the flashlight.

"Don't do it, Rod."

"Do what? I'm just cleaning up the campground because of those damn witches."

"In the dark?"

"I'll clean up when I damn well please. It's my property and you're trespassing."

"It's Marlton property and you murdered Lucille Foster."

He looked quickly around. "Who did you bring with you?"

Liv shrugged. "No one. The police aren't planning to look for the shawl until tomorrow. But when we were cleaning up after the jackass who vandalized the women, we found the shawl."

Rod growled low in his in throat.

"I was afraid Jon killed Lucille, but I wanted to make sure, so I could help him get away before they came to arrest him."

Rod snorted. "Him? You shouldn't have gone to the trouble."

"Oh, I know he didn't kill her," Liv said, stalling for time. Surely her backup was in place by now. "Because *you* killed Lucille."

"Think you're so smart."

"About this, I am. What do you plan to do with the shawl now, Rod? Burn it? Throw it in the lake?"

"I'll wrap it around your damn throat."

Liv took a cautious step back.

"You women are all the same. Take, take, take. Nothing I ever do is good enough. Amanda is on my back twenty-four/seven. Lucille was after me to leave Amanda. Ha. She was nuts to think I'd jump off that gravy train. I've been putting up with enough crap from Amanda. No way was I going to give up my chance of all that money when I was so close."

A chill ran up Liv's spine. "So close to what?"

"None of your business." He stepped toward her, the scarf wadded in one hand.

Okay, this was getting a little too exciting for Liv's comfort level.

"You're going to kill me just like you killed Lucille?" She didn't have to fake the tremor in her voice. *Confess already.*

"The silly bitch tried to run, tripped over her own feet, and knocked herself out. She didn't feel a thing when I wrapped these babies around her pathetic neck."

He raised both his hands. He was wearing driving gloves. "You, on the other hand, will feel plenty. And I won't leave the scarf around for the police to find in the morning when they come looking."

Dummy, Liv thought. *Come and get him now, please.*

He snatched the scarf in both hands, and before Liv could react, threw it over her head and yanked her forward.

Where the heck were those guys?

"Freeze." A.K.'s voice.

Rod froze but he didn't let go of the ends of the scarf. Liv knew exactly what he had in mind. Just before he lunged forward, she dropped to her knees, leaving the scarf wrapped around air instead of her neck. Rod stumbled over her—right into the arms of two Bayside Security operatives.

Floodlights popped on. Car doors slammed. Running feet, and the county police were on the scene, followed by a slow-moving sheriff.

A.K. pulled Liv to her feet. She brushed off her hands. "Cutting it a little close, weren't we?"

One side of A.K.'s mouth lifted and then as she watched, the other side lifted into a full smile. Liv nearly sat down again. That smile was lethal. She smiled back.

They were smiling at each other when Chaz and the rest of the crew crashed through the woods.

Chaz skidded to a stop. "Guess I missed all the fun," he said, looking at A.K. and Liv.

"What are you doing here?" Liv blurted.

"Doing my civic duty. I came for gossip."

"Yep, the good guys won again," A.K. said.

Chaz scowled.

"He confessed," Liv said, trying to defuse the standoff between the two men.

"And is on his way to jail," Bill added.

Chaz shoved his hands into his jacket pockets. "And did it occur to you that the Marlton money could pay a fortune to get him out on bail? And if he gets out, your life won't be worth a dime."

Liv had *not* thought about that.

"Well, let's ask her." Bill raised his chin toward the road. Amanda jumped out of the driver's side of Rod's jeep. She ran toward the group while Jon was still getting out of the passenger side.

"Looks like Amanda and your Manhattan swain to the rescue, a little late," Chaz said.

Liv shot him a quelling look, then waited as the police escorted Rod past the newcomers.

"It was you?" Amanda asked incredulously. "You? I let you have everything, including your women. Why did you kill her? Why?"

Rod shrugged. "I was sick of being stuck with both of you."

Amanda fists tightened, and before the police could take Rod away, she slugged him. His head snapped back. Even his two guards staggered beneath the strength of the blow.

"Whoa," Chaz said. "She packs a punch for such a little woman."

Amanda jutted her chin at her husband. "We'll see how you like having a court-appointed attorney to handle your case." Then she sagged; Jon put his arm around her as she started to cry.

"I guess we don't have to worry about Amanda getting him out of jail," Chaz said.

Jon caught Liv's eye, then looked to Bill. "I'll take her to the house, if that's okay with you."

Bill nodded, and Jon slowly led Amanda back to the jeep.

The rest of them stood where they were until the jeep drove away.

"Ted's going to be upset that he missed all this," Chaz said.

"He was manning the phone chain," Liv said.

A.K. rounded up his men. "Thanks for the use of your boat, Chaz."

Chaz nodded.

"Good work, Ms. Montgomery."

Liv nodded. She would have said something but she was beginning to feel a little shaky in the aftermath.

"I think a brandy would do wonders," A.K. said, but he was talking to Chaz.

"Wait a minute," Liv said. "Stop bossing me around."

"I think Liv could use one, too." Chaz grinned.

A.K. shook his head and left. Bill sent the rest of his men back to the station, then stopped by Chaz and Liv. "Come on, I'll give you a lift back to town. I promised Ted we'd tell him the whole story before the night was through."

"Not 'til I get there," Chaz said. "I just have to return the boat to the marina."

Liv slept in the next day. She figured she deserved it. She and Ted met in time for the opening of the Museum of Yankee Horrors. A ribbon-cutting ceremony by the mayor was accompanied by the zombie band, now back in their high school colors.

Bill walked back with them to town hall. He'd gone to yoga that morning and his sciatica was already feeling better. On the way, they stopped by the Apple of My Eye for some of Dolly's caramel apple cake and the Buttercup for two lattes and a tea.

"You two sure know how to enjoy the workaday world," Bill said. "If I'm lucky, I get stale donuts and motor-oil coffee."

"You're welcome to join us anytime," Liv said as Ted pulled up an extra chair to Liv's desk and laid out the morning fare.

"I have news," Bill said.

"Do tell." Ted handed him a china plate with a piece of cake.

Bill took a sip of coffee. "Got a call that the state troopers picked up Stanley Riggs yesterday morning. He was hitchhiking south on Route 87. When they picked him up he was incoherent and they took him in for psychiatric testing.

"He admitted to vandalizing the museum. But he kept insisting that the others weren't his fault because someone had made him do it.

"At first they thought he was talking about 'voices' in his head, but they finally realized that he meant an actual person. It seems he'd been camping out in one of the cabins at the fish camp."

"We saw the one where he stayed."

Bill nodded.

"Rod Crosby found him squatting and threatened to have him arrested unless he agreed to vandalize, for a fee, the Mystic Eye and Ernie's haunted house.

"And the fish camp?" Liv asked.

"That he did on his own when Rod refused to pay him what he thought he was due."

"Why did Rod want all the places vandalized?"

"Misdirection, I suspect," Bill said.

"But what about Lucille?"

"Well, according to Rod, who yo-yos between babbling and enforced silence . . ." Bill shook his head. "That's another nutcase.

"I guess he and Lucille went up to the fish camp to 'talk.' She was insisting he leave Amanda. He said no. She had a fit and he'd had enough. He grabbed her and she ran away. That's when she lost her shoes and scarf, and fell and hit her head."

"And he killed her while she was unconscious," Liv said. "That's just the worst."

"It was certainly the easiest," Ted said. "And it had the secondary feature of making the suspect list even longer. A lot of people could have strangled her easily when she was unconscious." Ted helped himself to another piece of cake. "Did he say why he threw Lucille's body in the vacant lot?"

"And why he used Jon's car?" Liv added.

"He used the Mercedes just because it was handy and he didn't want any evidence left in his jeep. Evidently Jon had left his keys downstairs. Rod didn't even have to hot-wire it."

"And it almost worked," Liv said.

"We would have gotten to the truth in the end."

Liv wasn't totally sure of that, but she wasn't going to quibble.

"And the vacant lot?"

"Pure serendipity. He was driving back to the town parking lot, where he planned to drop Lucille's body near her car. But as he passed Barry's Museum, he saw Riggs carrying the mannequins and dumping them in the lot. Rod said he just waited for Riggs to leave, then dumped Lucille along with the rest."

"And that's when Lola Bangs saw the Mercedes," Liv said. "That's diabolical."

"Certainly nasty," Ted agreed. "But why leave the shoes in Ernie's yard? More muddying the waters?"

"I think at that point it was just plain mean. He'd left the shoes in the car, he was going back for them and then had the brilliant idea of implicating Ernie. He actually chuckled when he told us that. If I hadn't been an officer sworn to uphold the law, I think I would have clobbered him."

Liv sighed. "Poor Amanda."

"She'll be better off without him."

"That's for sure." Ted said.

Bill reached for another piece of cake. "True. But women don't always reconcile their brains with their hearts."

"Bill," Ted said, "that was downright poetic."

"Yeah," Liv said. "But poetry won't buy us a new community center."

"You think Jon will turn us down?

Liv shrugged. "I don't know. We'll just have to wait and see."

They only had to wait until Monday morning to find out. Ted and Liv were reconciling the Pilgrim dinner sales with the number of tables and chairs that had to be confirmed for delivery when Liv's cell rang. "It's Jon." She walked to the window to take the call. When she hung up, she turned to Ted. "He's taking Amanda back to the city for a while and he wants me to meet him for a quick lunch at the inn. Do I look okay?"

"You look great for taking his money, but don't accept any job offers." He cleared his throat. "Or any other offers."

"Wouldn't think of it. Gotta go. Can you call the party supply place and confirm?"

"Doing it now." Ted picked up the phone.

Liv headed over to the inn.

When Jon walked her back an hour later, she had a note from Amanda in her messenger bag thanking her and the town. Plus a check for an additional fifty thousand dollars for a down payment on a new location for the community center.

And Jon had hinted that he would give a favorable report to the foundation committee.

They stopped on the sidewalk outside the town hall.

"So I guess this is good-bye for a while," Jon said.

"I guess so. Since I'm not on the circuit anymore."

"And don't intend to get back on." He smiled. A little wistfully, she thought. "You've found a home."

"Yeah, I guess I have."

"And you have your peeps."

He lifted his chin toward Liv's office window.

She automatically looked up. Chaz, Ted, and Bill stood at the window, looking down.

"They're obnoxious and annoying and drive me nuts, but they're definitely my peeps."

"They're lucky to have you."

"Yeah. They are."

"And they know it."

"You think?"

"Oh, I can tell. I'm a little jealous."

Liv laughed. "You?"

"All the best, Liv. Call me next time you're in the city. Who knows, maybe I'll be there, too."

He hugged her and walked back toward the inn.

Liv walked across the street to her office. She opened the door to Bill, Chaz, and Ted all looking guilty—but not repentant.

"Get an eyeful, boys?"

"Hey, we were just hanging out," Chaz said.

Bill stifled him with a look. "Liv, are you disappointed?

"Not at all. We got a big check from Amanda and a good word from Jon."

"What about your dapper boyfriend?" Ted said.

"He's an associate."

Chaz slapped him on the back. "Yeah, Ted, what would she want with some rich, educated, well-dressed New Yorker when she could have some homegrown boys like us?"

"How true," Liv said. "But you didn't have to be so infantile. At least I'm glad to see A.K. isn't here."

The outer door opened, and A.K. rushed in. "Is he gone? I got here as soon as I could."

"What's that you were saying about maturity?" Ted asked and burst out laughing.

"What?" A.K. asked.

Bill and Chaz joined in the laughter.

"Yep. Definitely my peeps," Liv said and she laughed, too.